WEAPON OF VENGEANCE

WEAPON OF VENGEANCE

MUKUL DEVA

A TOM DOHERTY ASSOCIATES BOOK | NEW YORK

WEAPON OF VENGEANCE

Copyright © 2011 by Mukul Deva

A Forge Book
Published by Tom Doherty Associates, LLC
175 Fifth Avenue
New York, NY 10010

www.tor-forge.com

Forge® is a registered trademark of Tom Doherty Associates, LLC.

The Library of Congress Cataloging-in-Publication Data is available upon request.

ISBN 978-0-7653-3771-9 (hardcover)
ISBN 978-1-4668-3570-2 (e-book)

Forge books may be purchased for educational, business, or promotional use. For information on bulk purchases, please contact Macmillan Corporate and Premium Sales Department at 1-800-221-7945, extension 5442, or write specialmarkets@macmillan.com.

Originally published in 2012 in slightly different form under the title *The Dust Will Never Settle* by HarperCollins *Publishers* India

First Edition: June 2014

Printed in the United States of America

0 9 8 7 6 5 4 3 2 1

This book is dedicated to those millions of people the world over whose lives have been disrupted by the senseless violence that mankind is so fond of inflicting on itself.

ACKNOWLEDGMENTS

This book would never have been possible if it had not been for certain people who came into my life at the right time. Al Zuckerman of Writers House, who was invaluable in giving the story shape and holding my hand from start to finish. Fran Rittman for selflessly connecting me with the right people at the right time. Avital, Idit, Gabriella, Jawad, Lilach, Ido, Karim, Amatullah, and Lynette, to name a few more, who shared their invaluable insights of their wondrous countries or various other aspects that totally flummoxed me. They made me feel emotionally connected to the characters in a special way. To each one of you I offer my humble and heartfelt thanks.

To my wonderful family for giving me the time and space to indulge in the (almost) solitary love of my life, writing.

To my comrades-in-arms in the Indian Armed Forces who were kind enough to ensure that I did not make any major blunders while writing about tactics, weapons, and weapon systems. However, I must stress that all technical data used in this book has not been provided by anyone; it is already in the public domain and available on the Internet and in libraries.

To the National Arts Council of Singapore for providing me the wonderful opportunity to finish this book in double-quick time. Singapore has been a fantastic breeding ground for me, freed me from so many worries and enabled me to focus single-mindedly on writing.

And of course, last but not the least, to each one of you, dear readers, who have egged me on with praise and criticism, by writing in to me, by blogging about my books, and of course, buying them. . . . ☺

Any errors, factual or technical, that still exist in this book are solely my fault or have been deliberately left in there by me to prevent any misuse of a technology or an idea.

AUTHOR'S NOTE

This book is a work of fiction, although some of the events mentioned here may have actually taken place.

All the characters, countries, places, and organizations described or mentioned in this book are fictitious or have been fictitiously used, and any resemblance to any place, organization, country, or person, living or dead, is absolutely unintentional.

In several cases, artistic license has been taken with the places mentioned in the book, distances between places, and the general topography.

In order to prevent an actual attack being carried out on any monument or building, the location and layouts of all monuments and hotels mentioned in this book have been suitably altered. Similarly the security arrangements of all places have been fictitiously described.

The technical details of the various weapons systems, the specifications and methodologies of bomb making and weaponry, as well as the tactics and security procedures employed by any police, military, intelligence organization, and/or militant organization, as also all criminal, forensic, and investigative procedures, have been deliberately kept slightly vague, inaccurate, and/or incomplete, once again to prevent any misuse, accidental or otherwise.

There is no slur or malice intended against any religion, race, caste, creed, nation, organization, or people.

PREFACE

Of all the books I have written, this is the one that gave rise to many conflicts within me. With every page I wrote or person I interviewed, I felt a strange, almost irresistible, emotional connection developing between the book, the characters, and me.

I must also confess that the success and publicity generated by the Lashkar series are weighing on me, and I await reader and media response to this book with some anxiety. This pressure has also been instrumental in ensuring I've put my heart and soul into this book, to make sure it lives up to, if not exceeds, the previous ones.

While researching and writing this story, it became clear to me that—race, region, and religion notwithstanding—the human race has displayed an inexplicable proclivity for violence. This is despite the fact that we facetiously call ourselves an *intelligent* life-form. Any species that is willing to kill so easily can scarcely be considered intelligent by any yardstick.

We, as individuals, teach our children the virtues of caring and sharing, yet as nations and religious groups show so little tolerance for others. That is why guns continue to roar, bombs go off every day, and the dust never settles.

Negotiate as if there were no war and fight as if there were no negotiation.

—Menachem Begin

WEAPON OF VENGEANCE

DAY ONE

The woman with the Mediterranean complexion blinked as she emerged from the aircraft into the bright Sri Lankan sunlight. Though early in the day, the light was already harsh. As was the medley of thoughts clashing in her head.

Lowering her wraparound shades over large, almond-shaped eyes to cut out the glare, she paused at the top of the stairs and surveyed Colombo's Bandaranaike Airport.

Stark brown fields with intermittent patches of green stretched away beyond the barbed-wire fence ringing the runways. Scattered along the fencing were security posts with tall, searchlight-mounted sentry towers. Grim reminders of the insurgency that had torn apart the island state.

Barring an odd airport vehicle and caterpillar-like luggage trolleys snaking around, the runway was devoid of life. An air of despondency hung all around. Not a good feeling. She gave a slight shiver, as though to shake it off.

As she descended toward the bus waiting to take passengers to the squat, yellow terminal in the distance, she watched a jetliner swoop down like a huge hawk, its blue and white Finnair logo sparkling in the sun. She heard a distant thud, followed by the smoky blistering of rubber as the jet's wheels made contact with the tarmac. The roar of engines faded as it vanished down the runway.

It was a short walk to the bus, but she could feel sweat in her armpits. Arriving from the London chill, she was annoyed by the heat, which caused her to hurry into the air-conditioned comfort of the bus. It did not take long for the bus to fill up. Soon they were on their way. Almost everyone was switching on mobiles, several already in animated conversations. The young girl standing beside her had tuned out the world with her iPod and was swaying to some unheard beat.

Conditioned by her training, the woman did yet another rapid scan with practiced eyes. She had done this many times during the flight, but compelled by habit, did it again. Her danger antennae remained quiet. Nothing out of sync. Yet.

Those who did not know her would have assumed she was just another thirty-something masking her femininity; though the baggy, almost masculine clothing did little to conceal her breasts and voluptuous figure. Those who knew her would have noted she was in battle gear.

The baggy black jeans and equally loose, full-sleeved, blue cotton shirt were not just to keep her cool. They would also let her swing into action should the need arise. She never wore skirts or dresses on a job; neither were practical, nor were they a good idea in the man's world she had occupied most of her working life. Also, skirts and dresses were not designed to carry the armory of an MI6 agent, which comprised a mobile, a BlackBerry, a weapon, spare magazines, and, very often, a secure digital radio. Nor could they conceal her backup, the .22 pistol in her ankle holster.

Today, of course, she was weaponless. Not good. She felt naked without them; the feeling intensified by her hyped-up state. Also missing was the protective, standard-issue Kevlar vest. Black, patent leather, rubber-soled, lace-up shoes completed her attire. The one-inch heels and rubber soles ensured she could move swiftly and soundlessly. Her black shoulder-length hair was neatly pinned back; ensuring no errant strands in her eyes. She wore virtually no makeup. On a job, she always dressed down.

As the bus swayed to a halt outside the terminal, she jumped out and headed for the immigration counters. She carried herself with the ease of a professional soldier. And she knew she looked good. Male heads turning as she passed confirmed that.

While waiting in line at the immigration counter, she ran through her operational checklist. She could not afford any mistakes. Time was short and there was a great deal to be done.

Nothing in her demeanor gave any inkling of the turmoil in her head. No one observing her could have imagined the immensity of the mission she was on. Not that she was dismayed by the obstacles that lay between her and her targets. Far from it. She wished she'd been able to run a detailed background check on her targets and her adversaries before leaving London, but there had been no time. Despite that, she felt ready and committed. She would pay any price to ensure she succeeded.

"Never forget your purpose in life." Her mother, Rehana's, words echoed in her head. "Never forget the blood your family has shed. Never forget what we have suffered . . . are continuing to suffer. No matter what, you must not let our sacrifice go to waste."

For a moment, the memory of her mother made her falter. The sight of her shattered, decimated body ripped at the woman's heart. But it was a fleeting lapse.

All these years, she had prayed for the day when she would finally raise her hand and strike down those who had inflicted so much misery on her people. And now the day of reckoning was almost at hand. Ten days more, and she would demolish the Israeli–Palestinian Peace Summit.

Ruby Gill strode forward. Eagerly. Completely focused. Nothing would stop her. She knew.

Ravinder Singh Gill, the tall, lean Inspector General of Police and head of the Indian Anti-Terrorist Task Force, was en route toward his third-floor office in Delhi Police HQ. Conscious he needed the exercise, Ravinder went past the elevators and took the stairs.

Though he was well past fifty, the years had been kind to him. With his neatly tied turban, flecks of gray spotting his mustache and beard, he cut a dashing figure in black pants, sky blue shirt, and patent leather shoes. A Montblanc pen peeped out from his breast pocket. Black cuff links embossed with the family's double-headed lion crest completed his attire. The lion had one paw raised, ready to strike. It resonated with his mood.

His day had begun with the never-ending mother–daughter discussion about marriage. These had been their sole agenda ever since their daughter, Jasmine, celebrated her twenty-second birthday. It took only minutes for them to degenerate into an acrimonious harangue. Today had been no exception. Not a great way to start the day. Ravinder was in a sour mood when he had left the breakfast table and headed here.

He sensed the day was not going to get better when he came out and saw the driver changing a tire on his Scorpio SUV.

"Sorry, sir," the man called out when he saw Ravinder emerge. "There must have been nails on the road near the Metro construction site. Both front tires are punctured."

"How long will it take to sort it out?" Ravinder controlled his irritation.

"About half an hour, sir."

"Damn! I am in a rush."

"Why don't you use our car?" his wife, Simran, called out from the door. "I will send the Scorpio when it is fixed."

"I guess I will," Ravinder replied, looking at the black BMW 750Li parked in the porch. Jagjit Singh, the family driver, in his bright red turban and pristine white uniform, complete with the family crest, was polishing it. Simran loved these royal-like trappings and ensured they were displayed wherever possible. Ravinder, though, preferred to downplay his wealth and royal background, not easy when being driven around in a spanking-new Bimmer. But he got into the car and they took off.

As he entered his office, Ravinder dragged his fingers back along his temples, trying to push away a budding headache. The phone rang. Ravinder reached for it, relieved to have something intrude on his dark mood.

"Mr. Gill?" The Indian Home Minister Raj Thakur's nasal, raspy tone was unmistakable. It felt jarring, which, Ravinder thought wryly, went well with the man's personality. Though new to this assignment, which had befallen him a few days back, when the previous ATTF chief's heart had suddenly given up on him, Ravinder had already had some disturbing meetings with the minister.

No! Ravinder shook his head. *Raj Thakur is not an easy man to like . . . or an easy boss.*

Though clueless about security, Raj Thakur had a know-it-all's self-confidence, which, coupled with his belligerence and eagerness to interfere in operational matters, could be dangerous. In their brief association, Thakur had already countermanded several orders given by Ravinder, generally without bothering to inform him. Consequently, Ravinder now felt he was walking around on eggshells, always peering back over his shoulders, wondering what would hit him next.

Still not fully settled in, and with his responsibility for the security of the Israeli–Palestinian Peace Summit and the Commonwealth Games that Delhi was hosting weighing on him, Ravinder so wished he had a more reasonable boss. And he was not the only one. Even the Prime Minister was said to be especially concerned. However, with Raj Thakur's negligible, Maharashtra-centric party holding some vital seats, the PM had had no option but to give him the Home portfolio to keep his majority in Parliament intact.

So be it, Ravinder consoled himself. As a professional cop, what choice did he have, but to go with whatever the dice threw up? With only ten days left before the peace summit *and* the Commonwealth Games, he had more concrete issues to deal with.

"Good morning, sir."

"I want you to come to my office, Gill. Immediately. I now have all the updates for the peace summit."

"Right, sir." Ravinder, with a mountain of urgent tasks to attend to, wanted to tell him to fuck off. *Alas!* "I will be there—" He checked his watch; it was a good one-hour drive to South Block, where the minster's office was. "—by eleven."

"Do that," Thakur commanded brusquely. "Bring Mohite with you." The minister rang off.

Ravinder was replacing the phone when, with a cursory knock, Deputy Inspector General of Police Govind Mohite walked in. Though not tall, Mohite had a well-muscled body. He was impeccably dressed in dark khaki trousers, a matching earth-colored cotton shirt, and brown suede shoes.

"You have a long life, Govind. I was about to call you. The Home Minister wants us right away."

"I know, sir. He called me half an hour ago." Mohite gave a wide grin.

"But I just got off the phone with him." The words were out before Ravinder could rein them in. He felt like kicking himself.

"Oh, you know how Thakur sahib is. . . ." Mohite pronounced the "sahib" with an elongated double-*a* sound, the way Maharashtrians tend to. "He likes to sound me out about everything. You see, we became close when he was in the Maharashtra cabinet and I was in the Mumbai Special Crimes Unit."

Ravinder heard him ramble on about what a great chap Thakur was; something Mohite was prone to doing. He wondered if Mohite knew what the meeting was about. Ravinder contemplated asking him, but shelved the thought. It would give the wrong signal. Ravinder was aware that Mohite was gunning for his job and he needed to watch his back, considering his chumminess with the minister. There had been rumors that the two had been in cahoots in several questionable killings of members of a particular crime mob. These had raised tons of media speculation, including insinuations that they had been carried out at the behest of another mob boss in Dubai and that large sums of money had exchanged hands, but nothing was proved. Ravinder shrugged. Whatever the bond, he knew it would be nasty. Since his predecessor had checked out without a formal and detailed handover, Ravinder also knew that he needed both his primary lieutenants, of which Mohite was one, till he had settled in properly.

"You are traveling in style today," Mohite commented when he saw the Bimmer. "Might as well come with you." Without waiting for a reply, he told his driver to follow and hopped into the rear seat.

"Why bring your car if you're going in mine?" Ravinder asked. "Why not save some gas and do your bit for Planet Earth?"

"Oh, just in case we need to come back separately afterward." Mohite gave an airy wave. "Thakur sahib might ask me to stay on. He likes to consult me on many things."

"Right." Ravinder kept the sarcasm out of his voice. Not that it mattered; Mohite was oblivious.

Tuning out Mohite's nonstop banter, Ravinder's thoughts returned to the meeting. The sudden summons had caught him unawares; he felt worried.

Her accomplice was waiting near the baggage carousel when Ruby emerged from immigration.

Over six feet tall, the oversized Mark Leahy occupied an unfair amount of space. Also wearing jeans and a cotton shirt, he had close-cropped, sand-colored hair and leathery skin, the hallmark of a man who spent most of his time outdoors. His Irish accent was so thick, one could cut it with a knife.

They had traveled on the same flight, but unlike Ruby, he looked rested and refreshed. Not surprising, since he was unaffected by her emotional turmoil.

Good! Ruby smiled. *At least one of us is cool.* She sure as hell was not.

"Feeling distraught is normal when one has been subjected to severe trauma," the agency shrink had told her when she returned to London after Rehana's funeral. Ruby's erratic behavior had prompted her boss to send her for therapy posthaste. "There is not much you can do about it. Just be aware that your mind may wander and try to control it. Everyone has a different way of processing grief. Apparently, this is your way."

Damn stupid way. Ruby frowned. But she'd had to cope. And live with it. *Try* to live with it. Especially since she had thrown away the medication as soon as she left the man's office. Having her mind stuck on a Prozac-shelf was not for Ruby. She now hauled herself back and concentrated on Mark.

Looking at him made her feel better. She'd thought of him the minute she decided to take on this mission, which was as soon as Uncle Yusuf had come to know about the peace summit. So much had transpired since then. She smiled as she remembered her conversation with Mark only yesterday.

"Hey! How are you?" He'd sounded so pleased.

"I am very well, thank you. How are things with you?"

"Same old, same old. There doesn't seem to be much happening. Certainly not the right kind of stuff . . . stuff that interests me *and* pays the rent. So I am catching up on life . . . tending to the garden and painting the fences . . . y'know . . ." He'd laughed.

Ruby knew Mark had quit the service a few months ago and was now freelancing.

"That can get kind of boring."

"Tell me about it."

"Well, I may have something for you."

"You? Naah. The government doesn't pay enough." She'd expected that. "Besides, haven't you heard, I quit working for them."

"Mark, this one is personal. Nothing to do with the agency. And the money is better than good." Ruby knew that, for the right money, Mark was the ideal man to watch her back—ruthless, resourceful, and ready to follow orders.

"Is it, now?" He'd made a humming sound. "Want to tell me more?"

Ruby knew he was on. "Not right now. You will have to trust me."

"I do. You know I do. Implicitly." Mark chuckled. "As much as you trust me. How many times have we watched each other's backs?"

"Often enough. Why else would I call you, Mark?"

"And here I was thinking you called because of my lovely smile and beautiful body!" They'd both laughed. "When and where do you want me? And how long will we be gone?"

Ruby's spirits had lightened when he said that. "We move out tomorrow. We should be back in two weeks."

"That's it, eh? Short assignment."

"Yep. Short and sweet. And lucrative."

"That's my type." A laconic laugh. "Where are we headed?"

"India, eventually." Momentarily, just the mention of India unleashed a whirlpool of raw emotions inside her; about her father . . . *a father who abandoned me . . . he means nothing to me.* Without realizing it, she made a dubious moue. *Doesn't he?* She pushed away the thought. *Not now!*

"India, eh? Exotic! Sounds good to me." He'd made that humming sound again. "Say, boss," Mark asked, somewhat bashfully, "we flying coach or—?"

"First class, Mark. Nothing but the best for you, *mon ami.* Your ticket will be in your mailbox shortly. Meet me at Heathrow a couple of hours before the flight."

She knew it was a happy Mark who'd put down the phone. He looked happy even now as they came out of the Colombo airport and headed toward the taxi stand.

Traffic in Delhi is never easy. These days, with construction taking place all over the city and the massive influx of games' tourists, it was maddening. To make things worse, Delhi had not seen such heavy rains, not in the last forty years.

As the car labored through clogged streets, Ravinder wondered what it was that the Home Minister wanted to discuss, hoping for no more unpleasant surprises; their first meeting had been one hell of a shocker. His mind fled back to that day.

"Have you heard the good news, Gill?" Thakur had greeted

them with a big smile when Mohite and he reached his office that day. "India is hosting the Israeli–Palestinian Peace Summit."

"We are?" Ravinder was stunned. One glance at Mohite's face and he realized the news was not news to him. *Damn the man! When will he learn to play for the team?* "The Israelis and Palestinians are talking? That's a surprise, considering the recent terrorist attack on Jerusalem! When did that happen, sir?"

"That's what triggered it off. The Americans . . . in fact the entire international community, has put a lot of pressure on them. Everyone is fed up with the endless bloodshed."

"And India will have the honor of playing host," Mohite chimed in. "Just imagine! We may help peace return to the Middle East."

"Yes, we are going to be doing exactly that." Thakur beamed. "Isn't it great?"

"When is it?" Ravinder ignored their euphoria, preferring to focus on the practicalities.

"Exactly two weeks from now." Thakur would not stop beaming. "This is our chance to showcase India. . . . It is going to be the most critical and game-changing event of our times."

"Two weeks?" Ravinder was floored, but the other two were so caught up in their enthusiasm that they missed it.

"Precisely. It starts on the thirteenth of October."

Thirteenth! The number sent a shiver up Ravinder's spine. Too much had happened to him on that particular date . . . and none of it good.

"But that is exactly when the Commonwealth Games are due to start, sir. Such an event will require massive security, and we are already hard-pressed for resources."

"Resources are never available, Mr. Gill"—Thakur waved dismissively—"we have to find them. Don't you see what this summit will do for India's prestige?"

"I do, sir, but don't you—? I mean . . . one must account for the fact that so many terrorist groups will strive to disrupt it. Palestine is the one cause that all the jihadis use to pull in money and recruits. They will never allow this."

"All that is fine, Gill, but we have to make it happen. Maybe things will be simpler if we can keep it secret and low-key."

"Sir, with the recent attack on Jerusalem, the whole world has its eyes on the Middle East. There is no way we can keep such a momentous event secret."

"Well, regardless, we have to make it happen." Thakur's tone was firm. "We have no choice; the decision has been made. It is now a matter of national pride."

"The security requirements will be a huge challenge, sir. What if the summit gets attacked? The stakes are so high for the jihadis; they will definitely try to strike."

"No, Gill. Nothing must be allowed to disrupt it," Thakur retorted. "I want you to personally take charge of the security."

"But I also have the Commonwealth Games at the same time, sir," Ravinder objected.

"No, you don't." Thakur had then sprung the second, ugly surprise. "I have put Ashish Sharma in charge of the games."

DIG Ashish Sharma was Mohite's peer; they both reported to Ravinder. Now to his dismay, Thakur was directly delegating work to officers under his command. Ravinder opened his mouth to protest once more, but stopped. Pointless; the man *was* the Home Minister, after all. Confrontation would serve no purpose; nor would it be a career-enhancing move.

"I don't see the problem, Gill." Thakur continued, "The arrangements for the games are in place. Sharma just has to keep things going."

"Then why not put Mohite in charge of the peace summit, sir? That way I will be able to run oversight on both events."

"I thought about that, Gill. I trust Mohite totally, but I think the summit is too important for any one man. Do you have any idea of the consequences if something happens to the delegates? India's reputation would be shot to hell . . . not to mention the carnage that may be unleashed in Israel. No. I want you in charge. Of course, Mohite will assist you."

"Of course I will, sir. You know we will never allow anything to happen to the summit." Mohite was quick to spot an opportunity, one where he would be able to take credit if things went well, yet not be responsible if there was a screwup. He turned to Ravinder. "Am I right, sir?"

Ravinder caught his grimace in time, marveling at the man's cheek.

"True, sir," Ravinder replied with a silent sigh. "How come we got to host the summit?"

"Because the Israelis did not agree to any venue that was acceptable to the Palestinians," Thakur was eager to explain. "And the Palestinians refused to agree to any of the Western countries. That did not leave many options. India was a logical choice, since we are on a good wicket with the Israelis, the Palestinians, and the Arab world."

"They met at Oslo the last time," Ravinder mused.

"Yes, but both have a problem with it this time," Mohite jumped in again. "Apparently both sides feel that Oslo is jinxed. That is why when the PM asked Mr. Thakur if we could host it, I advised him to accept."

Ravinder resisted the impulse to give Mohite a solid kick. Instead, he gave a politic smile. "Wonderful. I am so glad you are going to help me secure the summit, Govind."

"But of course, sir." Missing the sarcasm, Mohite gave another bright smile.

"So we all agree that we must keep it a secret?" Thakur asked, failing to mention that he had already spoken about it to at least ten people in the three hours since the PM had informed him. In fact, if he had his way, he would have held a press conference and shouted it to the world. This could be his moment in the sun, and he was loath to keep it under wraps. "I figured Delhi would be ideal. With the Commonwealth Games taking place, we already have a flood of VIPs and athletes, and security is already functioning at peak level."

"That is what I explained to Mr. Thakur, sir," Mohite rejoindered. "It will make our task so much easier."

Ravinder looked at both men, doubting even they believed that. On the other hand, for Thakur this was a once-in-a-lifetime opportunity to showcase himself on an international platform. And for Mohite, a heaven-sent chance to latch on to the minister's coattails and try to grab the limelight.

Got to watch my back, Ravinder reminded himself again. Given half a chance, Mohite would deliver him to the wolves.

"I know I can rely on you, Govind." Thakur gave Mohite a cordial smile, then realizing that Ravinder was also present, added, "and you of course, Gill." He wagged a finger in the air. "Now, remember, we simply cannot fail. If anything bad happens, it would be a shame for India and it would also put an end to all hopes of peace in the Middle East."

Ravinder was in a somber mood as he listened to the two prattle on. Obviously, neither had given any thought to the practicalities of securing such an event. The whole thing was fraught with danger.

Ravinder's memory spool ran out as their car halted in the South Block parking lot. He led the way toward the minister's office, wondering about today, what new shocks awaited him.

Watching Mark move into action, Ruby smiled again. The efficiency with which he organized a car and driver made her feel good.

She beheld a sturdy silver, almost-new Nissan van, with a solid air conditioner. The driver, whose name she couldn't get, spoke more Sinhalese than English, but seemed pleasant and presentable. They threw their bags into the rear. Both were traveling light. Moments later, they were headed north.

Ruby glanced at her watch. It was ticking fast. Reminding her that time was short. A pulse of urgency raced through her.

For the *n*th time, she wished she had been given the heads-up about this summit sooner. And again she cursed Pasha, the Lashkar-e-Taiba commander who had told her about this summit. And also e-mailed her the gory video of Yusuf, her dead uncle.

Its images had become a nightmare, returning every night.

By now she'd become scared of switching off the lights and laying her head on the pillow.

The murderous bastards had even chopped his hands off.

Pinpricks of wetness pushed at her eyes. She kept them at bay, knowing she could not allow them to be seen by Mark. In their world, tears were weakness . . . and weakness was death.

Shaking off the gory images of Yusuf's dismembered body, Ruby mentally urged the driver to go faster. She *needed* to be in motion. Motion was important. It kept the nightmares away.

They hit the first security checkpoint on the outskirts of Colombo. Fortunately, only a few cars were ahead. It took only seven minutes to get past it. A second one, a few miles out of town, took a tad longer.

Then the road stretched out before them. Long. Narrow. Lonely.

Ravinder noted that Thakur seemed excited when they entered his office.

Large and well appointed, it was tastefully decorated, in contrast with Thakur's abrasive personality. Lemon-colored walls set off the Persian carpet in the center. To one side was a burnished teak table with a high back, deep-brown executive chair on one side and four matching leather guest chairs on the other. In the far corner, a trio of single-seater sofas was placed around a smoked-glass center table that held several coffee table books. Large paintings rode high on the walls on either side of the table. He could hear the soft hiss of air-conditioning. The aroma of room freshener reached out to Ravinder.

Lavender. One of his favorites.

"Ah, there you are, Gill." In his mid-fifties, Thakur wore the trademark white kurta pajamas that found favor with most Indian politicians. A Nehruvian cream cotton jacket completed his attire. Thakur did not bother to get up. "Come, come. How are you two?" Without waiting for an answer, he launched off.

"How are the preparations for the summit and games coming along?"

"They are coming along just fine, sir," Mohite butted in before Ravinder could reply. "We have taken over the top two floors of Ashoka Hotel, and our teams have started installing top-notch equipment to secure the summit. We have also started putting checkpoints and roadblocks around the hotel."

"That's good." Thakur rewarded him with a paternal smile.

"We have also broken three terror cells and have information about two more sent in from Pak-Occupied Kashmir to attack the games. We hope to catch them before they get anywhere near Delhi."

"Hope to?" Thakur raised an eyebrow. "No hopes, Govind— just get them."

"We will, sir." Mohite again.

"Amazing." Thakur tapped his table. "These damn terrorists never give up, do they?"

"No, sir, they don't," Ravinder replied. "The ISI has given them carte blanche, sir. They will do everything possible to hurt us."

"Yes, I can see that." Thakur's smile slipped. The full implications of the threat now dawned on him.

"But don't worry about it, sir. We will not allow anything to happen," Mohite jumped in, ever eager to keep the boss happy.

"Excellent." Thakur's smile returned. "I know I can rely on you, Govind."

Ravinder held his peace, not wanting to rain on their parade and point out that it was impossible to stop every terror strike. Somewhere, somehow, someone would always manage to break through any security cordon . . . the law of averages made that a certainty.

"Here." Thakur pulled out two slim brown files and slid them across the table. "A list of the thirteen summit delegates, with their complete details."

Damn! Thirteen again! Ravinder frowned; his unlucky number seemed inextricably linked to this ruddy summit. *I just hope it is not—*

The minister's voice intruded. "Each delegate is accompanied by two personal security officers. Considering the special circumstances, we are permitting the PSOs to carry weapons."

"Foreigners running around with guns in our capital?" Mohite looked up, surprised.

"Yes, Govind. And . . . oh, that reminds me—to assist us, the Americans and the British both have sent across an agent each."

"Why? What do we need them for?" Mohite half rose, his agitation palpable. "We are more than capable of handling our own turf."

"Calm down, Govind." Ravinder waved him down; although having foreign agents mucking around was the last thing he wanted to worry about. "We will need all the help we can get."

"Yes, but . . ."

"Orders from on high, Mohite." Thakur glared, upset at being challenged by his crony. "They will be coming to your office later today, Gill. The Israelis are also sending an agent to brief us about the threats they anticipate. He should be here in a day or so."

"Don't worry, sir," Ravinder reassured him. "We will ensure things go smoothly. Anyone . . . and anything that helps us get the job done properly is more than welcome."

"Good attitude, Gill. Now for the most important thing: The PM will be coming on the first day of the summit. I got the call this morning; the PMO wants the security plan immediately."

"Today?"

"Why? Any problems with that?"

"None at all, sir." Ravinder kept his chin up, knowing the rest of his day was going down the shitter; PM's own security was paranoid and would question everything till the cows came home. *Oh well! Maybe that will keep Mohite busy and get him up to speed.*

"Good, then send those plans to me as soon as possible, and I'll forward them to PMO."

Minutes later, they left and headed back to Police HQ.

"Let us use this time to firm up the details we have to send to PMO," Mohite muttered as he hopped into Gill's car again. "I will ask my car to lead. Too much bloody traffic. The siren will clear the way for us." Poking his head out, he yelled instructions to his driver.

They headed out with Mohite's staff car leading; its flashing red light and madly whooping siren carving a corridor through the traffic. Ravinder detested the siren and would have liked to minimize the time he spent with Mohite, but recognized that now he had made useful suggestions.

"Did you notice this, sir?" Mohite tapped the file in his hands a few minutes later.

"What about it?"

"Look at the delegates list; the Israelis are sending Ziv Gellner, Yossi Gerstmann, and Shahar Goldstein. From the Palestinian side, we have Hisham Gheisari from Hamas; Mullah Ghassan Ahmed Hussein, the head imam of the Al-Aqsa Mosque; and Ghazi Baraguti from Fatah."

"Interesting," Ravinder commented as he ran through their profiles.

Thirteen delegates! Again that bloody unlucky number. But he shrugged off the foreboding that snaked through him and nudged his mind back to the profiles.

Ziv Gellner, a former aide of Yitzhak Rabin, the Israeli premier, was now a staunch Kadima man and one of the chief proponents for a peaceful solution. Originally a hardliner, he'd lost his wife to cancer and later his firstborn son, David, in an Arab attack on the Yitzhar settlement. Mourning his son, he'd adopted Ean, a boy who survived the raid but lost both his parents during it.

When Rabin was gunned down, Ziv's feelings had converted him into a staunch pacifist. Ziv had been right there, a dozen feet from Rabin. Right in front of his eyes he had seen all hopes for peace disappear, blown away by an assassin's bullets. All the euphoria and hope that the Oslo talks had generated evaporated.

"Damn! Did you read this?" Ravinder pointed at Gellner's profile. "He also lost his adopted son, Ean, in the recent terror attack on Jerusalem?"

"Really?" Mohite perused the profile. "Hmm . . . I wonder how he will handle this summit." Both men pondered that. "Strange! Another coincidence," Mohite pointed out a moment later. "Like Gellner, Yossi Gerstmann also lost his son and wife during the same Arab raid on Yitzhar."

Ravinder found Gerstmann's résumé fascinating. A hotshot intelligence professional, he'd been earmarked to head up the Mossad one day. But a counterterrorist operation led by him went wrong, resulting in a bloodbath; putting paid to a promising career. Now a political advisor, Gerstmann was a staunch right-winger who strongly believed that Israel should not part with an inch of land. He was obviously a logical choice for the hardliners and a counterbalancing foil for the pacifist Gellner.

The third Israeli, Shahar Goldstein, often known as the Prince, the son of a former Israeli premier, was a respected Likud man. Due to his legacy, Goldstein carried weight in most sections of Israeli society and could be expected to maintain a balance between the opposing viewpoints of Gellner and Gerstmann. His presence would ensure that whatever solution was recommended might well be acceptable to the Israeli public, which still held his late father in awe.

Of the Palestinian delegates, Hisham Gheisari, a Hamas man based in Gaza, had done a lot of community-development work and made life easier for the Palestinians. He was reputed to be above corruption, and a dozen schools and hospitals in Gaza owed their existence to him. It was men like him who had helped put an end to the corrupt Fatah regime. Though a staunch Hamas man, Gheisari was also a known dove.

Mullah Ghassan Ahmed Hussein, the Head Mufti of Jerusalem, respected in all circles Islamic, Jewish, and Christian, would also be able to play a pivotal role with the Palestinians, especially in light of the recent terror attacks on Jerusalem. In a way, he was Shahar Goldstein's equivalent, whose presence might make a solution palatable to his people.

However, the third Palestinian, Ghazi Baraguti, a Fatah man until now languishing in an Israeli jail, was a surprise. For several months, there had been debate in Israel about setting him free as a goodwill gesture. But it had ended abruptly when Fatah terrorists made the mistake of capturing some Israeli soldiers and demanding his release. All talks of release had died away.

"Do you see the point I was making?" Mohite asked again. "From Egypt we have Atef Aboul Gheit, a retired diplomat. Jordan is sending Ghafar al-Issa, an advisor to their ministry of Foreign Affairs. Ghada al-Utri, another senior diplomat, is representing Syria, and from Saudi Arabia we have his Royal Highness Prince Ghanim Abdul Rahman al-Saud."

"And from America we have Senator George Polk," Ravinder added, flipping the page.

"Isn't he known as a loner and prone to marching to his own drumbeat?"

"The very man," Ravinder replied, double-checking the senator's profile. "No one can be sure what his stance is, though odds are that he'd be biased against the Israelis."

"Surprising. Very surprising." Mohite made a clicking sound with his tongue. "Right. And from Britain it's MP Sir Geoffrey Tang, and lastly we have the Norwegian, Sigurd Gaarder."

"Like Polk, Tang too is a wild card, though he's more likely to be sitting in the middle. As for Gaarder . . . he was one of the original Oslo negotiators and could bring in invaluable expertise."

"Well, yes, but did you notice this?" Mohite grinned. "Each of the delegates has a name starting with *G* . . . either the first name or the family name." He looked up. "Even both of us." The grin broadened. "We should code name this the G-string Summit."

Ravinder could not help smiling. He had to admit; this was a good one . . . even for Mohite . . . *especially* from Mohite.

"Nice, Govind! Now, let's work on keeping that damn G-string intact. We've got a lot to protect and not much to do it with. Every damn terror group in the world must be panting to take a shot at us."

"True." Mohite's face turned grave. "Like you said, bringing peace to the Promised Land will take away a major raison d'être for the jihad." He may be an ass-licking busybody, Ravinder thought, but he was no fool.

The two-car mini-convoy slowed as they turned onto the road leading to the MSO Building, which housed Delhi Police HQ. The traffic was awful, and despite the siren, they were barely crawling.

That was when Ravinder saw the man. Medium height. Clean-shaven. Mid-twenties. Perhaps it was the purposeful manner of his approaching Mohite's car that caught Ravinder's attention. Or perhaps . . . *Yes, that's it, why is he wearing such a bulky overcoat? It's not that cold.*

An alarm clamored in Ravinder's head. Tersely ordering his driver to stop, he pulled out his 9mm Browning. Leaping out, Ravinder headed straight for the man. Mohite and the driver were gazing at him, perplexed.

The man was now fifteen feet away. Perhaps his instincts too were working overtime or he had spotted the blur of movement. He swiveled and saw Ravinder rushing toward him. For a nano-second, he froze, then threw open his overcoat and began to reach inside.

Ravinder saw the coat fly open; saw the bomb strapped around the man's waist. Instantly his right hand rose up, but mindful of the crowd, he took aim and fired. Just once. It was enough.

The man came to an abrupt halt, as though he'd run into a brick wall. For a second he was upright, and then flung backward, his head a mass of blood.

Ravinder had gone for the headshot. He could not have let the man detonate the bomb; the casualties on the crowded road would have been horrendous.

It was over as swiftly as it had begun.

It took but an hour to sort out.

"He was Mir Kasab, from the Jaish-e-Mohammed. A known terrorist . . . we have a thick file on him. Came in from POK last week," Mohite reported to Ravinder. "We found a map of this area in his pocket and the numbers of three cars: yours, Ashish's, and mine. Apparently, he'd been tasked to take out senior ATTF cops."

"Looks like the terrorists want us out of the picture at this juncture."

"I guess so." Mohite's tone was grim; he was still sweating. Ravinder could see that he had been badly shaken. He himself wasn't feeling so bright either.

"Don't think too much about it, Govind. It could well have been my car. Or Ashish's . . . He would have gone for whoever he reached first." There was a silence. A shitty feeling. "The luck of the draw, my friend. . . . Who knows when one's time is up." Ravinder had to lift the mood, Mohite's and his own. "Look at the bright side; we got the bugger before he got us."

But the words had little effect. On either of them. Both knew that the next time the tides might well favor the other side.

"There is more, sir. He was not alone," Mohite almost stammered. "He was part of a cell of three men."

"Who are the other two? Find any clues on him?"

"Yes, most probably Javed Khan—we already have a file on him—and an unknown called Aslam. They came from POK together. Most likely the other two are out there"—Mohite stared out the window—"somewhere in Delhi."

"We have to find them." Ravinder controlled a tremor.

"I have already issued an APB and also alerted the int agencies."

"We'd better find them . . . before they find us." Ravinder thought for a moment. "Have the guards doubled. At the office and all three residences."

Mohite ran to the phone.

Ravinder knew there was nothing more they could do. Not

right now. "Now let's focus." He knew that work was the best distraction. "We have a summit to secure, Govind. The PM's office is waiting for our security plans."

Had it not been for their car's air-conditioning, the seven-hour drive to Vavuniya would have been miserable. The dust from the potholed road added to their misery. Though tougher, Mark was not handling the heat and dust well. He took every opportunity to sleep it off. Ten minutes into the drive, and he was sprawled against the car door, tucked away in dreamland, snoring lightly. Every so often, Ruby saw him smile; obviously having pleasant dreams.

Oh well . . . at least someone is. A mirthless smile creased her face. He was looking good, if a trifle uncomfortable with his head knocking against the window every time they hit a bump. *Pity he is gay! All the good ones . . . either gay or married.* Ruby sighed; she could do with some comforting. It had been a while since she had enjoyed being held . . . not since Chance had gone. Wondering where he was right now, Ruby felt a tug. She missed him.

For a moment she dwelled on the contrast between Chance and Mark; it was huge. Physically they had a lot in common; both tall, well built, and fair, with similar close-cropped hair. But that's where it ended. Chance was so much more sensitive and caring . . . and his sense of humor . . . Ruby smiled. Whereas Mark was not cerebral, liked to plunge into action without much thought. *Well, that is what I need right now . . . someone who will simply follow orders.*

Ruby couldn't sleep; she felt hyped up, as though pumped with pure oxygen. She sat on the edge of her seat, watching the countryside fleeing by.

Barring small, occasional green patches of cultivation, she saw only bleakness. The color brown predominated. Like the narrow potholed road, the bleakness got worse the farther north they moved from Colombo. So did the presence of soldiers and small army camps surrounded with barbed wire, grim reminders of the recently ended insurgency.

The driver stepped on the gas now, going as fast as the road would allow. Enjoying the speed. Ruby was about to try to catch some shut-eye when they hit another checkpoint. A long line of vehicles waited to cross it. The soldiers were in no hurry; they searched each vehicle thoroughly, with the trucks, of which there were several, taking a lot of time.

Sleep forgotten, Ruby sat back, exasperated, watching the vehicles inch forward. Her mind wandered away, to Palestine, to another such checkpoint.

"That day too the line had been long." Rehana's oft-told story echoed in her memory. Her voice, clear as a bell; as though it were she, and not Mark, sitting beside Ruby in the car.

The Israel Defense Forces checkpoint at Huwwara, one of the main "Inner Checkpoints" of the West Bank, lay deep within Palestinian territory, just south of Nablus, at the junction of Routes 57 and 557, between the settlements of Bracha and Itamar, standing between Nablus and the satellite communities that depend on it.

"About six thousand people pass through Huwwara every day," Rehana narrated, "some to work, go to hospital, visit relatives, or to do their shopping."

Like all such checkpoints, passing through Huwwara involved a meticulous process. It was not uncommon to take up to two hours to get through. And the rules were never predictable, adding further to the confusion and delay.

Men line up in a closed waiting area, while women and children go through a separate pathway. The area for men was an open shed with a corrugated roof. Waist-high walls demarcate the area into aisles. The roof trapped the sweltering heat.

"*Wuakef!*" (Stop!) "*Jubil aweah!*" (Show me your identification papers!)

One by one, the men trudged up to the barred window and

handed over their papers. They lifted their shirts and rolled up trouser legs to confirm no weapons or bombs. The women and children were also frisked. And arrays of scanners were also at work.

The procedure for cars was more tedious, with all passengers getting out and standing clear while a search was carried out using undercarriage mirrors, detectors, and sniffer dogs.

Bilal, Rehana's brother, thumped the steering wheel, his frustration evident. Half an hour had passed, and only two cars had been cleared—with three more still ahead of them. Bilal, the eldest and usually the calmest of the three siblings, was getting jumpy; perhaps his diabetes was acting up. In their hurry to rush their mother, Salima, to hospital he had not eaten. Eventually, driven by his anxiety, he got out and went to speak to the IDF soldiers.

"You! *Wuakef!* Stop right there!" The Galil AR multipurpose rifle in the hands of the soldier yelling came up. "Where do you think you're going?"

"Soldier, my mother is ill," Bilal replied.

"I don't fucking care." The beardless twenty-year-old yelled, "Get back to your car and wait your turn. *Now!*" His rifle pointed straight at Bilal, rock-steady, confirming his willingness to use it. "Don't come any closer." He pointed at the security line painted on the road, meant to keep the soldiers safe from suicide bombers.

The neatly painted BORN TO KILL shining whitely across the front of his helmet and his badly accented Arabic added to the menace.

Cursing under his breath, Bilal returned. Another fifteen minutes slithered by; only one more car got cleared. Then another bout of coughing shook Salima. More blood sprayed out; by now the sheet covering her was splattered with red dots.

"Mother had been terribly ill when she woke up that morning and had started coughing blood. She was so bad that your uncles Bilal and Yusuf immediately decided to rush her to hospital. I too went with them." Rehana began to cry as she told the story to

Ruby. "By now, mother was barely conscious. The fever had sky-rocketed. I could feel her body burning."

Sitting in the front passenger seat, the more hotheaded Yusuf looked explosive, but also on the verge of tears.

Bilal could not take it anymore. His breath was short, and his hands had begun to shake as the level of glucose in his body plummeted and hypoglycemia began to take hold. That, coupled with his mother's increasing distress, shattered his control. He jumped out of the car again.

"What the fuck is wrong with you?" BORN TO KILL screamed. "Get back inside your car."

"Come on, soldier," Bilal yelled back. "Look! She is losing so much blood. Let us through."

"Yeah right!" The anger in BORN TO KILL's voice matched his raised weapon. "Get back to your car and wait for your turn."

"Please, soldier!" Bilal was begging.

It had no effect on BORN TO KILL. "Back in line."

"She seems to be really sick." A younger soldier standing be-side BORN TO KILL whispered. He had peered inside the car while the heated exchange was taking place. "Why don't we let them through first?"

"You shut your fucking mouth, wimp." BORN TO KILL hissed, "You don't know these bastards. That is exactly what a pregnant woman said to my father. They were about to let her through when she blew herself up . . . taking my father and four others with her."

The recruit, Ean Gellner, subsided. This was only his fifth week in uniform and his first day on checkpoint duty.

The other soldiers snickered.

Their words meant nothing to Bilal, since he did not under-stand Hebrew, but those snickers jump-started him. Hot anger enveloped him. Shaking an angry fist, he leaped forward.

"Stay back!" BORN TO KILL's strident yell fell on deaf ears. "Stand back, you moron!" Another yell went unheeded. "Do *not* cross the line!"

Tension suddenly escalated.

To Yusuf and Rehana, watching from the car, everything speeded up and slowed down; too fast for them to do anything yet slow enough to see every nuance.

As Bilal crossed the line, the rifle in BORN TO KILL's hands emitted a sharp flat report. Then, a second later, another shot exploded out.

The gunshots echoed bleakly in the silence. Jews and Arabs alike, not one could believe shots had been fired. The disbelief was shattered by Bilal's howl of pain. The first bullet gutted him. He was falling when the second hit him. He swayed, and then slumped to the ground. A shocked Yusuf jumped out and rushed to his brother's side.

Yusuf's move broke the frozen tableau; people scattered frantically, racing to get out of the line of fire.

BORN TO KILL stood, still as a statue, with his rifle pointed at Bilal, a confused expression frozen on his face. Like the others, even he was shocked.

Ean Gellner, the recruit, looked as though he was about to burst into tears.

Life paused, breathless.

"What the hell have you done?" a soldier on BORN TO KILL's right yelled, dismay plastered on his face.

"What could I do? Didn't you see he was rushing me?" There was a sick smile on his face.

At that moment Yusuf, kneeling beside his dying brother, looked up. He saw BORN TO KILL's smile. He did not see the fear that went with it. To him it looked as though the murderous bastard were smirking. An animal-like howl of rage burst out. Yusuf leaped up and ran toward BORN TO KILL, needing to wipe that ghastly smile off his face. From the rear of the car, Rehana saw Yusuf lunge forward. She screamed, a long futile scream; Yusuf had already broken past the line.

BORN TO KILL saw him. His finger was still on the trigger. The finger tightened as his mind emitted a silent scream of alarm. In an instant, almost half the thirty-five-round magazine had emptied itself.

Two of the bullets slammed into Yusuf's right shoulder, spinning him around and dropping him. One of the other bullets shattered the windscreen of their car and found his mother's jaw. It bored into Salima's face, replacing the already quivering, bloodstained lips with a red, gaping hole. Three bullets found two more victims in the fleeing crowd. The others slammed harmlessly in the cars and the milling dust.

"There was so much blood . . . all around me. . . . I can feel it . . . even now. . . ." Remembering those moments, Rehana shuddered. Her fingers were making an involuntary rubbing motion, as though trying to wipe the blood clean. "No outsider can ever understand why our youngsters are so ready to seek martyrdom. Ruby, they don't understand that we have no choice. We either die in a blaze of glory or slowly . . . inch by inch . . . one day at a time . . . but we die . . . and continue to die . . ." Her voice trailed away. "And still nothing changes." Rehana's cheeks were wet with tears, her voice barely audible. "Nothing changes . . . nothing . . . Ruby, *we* have to make it change. . . . We *have* to do something. . . ."

Harsh popping sounds shattered Ruby's bloody march down memory lane. Her head hit the window with a crack, jolting her awake. The heavy tires of the Nissan van ground over loose gravel. Pebbles flew out with sharp, flat reports as the driver brought the vehicle to a halt. Except for puffs of dust swirling around, everything was still and silent.

Ruby looked around befuddled, her mind still trapped in her mother's violent memories. It took a moment for the red and yellow signboard across the building to register.

DIYA DAHARA RESTAURANT.

Its paint had seen better days.

"You must try the food here." The driver had twisted to face them. "This place is famous."

"Why don't you help us with the menu?" Mark took the reluctant Sri Lankan by his arm and led him to a table below a fan.

"And tell them to go easy on the spices," Ruby added.

He was plainly uncomfortable, but he ordered a copious meal.

The service was efficient, but not surprising, since there were just a handful of customers. They had just cooled off with a chilled glass of King Coconut when the waiter carted in an array of steaming dishes.

"You have ordered food for the whole restaurant?" Ruby smiled as dish after dish arrived, soon covering the entire table.

"I did not want you to go hungry." The driver smiled, hungrily eyeing the food; making it clear that he certainly wouldn't. For him, this had to be a great luxury.

The aroma of yellow rice flavored with spices wafted out as the white-liveried waiter removed the lid from the first platter. Next he displayed fried chicken, crab curry in coconut gravy, deviled cuttlefish, white cashew curry, and coconut sambol. Their driver must have briefed the waiter to go easy on the spices, since Ruby was able to relish every dish, without breaking into hiccups. The wattalappan dessert she thought was to die for.

Mark, though he cast several covetous glances at the bottles of Three Coins beer chilling in the cooler near the cash counter, made no move to order one. He knew Ruby seriously enforced the no-drinking-on-the-job rule.

The most amazing aspect of the meal was the bill. Ruby couldn't believe it was just a tad more than what they would have paid for a sandwich back home.

"So why are we here again?" Mark asked when the driver went off to tend to the vehicle. "I thought you said this assignment was in India."

"It is, but we first need to meet a man and pick up some equipment."

"Well, okay."

"We also need to recon our extraction route. In case we need to leave India by less . . . umm . . . conventional means."

Mark nodded, satisfied. That he understood. Physical recon of an escape route was smart. He liked that Ruby was thinking through to the end. Her recent, long silences had made him uneasy.

"Tell me about the team I asked you to put together, Mark. . . . Who are the three guys you picked?"

"Solid, reliable hitters . . . just like you wanted. Experienced blokes who don't ask too many questions. They take orders and have no qualms in executing them."

"Perfect."

"Yeah. Not the fancy, brainy, officer types." He could never resist a dig at authority.

Ruby laughed. "Any of them have criminal records?"

"Nope."

"Perfect. Can't have any flags coming up when they cross borders."

"Don't worry about it." He waved airily, but Ruby could tell something was bothering him. Mark brought it up before she could ask. "Say, boss, any chance that they may not be coming back at all?"

Ruby shrugged. "Depends on them . . . how things pan out . . . and how they handle them."

"Fair enough." He cleared his throat. "I see what you mean." Another pause. "Well, the first two are a couple of Aussies, Gary Boucher and Shaun Ontong currently operating in South Africa, and the third, Rafael Gerber, is from Germany. All three are clean and perfect for the job."

"Did they have any questions?"

"Not the Aussies, but the German did . . . he is a bit anal. Wanted to know who he'd be working with, so I had to give him a brief about the Aussies. He was happy when he learned they're operating in Africa. He's been there several years and thinks it's the best training ground."

"Nothing about me, I hope?"

"Not a peep about you." Mark smiled reassuringly. "In any case, his primary concern had been only one."

"Which is?"

"*Wie was das Geld ist?*" (What is the money like?)

"*Das Geld ist gut,*" Ruby replied firmly. Knowing what she had told Mark to offer them, she knew the money was more than good.

"Yeah." Mark grinned. "That's exacty what I told him. Half payable on reaching Delhi and the rest when the job's done. He had no further questions."

"Hmmm . . . *hoert sich gut an.*" (That sounds good.) They both laughed. "Did you set up the communication protocol with them?"

"I did. They are packed and ready. One text message and they'll move to Delhi."

"Perfect."

Twenty minutes later, they were off again. The A9 highway seemed to be getting even worse. As did the condition of the buildings and houses they passed.

Ravinder and Mohite had finished hammering out the details of the security arrangements for the peace summit and shot it off to Thakur when Gyan, Ravinder's office runner, entered.

He'd been with Ravinder for several years. Though less than brilliant, Gyan was rock-solid and totally devoted to Ravinder. The bond between them had grown ever since Ravinder, learning about Gyan's cancer-stricken seven-year-old son, had ensured that Gyan was always posted where the best possible medical facilities were available and had ensured that Gyan received aid from police welfare funds to care for his son.

"There is a visitor for you, sir." Gyan's gentle tone was a nice contrast to his massive size. A moment later a tall, well-built man with close-cropped blond hair and bright, blue gray eyes walked in.

"Mr. Gill?" Dressed in a smart gray business suit, he appeared slightly ill at ease. "I am Chance . . . Chance Spillman. I'm with the agency." His British accent made it abundantly clear which agency.

"Ah! Mr. Spillman." Stepping forward, Ravinder extended his hand. "The minister told us to expect you. How are you?"

"Very well, thank you, sir. It is a pleasure to meet you." After withdrawing a letter, Chance held it out. "Our director asked me to convey his regards."

Ravinder took the letter. "And how is my friend Edward?"

"He is well, sir." Chance understood that Ravinder was referring to Sir Edward Kingsley, Director of MI6.

"Did he mention that we had been at college together in London?"

"I don't believe he did, sir." Chance smiled—it was an easy, pleasant smile. "Not that I meet him very often." Another easy grin. "I am still at the lower end of the food chain."

Ravinder felt himself warming toward the man. "Right." Ravinder laughed. Then turning to Mohite, who had a frown plastered on his face. "This is DGP Govind Mohite, my deputy." The two men shook hands warily. The vibes between them were not good. Hostility emanated from Mohite. Ravinder moved to smooth things out. "When did you get in, Mr. Spillman?"

"Just this morning, sir." Then he added. "Chance is good enough for me."

"Chance it is." Ravinder acknowledged. "An unusual name if you don't mind my saying so."

"Well, that was my dad for you." Chance smiled. From the way his eyes flicked away, upward and to the right, Ravinder could tell that his mind had skipped into the past. "He always believed that everything that happened was purely a matter of chance . . . just that." Pause. "I like it."

"The thought or the name?"

"Both." Chance smiled back.

"It is unique." Ravinder decided that it was not polite to leave it there and added. "It is very nice too."

Chance's grin broadened.

A longer pause ensued. Ravinder continued before it became awkward. "I want you to know, Chance, that we really appreciate your government sending you down to help us."

Chance picked up the cue and responded. "I would like to assure you that I will do my best to make things work in whichever way you want them to. We understand this is your turf and—"

"I am glad you understand that, Mr. Spillman." Mohite made no effort to keep his tone polite. "India has been fighting terrorism for over thirty years, and we don't need anyone to tell us how to do things around here."

Ravinder groaned inwardly, but the damage was done.

Luckily, at that moment there was another knock and Gyan entered. He had an attractive, fair, auburn-haired Caucasian woman in tow, medium height, in her late twenties or early thirties, with curves in all the right places. Like Chance, she too was dressed in a gray business suit. Despite her physical attributes and chiseled facial features, everything about her screamed secret agent; only the earpiece and dark glasses were missing. Her nasal twang defined her nationality.

"I am Special Agent Jennifer Poetzcsh." She shook hands with the three men, a strong handshake, the kind women adopt when working in a male-dominant field.

Ravinder noticed the appraising look that she gave Chance. When they shook, her gaze lingered on his wedding finger, noting the absence of a ring. It was obvious she found him attractive. Chance also seemed taken by her. Then she too presented her CIA credentials to Ravinder.

With pleasantries behind them, Ravinder got busy. "As you both know, we have just starting preparing for this summit, so may I suggest you two spend a couple of days getting a feel for Delhi while we complete the arrangements."

"Very well, sir." Chance nodded. "If there is anything we can do in the interim, please call us."

"But of course, Chance, thank you." Ravinder was beginning to like the professionalism of the young MI6 man. "Where are you two staying?"

Both named different hotels.

"Then may I suggest that both of you shift to the Ashoka, since that is the venue for the summit and you can get familiar with it. Govind will put in a word with the hotel. They will give you rooms on the seventh floor, where we all will be staying." He noted their quizzical expressions and added. "We are sealing off the top two floors for the summit, the seventh for security and admin and the eighth for the delegates. You two will have adjacent rooms on the seventh floor."

"Excellent, sir. I will shift tomorrow."

"Me too." Jennifer nodded. She shot another glance at Chance, clearly pleased to be staying closer to him.

"Lastly, may I also request you to contact your agencies and get us whatever intelligence they have . . . anything that may affect the summit would be much appreciated."

"Well," Jennifer chipped in, "we do have indications that a terror strike on Delhi may well be under way, but still no way of knowing if the target is the Commonwealth Games or the peace summit."

Everyone absorbed that.

"Anything specific?" Ravinder asked when he realized she was not going to continue. "What is the source?"

"It's classified," Jennifer countered, displaying none of the subtlety he thought Americans were famous for. "Just that we have electronic intelligence to believe that mercenaries, probably from England, appear to have been hired by the Lashkar-e-Taiba. I'll let you know as soon as we have anything more."

Her words and how they were delivered created tension in the room. Mohite's face displayed increased hostility. Even Chance looked uncomfortable. Ravinder masked his irritation; though he had half a mind to remind her that with Pakistan as a neighbor, terror strikes on Indian cities were something they expected almost every day.

Minutes later the meeting broke up. Not on a great note.

The A9 highway from Colombo to Vavuniya got worse and worse. Ruby saw little cultivation on either side of the road.

Brown stubble predominated. Barring an odd civilian vehicle and more frequent army trucks, there was little traffic.

Lounging in the rear sear, Mark had again dozed off. Though tired, Ruby was wide awake, her mind boiling with thoughts that would not let her sleep.

The sight of soldiers and their surroundings felt strangely familiar to Ruby. Then she knew why. The bleakness was so similar to what she had recently encountered in the Congo.

Again her mind flew back . . . to the last time Mark and she had operated together. That day too, they had been in a similar vehicle.

Ruby folded the newspaper she'd been speed-reading and let it fall to the floor of the five-door, eight-seat Toyota Alphard. The engine was running so the air conditioner could beat back some of the stifling Congo heat. She threw a glance at the house across the street before checking her watch again. Only an hour had bled away. It felt like longer. Tired of sitting still, Ruby shifted, trying to make herself more comfortable.

"The wait is always a bitch," Mark, sitting beside her, murmured; as usual he didn't miss a thing.

"It is these bloody vests," Ruby muttered, trying to wipe away the sweat that was making it stick to her skin.

"Yeah! But I'd rather be hot than not have these babies when there's lead flying around."

Ruby was about to reply when her Motorola, a frequency-hopping piece of work, crackled to life.

"They are coming out now." Mission Control had a clipped and calm voice. It was very upper crust, very British.

The words unleashed a jolt of adrenaline in Ruby. Her spine straightened. Her brain craved more oxygen. Hands grabbed up her weapon.

Like Mark, she was carrying a 5.56×45mm NATO, thirty-round Heckler & Koch G36K. She loved its heft; a lightweight and low-maintenance weapon, it was constructed almost entirely of tough carbon-fiber-reinforced polymer. Its barrels had been exchanged to give it a carbine profile, making it more useful for close-quarters use, where long-range accuracy was not a requisite. The fight ahead was likely to be up close and personal. And bloody.

"Nitpickers?" Mission Control again, asking and alerting them simultaneously. The code word showed MC's kinky sense of humor.

"Ready to nitpick." Chance Spillman's voice carried the undercurrent of a man readying for action. Despite its tautness, it ignited a storm of feelings in Ruby. Desire. Regret. Confusion. The nagging feeling of something left unfinished, unresolved.

How in hell did Chance manage to slip past the guard and get to me . . . to the real person behind the façade I maintain? Ruby had always worked to ensure no one ever got under her skin. She had always kept her heart secure, merely allowing the body to fulfill its needs with casual, meaningless flings. *Despite that, Chance managed to touch my heart. Damn! It does not matter. He did . . . now I have to deal with it . . . the why is no longer relevant . . . What do I do now? I want him back in my life, but . . .*

"He is the enemy, Ruby." Her mother's voice tugged at her. Rehana had been miffed when Ruby told her she was moving in with Chance. "You are forgetting your purpose. He will never understand or accept what our people have suffered."

"But I love him, Mom."

"More than your people? More than our cause? You are ready to throw everything away . . . everything that we suffered to ensure you are trained and ready when the time comes for you to act."

Unsure, conflicted, Ruby had faltered. Love, a deep caring and wanting she had never experienced before, pulled her to Chance. Love for her mother and her cause pulled her away from him. It had torn her apart. Not allowing her to commit and yet trying to cling to him.

She knew she needed to sit down and talk with Chance. Something they had not been good at doing even when living together.

So many unsaid, unfinished things still hanging between them. Chance had to be aware of them too. Yet, of late, it was he who was avoiding talking, something that had been her choice earlier.

What goes around comes around. The thought discomfited her. Ruby pushed it away. *Wandering minds get people killed.* Too many people had drilled that into her. She focused on the mission and checked the deployment again.

Chance was one of the five MI6 agents here, the one controlling the four snipers ranged around the house. She thought it was a clever deployment.

Ruby rewarded herself with a proud grin; she was the designated Operational Commander for this mission, and it had been her plan.

The target house was a sad-looking, dilapidated bungalow on the outskirts of Kinshasa, the capital of Congo, known until 1997 as Zaire; the third-largest country in Africa by area and the fourth most populous. Torn apart by warfare since its inception, the vast land had made no progress, and was one of the poorest countries in the world. Estimates were that even today about 1,250 people died daily due to war and related causes, like hunger and malnutrition.

In better times, the bungalow, with its red-tiled roof, would have housed some high-ranking Belgian official. However, most of the tiles had fallen or broken, leaving ugly gaps, like missing teeth. Now it was occupied by a handful of Lord's Resistance Army terrorists . . . kidnappers, actually.

Ruby knew the LRA, despite its grand-sounding name, was a small group of about one hundred men, women, and adolescents, who usually operated in Congo's northeastern province of Orientale. The group had come to the attention of MI6 because it had managed to lay hands on the British ambassador and his wife, and were now holding the couple hostage for a large ransom and for freedom for their thuggish colleagues languishing in Congo jails. The kidnap had been pure luck (for the LRA) and sublime stupidity (by the ambassador, who had disregarded basic security).

And now we're in this hellhole to bail out the nerd and his wife.

Ruby's fingers instinctively checked her weapon's load and confirmed it was set on single-shot fire mode, since the semiauto- or auto-fire mode would not bode well for the health of the kidnap victims. Her feet began to flex inside her black, rubber-soled, lace-ups, getting ready to fly toward the target. Her fingers checked the weapon's magazine again; the only visible sign of her insecurity.

Up ahead, the door with peeling paint opened and two men tentatively emerged. Both young; the one in front barely out of his teens. Both were toting AK-47 automatics; not surprising. Cheap and easily available, it was the weapon of choice of Terror Central. They halted on the porch, surveying the area outside.

The porch ran right around the house. Beyond it was the so-called garden, mostly overgrown grass. The garden ended in a six-foot-high wall, which like the rest of the bungalow was also in disrepair. Beyond it ran the road on which Ruby and her team were deployed. The road was bereft of traffic. In the distance, half a klick away, a handful of children were playing, and occasional shouts of laughter carried with the wind. In closed, air-conditioned cars, none of the agents or paramilitaries heard them. The two terrorists must have heard them, since the children held their attention for a moment before they shifted their attention elsewhere.

"Bloody amateurs!" Mark snickered, the G36K almost lost in his huge hands, noting that the scouts had their rifles slung on their shoulders and not carried in the half-port position, so they could swing into action instantly, should the need arise. And the need was going to arise. Soon.

Ruby nodded agreement; no place for amateurs.

The two kidnappers did not venture out to the road, something any scout worth his salt would have done. Even if they had, unlikely they would have spotted the two concealed cars, one on either side of the road. The vehicles on the other three sides of the bungalow were also safely tucked away.

It was several minutes before the two scouts were satisfied. Then the younger one went back inside; again with that same casual gait. Another minute ticked away before he emerged again. Following were two more gunmen, also barely out of their teens, but this pair held their rifles in battle positions and appeared more alert.

They will die first. She was certain that Chance would ensure that; it was the expedient thing to do.

Following this pair came a short, portly Caucasian man, standing out whitely among the blacks. He had his arm around an equally short but slightly built Caucasian woman. Judging by her halting gait and how the man supported her, she seemed to be sick. *Or wounded.* Ruby noted.

"That's our man," Ruby breathed as she recognized the ambassador. No one replied. Each was now readying for action. They knew the signal would be coming any second. Nerves drew tauter. Breathing began to even out, as precombat jitters settled down.

Eight more gunmen emerged. Gun women too. This latter lot arrayed themselves around the hostages and moved toward the yellow minibus parked outside the gate. A handful seemed alert, but none were all that careful. Sure, no one would have known where they were if it had not been for one of their lot who had turned Judas for the silver thrown at him by MI6. Of course, it had been a rather big bag. Ruby wondered which, if any, of them it was.

Will he live to enjoy the loot?

"Now!" Ruby half whispered as they stopped near the minibus, trying to second-guess Mission Control, who was located with the sniper facing the main door and would have a bird's-eye view of the bungalow. Once they got into the vehicle, the job would become much more difficult.

"Sundown!"

She was right.

The code word cracked out of the radio. The Controller's voice retained its British cool, stiff upper lip.

A scant second later, the sharp crackle of the team's sniper rifles rang out. The four kidnappers closest to the hostages fell; the two extra-alert ones among them.

Nitpicking had begun.

Four down. Eight to go.

That was the last thought in Ruby's head as she levered open the door and flew out, her weapon in her left hand—which was not her master hand, but that did not bother her, she had long ago trained herself to marksman standards with both hands, just one more of the prices she'd had to pay for being a woman in a man's job.

She had barely exited when a battered maroon van turned the corner and began to nose its way down the potholed road.

At the same time, three women on foot came around the bend to the left; they hit the road just meters away from the terror cluster.

Damn! Ruby cursed. Collateral damage would not go down well on her record.

She was on her third stride when the first shot left her weapon. Though almost flying, her shot did not miss. Beside her, Mark's weapon spit lead a millisecond later. Another kidnapper fell.

The team's sniper rifles crashed out again. More terrorists fell. The odds were improving. Every inbound agent was firing as fast as they could.

The terrorists still standing had turned to face their attackers and their guns thundered too. So none of their bullets were aimed at the hostages.

Reacting smartly, the ambassador had dropped to the ground, dragging his wife down with him.

The terrorists' lack of training was evident; they were firing blindly before they had even registered their targets.

But there was nothing amateurish about the bullets that zipped past her. However, with hyped-up nerves and the kill-or-be-killed instinct overruling everything, Ruby and her team raced in. No other options; they had to kill before they were killed.

The maroon van, seeing all hell break loose ahead, screeched to a halt and began reversing as fast as the driver could make it go. The three women huddled in a screaming cluster on the dirt. One stopped screaming as a passing bullet found her. The screams of the other two grew louder, but were now no more than a part of the background, as were the gunfire and screams of the dying.

By time Ruby fired her third shot, all twelve terrorists were down. Two, a thirty-something man and one of the younger women, were writhing on the ground, moaning. She shot both of them, putting one bullet through each head as she weaved past to the ambassador.

He was huddled in the dust, his arms wrapped around his wife. She was screaming, an ululating, keening sound that set Ruby's teeth on edge. Controlling the urge to slap her into silence, Ruby reached down to grab him. She did not see the beardless teenager, with blood staining his chest, fallen beside the ambassador, reach for the pistol in his waistband. She became aware of him only when Mark's weapon crackled to life behind her and he died with a sharp, short scream.

Ruby froze.

Damn! That was close.

She cursed herself before throwing a grateful look at Mark. He gave a fleeting half salute as he continued checking the others for signs of life. Another must have been showing some, since Mark's weapon spit again, the shot echoing away in the now silent surroundings.

Ruby hoisted up the ambassador; his wife followed in tow as he clutched her. They hustled toward the Toyota, which had shot forward as soon as the last shot faded away.

The two women passersby huddled down on the road had stopped screaming. Shell-shocked. The playing children had faded away. The maroon van was gone. Barring the thrumming of Toyota engines, the silence was complete. And it felt deafening.

Just eighty-seven seconds had elapsed, and twelve kidnappers had forfeited their lives.

Score one for the home team, Ruby thought triumphantly as she did a quick visual check and saw that her team was intact, so lucky to have come out unscathed; losing someone always hurt. Nor did it look good on the Operational Commander's scorecard. That was something that Ruby, keenly aware of her double life, was always concerned about. Like Caesar's wife, she always wanted to be above reproach.

Seconds later, the Toyota was racing away with its twin prize safely seat-belted inside. The ambassador's wife had stopped screaming and gone into the never-never land of shock. Ruby did not care a rat's ass about that. She only had to get them back alive. Cuckoo or sane, didn't count.

The Toyota raced past where the children had been playing. Ruby spotted one of them staring openmouthed from around the corner of a hut; he would have stories to tell for a long time.

Or maybe not. This was Congo; he may have seen worse.

They had gone half a mile when the other five vehicles caught up. The convoy pelted down the narrow, potholed road.

"We have them." Ruby heard the driver bark into the radio as she replaced the half-empty magazine of her weapon and began to reload. Beside her Mark was doing the same.

"Jolly good show. Right behind you," Mission Control intoned, his Brit stoicism intact. "Extractors inbound."

Minutes later, the vehicles pulled off the road and ground to a dust-churning halt in a flat, open field. The vehicles drew up in a wide circle; like wagons readying to meet an Apache attack. Kevlar-clad agents spilled out and took positions behind their vehicles, all facing outward. Not that they expected trouble, but security drills were what kept them alive.

The dust had yet to settle when three choppers swept in. Two of them headed straight into the secured clearing while the third, its guns ready, started circling overhead in a wide loop to ensure nothing on the ground interfered with the extraction. And, though the agents could not see them, high up in the sky, a sortie of RAF fighters ran a protective Combat Air Patrol, just in case air cover or heavier fire support was required.

The ambassador and his wife were hustled into the first chopper with Ruby's team. She saw Chance and his sniper team jump into the next one as hers lifted off.

Clawing upward, the birds raced away.

Mission Complete!

There were smiles all around.

Ruby leaned back and let the stress drain away. Momentarily, the faces of the downed terrorists she had shot flipped into her mind. She shrugged.

The fuckers should have realized what they'd signed up for. She shrugged again. *They are wrong. I am right. Well . . . if not right, at least on the good team. Isn't that reason enough for me to pull the trigger? Isn't it!* The thought troubled her only briefly. *Of course it is. That is all there is to it . . . nothing to fret about.*

Closing her eyes, she shut out the clamoring roar of the rotors.

As the Nissan van halted again, Ruby startled back to the reality of Sri Lanka.

The man whom Ruby and Mark had traveled halfway across the world to meet was waiting when they pulled to a stop outside a seedy hotel in Vavuniya. He was one of the contacts passed on to her by Pasha; she had called him before leaving London.

Barely five feet, the dark-skinned Chanderan was roly-poly, and like most men Ruby had seen on the streets, he wore a blue-and-white-checked cotton lungi and a white cotton half-sleeves shirt, with its buttons undone almost to the midriff. He led them proudly to the reception desk, a tiny wooden table adorned by a large, thumb-worn guest register and a pink flower vase with plastic flowers sticking out from it. Like the table, both the flowers and the vase had seen better days.

"It is all taken care of." He announced grandly. Though afflicted by the typical islander accent, his English was okay. "I will wait while you freshen up."

"No worries." Ruby was in no mood to tarry. "Come on up to the room with us." She threw a glance at Mark, making it clear that he was to stick with her.

The first-floor room Chanderan led them to was about the size of two prison cells. It had a queen-size bed in the center, a minuscule wooden table near the window, which overlooked the noisy street outside, and had a chair pulled up against it. The bed was covered with a flowery, cotton bedspread. A stale smell hung in the air, making it obvious that the hirers of these rooms usually took them by the hour, and it had been a while since the room had seen any housekeeping services. With the three of them in it, the room felt claustrophobic. Mark threw an amused look around. No air conditioner. Just an ancient-looking fan slowly churning overhead. Ruby thanked her stars that they were staying just the one night. She waited till Mark closed the door. "Our mutual friend said you could be relied on to get us what we need."

"He is most kind. I will try my best." She saw nothing about this Chanderan that convinced her he had been the primary weapons supplier to the Liberation Tigers of Tamil Eelam, the terrorist group that had held the island captive for two decades. Of course, with the group now destroyed, Chanderan's business had nosedived. Ruby had been given these inputs by Uncle Yusuf when he called her from Dubai. The memory of what had since happened to him overwhelmed her; the ghastly manner in which he had been killed filling her with fury. She pushed it away.

This is not the time. I must focus. That will be revenge enough. His death will not go to waste.

She saw Mark watching her as she focused again on Chanderan.

Yes, he would be delighted to supply them with whatever they needed.

"This is what I need." Ruby handed over a short list to him. He scanned it, all at once mutating from bumbling hotel manager to seasoned arms supplier. Ruby could see why he had survived.

"The rocket launcher and the rockets to go with it are not a problem." Chanderan looked up. "The Glocks will take some time."

"How much time?"

"Two weeks at least. Maybe even more. I will need to check. New stuff stopped coming in a while ago . . . ever since . . ." He shrugged.

Damn! "I don't have that much time."

"Maybe I can give you something else in that category?"

"No." Ruby shook her head; the Glock 17 was crucial. With 17 percent of it high-tech plastic polymers, it was almost undetectable. If unassembled, it required an expert manning the detectors to ascertain its presence. And its seventeen-shot magazine capacity offered a huge advantage. She'd need that for the thirteen targets to be taken down. Not to mention the security men between her and the targets.

Chanderan was about to say something when Mark spoke. "Boss, can I have a word with you?"

Chanderan took the hint. "Why don't I organize some refreshments for you . . . while you two discuss things." He left.

"How badly do we need them Glocks?" Mark asked softly as soon as they were alone.

"We need them for sure."

"I know a guy, way bigger and more organized than him"— Mark nodded toward the door through which Chanderan had exited "—who can get them for us in India."

"You sure?"

"As sure as I can be. I have dealt with him." Mark shrugged. "In any case, what have we got to lose? This guy doesn't have them for sure. So even if the chap in India doesn't, we go for the next best option."

Ruby nodded. "Fair enough."

"We can even get all the rest of the stuff in India . . . why cart it all the way from here?"

"No, we need him to get us out," Ruby explained. "This guy is also our fallback escape route so this is money well spent, just in case things go badly in India."

"Makes sense."

When Chanderan returned, it took another twenty minutes to seal the deal. Ruby did not bother to negotiate on the price, even though she knew he was charging way too much for stuff that he'd never be able to sell for years.

"But, for that price," Ruby said flatly, making it clear that her demand was nonnegotiable, "you will need to deliver our materials to India and also organize a boat for us." Her guess had been right: Chanderan needed the business; he agreed without a murmur.

With everything going according to plan, Ruby should have slept well that night. But she didn't. With sleep came the recurring dream.

Once again that faceless, formless man appeared, urging her on, pleading to her. She was feeling nauseated when she jolted awake the sixth or seventh time. Gulping down a glass of tepid water, she reached inside and drew on her inner resources, the way they'd taught her during training. However, it was a while before her calm returned, bringing with it a renewed sense of purpose.

When she finally fell asleep, it was a deep, dreamless sleep.

By time Ravinder finished checking the games' village security and returned home, it was almost eleven. The road leading up to his house was in near darkness; the power supply had failed again.

Ravinder noted the two additional security guards, one patrolling along the boundary wall and the other backing up the gate guard. They seemed alert; Mohite had gotten this one right.

First thing tomorrow I must caution Simran and Jasmine to be extra careful till those Jaish terrorists have been captured, Ravinder reminded himself as he let himself into the almost dark house. He'd already called Simran earlier that evening and knew she wouldn't be waiting up for him.

DAY TWO

Ruby awoke feeling rested. The bright Sri Lankan sun, streaming in through the thin curtains, warmed her face. Somewhere in the night her mind had scaled a plateau. She felt alive again. Her life had purpose. She felt a spring in her step when she exited the seedy hotel room.

Mark took note of her buoyancy. He did not say a word, but he was relieved. Her brooding silences were new to him; they had begun to worry him.

After a hurried breakfast, they moved on. Chanderan sat toadlike in the front passenger seat. Now upbeat and perked up, Ruby could not keep still. She kept up a barrage of questions, querying everything they drove past.

But that did little to dispel the quiet tension that rode with them.

Simran was in the living room when Ravinder came down. The Gill family lived in a two-level government bungalow on Satya Marg, allocated to him by virtue of his designation as ATTF chief. Though they could have stayed in their family-owned farmhouse at Chhatarpur, a huge eight-bedroom place with swimming pool, tennis court, and gym, Ravinder preferred it here; it was a much easier commute and it relieved him from having to go around explaining to everyone how he, a cop, could afford such an extravagant home.

On one wall of the rectangular living room there was a bright, cheerful painting of a young boy running with a kite; the painter had caught the boy's excitement. Contrasting with it was a somber, much darker mountainscape on the opposite wall, with small houses caught in the dying rays of the sun. Both paintings were large and added vibrancy to the room. On a third wall was an array of photographs: ancestors in their regal finery; the large family home in Patiala; men in uniform, with the family crest clearly visible. Ravinder referred to this as the family's vanity wall; a reminder of their royal legacy. A massive Persian carpet, two big, well-polished brass lamps, one on either side of the sofa, and an abundance of antique wooden furniture added to the room's rich feel. Ravinder always felt a soothing sensation when he entered this room; which was not often. In fact, barring the monthly dinner, which Simran hosted for close friends and family, he always found himself with no time to just unwind and smell the roses.

Dressed in a fawn-colored sari with an intricately embroidered border, with her waist-length hair neatly tied in a bun, Simran was a handsome woman and carried her years well despite a few extra kilograms. There was an elaborate tea service placed on the round, dark coffee table in front of her. It was also antique and went well with the camel-colored sofa set. The tea was one of the rituals she had carried over from her father's house; associating these rituals as something royalty indulged in, despite the fact that in independent India, kingdoms and fiefdoms were things of the past. Scattered across the table were also some photographs and papers. When Ravinder strode in, she was busy with one of them, her lips puckered in concentration.

"You are just in time." Simran looked up. "Come and give me your opinion on these."

"What are they, my dear?"

"You never listen to me." Simran made an exasperated clucking sound. "All these days I have been telling you that we need to find a nice groom for our Jasmine."

Ravinder's sigh was inaudible; he knew he was again going to be drawn into the running battle going on between his wife and daughter.

Simran was adamant Jasmine was now at the age where Sikh girls from her (royal) background got engaged, if not married immediately.

But Jasmine, at twenty-two, cut from the same stubborn cloth as her mother, was equally adamant. She was not going to marry till she had finished law school, completed her master's, and worked for a couple of years.

The idea that her daughter would go out into the world and work was anathema to Simran. *Girls from our family don't do that.* She had been harping on it daily for weeks.

Ravinder felt caught in the cruel cross fire between mother and daughter. Despite his efforts to stand up for Jasmine, he was not making headway; Simran had the unnerving ability to hear only what she wanted to hear and had been poring through the files of all Sikh royal families that she could lay her hands on. The papers and photographs before her, Ravinder guessed, were the results of her painstaking research.

"Simran," he said, sitting down beside her. "Why bother? You should know your daughter by now. Jasmine is not going to agree to any marriage proposal. Let her finish her studies and—"

"What does *she* know?" Simran repeated her exasperated clucking. "She is a child. It is our job to instill the value of customs and tradition in her." She waved her hand at the clutter of paper and photos. "Don't you realize that these boys are the best we can find . . . and they are all from good, royal families—"

"The pick of the litter, are they?" Ravinder could not resist the quip. It earned him a cold, angry glare, lately her expression of choice for him. He regretted it immediately.

"Be serious! Our daughter's future is at stake."

"Sorry," Ravinder waved placatingly, "that was uncalled for, my dear."

Before he could go on, his mobile chimed. Grateful for the excuse, Ravinder took the call, walking out to the garden. It was a telemarketer trying to sell him a credit card. He wanted to thank her for calling when she did. Cutting the call, he was returning to the living room when the phone chirruped again.

"Good morning, sir." Mohite sounded angry. He launched off without waiting for Ravinder to respond. "I have no idea how to deal with these bloody foreign agents."

"What happened, Mohite?" Ravinder knew that it was going to be one of *those* days.

"I have spent the whole of yesterday going over the security arrangements at the hotel with both of them, but that bloody Spillman is not satisfied with anything." He spluttered. "As for that woman . . . Jennifer . . . I have never seen anyone nitpick so much. . . . She has a problem with every fucking thing."

"Okay." Ravinder was familiar with Mohite's exaggerating and knew he needed to get him focused. "What are the precise issues?"

"There are so many," Mohite spluttered, "where do I start?"

"Start with the big ones, Govind."

Ravinder spent the next twenty minutes listening. As he'd expected, they had more to do with Mohite's hostility toward the two foreigners than with any practical issues; most of the points raised by them appeared valid to Ravinder. So, realizing he needed to deal with these and also maintain morale in his organization, Ravinder diplomatically talked Mohite through them one at a time.

"You're asking me to give in to them on everything," Mohite complained.

"Govind, this is not about them or us. . . . It is about ensuring the damn summit goes off smoothly." Ravinder then played his trump card. "Remember how much Thakur sahib trusts you? Can we afford to let him down? How would he feel if these guys complained to him?"

He listened through the long pause at the other end. "Right, sir, if that's what you want, I will do it." Mohite did not sound happy.

"So where are they now?"

"I told them to take a hike and go see the city for the day . . . while I fix the problems," Mohite replied, now in a satisfied tone.

Ravinder wondered why they called people like him civil servants; there was hardly anything civil about Mohite and nothing even remotely akin to the desire to serve present in him, except in pursuit of his own interests.

But we have to work with what we have. No point in bitching. Just deal with it.

"Fine, you work on the issues we have discussed. I will swing by later, once I've met Ashish."

By the time the call ended, he felt drained, and the day had only begun. And, knowing Mohite, he also felt sorry for the two foreign agents.

"Don't forget that we have to go for Navjyot's wedding reception tonight," Simran called after him as he returned inside, and grabbed his laptop.

"Navjyot?" Lost in thought, Ravinder gave her a blank look.

"My cousin's daughter, Ravinder." Simran voiced her exasperation: "When will you remember that there is a life outside your office also?"

"Oh, I'd clean forgotten." Ravinder thumped his forehead. "That's tonight?"

"Yes. Eight P.M. at the Claridges. Come straight there if you're getting late."

"Right. I think I'll do that." Ravinder waved a hurried bye.

"I know, I know. It's too much to expect you to come home and go with us." Her exasperation followed him to the door.

Chance and Jennifer were already in his office when Ravinder walked in. Chance was sitting, but Jennifer was wearing out the carpet, her agitation evident.

"Mr. Gill!" she burst out in frustration. "You really need to look into this. Your Mr. Mohite does not seem to understand the basics of security, and he is so rude."

"Tell me about it, Jennifer." Ravinder kept calm. "Why don't you sit down? Would you like a cup of tea first? Or coffee?"

"I think that is a good idea, Mr. Gill," Chance interceded, realizing that Ravinder was trying to cool her down. "Jennifer." He pushed the chair beside him toward her.

She gave him a long look. "You do realize that we will be put out to pasture if these guys don't get their act in place," she muttered as she sat.

"Getting worked up is not going to help," Chance whispered back.

"What is the precise problem?" Ravinder asked after instructing Gyan to get some tea for Chance and himself and coffee for Jennifer.

Chance took the lead. "We don't want to be difficult, Mr. Gill, but Mr. Mohite will not share any information. We have no idea what your security plans are. So how can we confirm to our superiors that our people will be safe?" Struggling to find the right words, he went on. "Please understand that we also are under a lot of pressure. Our agencies will hold us accountable if . . ." His voice petered away, unwilling to state the bad stuff.

"I understand, Chance." Ravinder met his gaze evenly. "Let me assure you that I will personally look into things and make sure you are in the loop at all times. Give me a day to sort things out."

"Fair enough, Mr. Gill."

Jennifer looked unconvinced, but she caught the look on Chance's face and subsided.

"Thank you." Ravinder stepped in smoothly again. "While I put together a document for you, why don't the two of you take the opportunity to do some sightseeing? Delhi has a lot to offer. Check out the Qutab Minar, Jantar Mantar, Red Fort. . . . You won't regret it, I promise you. . . . It's a lovely walk down history." He smiled.

"Seems like a good idea." Chance returned the smile.

Jennifer visibly perked up. She appeared eager to spend some personal time with Chance; the attraction between them was evident. They left.

Ravinder sat down and began to work out how to resolve the issue without ruffling more feathers, either with Thakur or his crony Mohite.

T he paperwork put together by Ruby, passing them off as volunteers working with a British aid group, got them through the checkpoints, but the delays irritated her.

It was past noon when they entered Vellankulam, a clutter of houses and huts amidst clusters of palm trees, some of brick, but mostly mud-walled.

The sun was almost directly overhead, but the heat was mitigated by a sprightly sea breeze as they alighted outside a small house by the sea with faded wooden doors and windows. Several windowpanes were missing; the gaps boarded over with cardboard and yellowing newspaper. The house was screened off from all sides by trees.

On the Sri Lankan eastern coast, Vellankulam was historically a convenient, though illegal, jump-off point to India. During the war years, it had been an established staging post for men and warlike matériel. So it abounded in fast-moving speedboats and men who plied this risky trade. It was one such man to whom Chanderan had brought them.

They were expected; he stepped out to meet them as their vehicle navigated through the narrow wooden gate.

Though he was a few inches taller and several kilograms heavier, there was not much difference between him and Chanderan. Neither told them his name. They both wasted no time in pleasantries.

The cargo sought by Ruby was already loaded on the dull gray speedboat lashed to the jetty. Mark checked each item.

The rocket launchers were Swedish 84mm Carl Gustav, easy to use and effective. Both were wrapped in oily polythene. Accompanying were two containers of rockets: the first had two high-explosive rockets and the second two high-explosive anti-tank rockets.

"Everything seems to be in order," Ruby told Chanderan when Mark gave her the thumbs-up.

"Of course it is," he replied with a smile. "Should we move, then?"

Ruby nodded. They clambered into the speedboat and after covering the items with a tarpaulin took off.

The sun bounced off the water, blindingly bright. There was a lively breeze, but that did not affect the high-powered boat, since it was literally skimming the surface.

For the first few minutes, Chanderan tried to point out places on the coastline receding behind them; however, the wind made talk impossible. And neither Ruby nor Mark was in the mood for a guided tour. Both were aware of the danger of being intercepted by the Sri Lankan or Indian Coast Guard. Though Chanderan had assured them they could outrun anything that either government could throw at them, which had not been reassuring. Both knew that outrunning another boat was one thing; outrunning bullets yet another.

Ruby shrugged. *But this is the best we can hope for. Reconnoitering the escape route is important . . . worth the risk.*

Soon the sun was dropping toward the horizon, casting a deep red glow over the waters. As darkness closed in, lights began to flicker on the approaching Indian coastline.

Ruby's mind had begun to spiral away when they made land and the engine was cut. Though slowing, the boat slid forward due to its momentum. Chanderan and his taciturn accomplice leaped into waist-deep water and hauled the boat ashore.

Ruby felt an admixture of pain and anger jab at her as her feet hit Indian soil. *The land of my father . . . this is not the way I ever imagined coming here.* It was an unsettling feeling. Confused, she pushed it away.

It was a quiet sliver of beach. Perhaps cleared by Chanderan's local contact. Perhaps the fishermen knew better than to be around. Here and there nets had been hung out to dry.

A yellow bulb from a nearby temple cast eerie shadows all around.

A man who had been waiting for them emerged out of the shadows. Once again, no introductions. The cargo was offloaded.

"He will have them trucked down to Delhi and stored. They'll be there by the end of this week. You can collect them from the address I gave you. They will be expecting you."

"Have you explained to him about our return?"

"Of course. He will wait for you at the guesthouse in Chennai. It is perfectly safe. . . . My cousin owns it. You just reach there and he will get you back."

"And him?" Ruby gestured at the boatman.

"He will wait for you here. . . . Remember this temple." Chanderan pointed. "It is an easy landmark. Even if you have to come on your own, just ask for the Devipattinam temple."

"Spell that out, please." Both Mark and Ruby took note of the long, unfamiliar name.

"From when to when?" Ruby double-checked.

"As you wanted, for four days, starting from the fourteenth of October."

"Right." Ruby exchanged glances with Mark; he nodded, confirming he had taken note of everything . . . just in case they got separated . . . or if one of them did not make it back at all. "That's it, then. Thank you. Let's go."

Minutes later, they were off again, heading back to Vellankulam. Their escape route had been physically reconnoitered. The heavy weapons were being delivered to Delhi.

By now the darkness around them was almost complete. Barring the rhythmic throbbing of the powerful Yamaha outboard motor and the sound of water swishing past, silence surrounded them. It was almost spiritual. The dark skies, the overwhelming magnificence of the ocean, and the wind zipping past; all came together in harmony. Soon, the reddish glow of the dying sun vanished, plunging them into darkness. The darkness gathered strength, now broken only by the twinkling lights of some distant coastal village, or passing ship.

Their boat rode without lights.

Ruby felt a comforting calm. It began in her heart and slowly spread through her, enhancing the strong, positive feeling she had woken up with that morning. Despite that, somewhere deep inside, the sight of the receding Indian coastline unsettled her. She knew that somewhere out there, in that massive land of millions, was the man who had sired her . . . *and abandoned me. Where is he? Will I run into him?* Then, a bit later, *Does he think of me? Ever?*

All at once she wished they would never stop moving.

But they did.

Soon they were rushing through the night, back to Colombo. They had a flight to catch. To Delhi. Ruby did not want either of them to enter India illegally.

It was pushing midnight when the cab brought them back to Ashoka Hotel. Chance paid the driver and followed Jennifer in. Both had rooms on the seventh floor, in the zone that was being secured.

The encounter with Mohite that morning had soured the start of their day. But then, realizing they needed to give Ravinder time to sort things out, they'd taken his advice and gone sightseeing.

They'd had an exciting time traipsing through the Qutub Minar. Though access to the upper reaches of the world's tallest brick tower was no longer allowed, they had fun browsing around it. Jennifer also tried to encircle the famous iron pillar with her arms when their guide told them anyone who managed to do that would have their wish fulfilled.

Watching her trying, Chance wondered what she would have wished for. Then, out of the blue, the thought of Ruby dropped into his mind. He wondered where she was . . . how she was doing . . . what *she* would have wished for.

What would I have wished for?

It was an uncomfortable thought. He pushed it away, declining to try the pillar when Jennifer asked him to. He was not feeling gung ho as Jennifer laughingly led him out of Qutab Minar. Ruby's shadow between them had lengthened.

The ultramodern Lotus Temple was a change from the historic Qutab Minar, its exquisite construction and serene gardens holding them enthralled. Their guide then led them into the Jantar Mantar, a collection of architectural astronomical instruments built by Maharaja Jai Singh II. They were amazed at the sophistication of the eighteenth-century monument. Then they spent a couple of hours wandering through Jama Masjid, Delhi's oldest and most famous mosque, built by Emperor Shah Jahan, who'd also built the Taj Mahal. They were exhausted by the time they arrived at the *son et lumière*, the sound and light show at Red Fort, but ended up feeling rejuvenated by the time the brilliantly choreographed show ended. The finale was an authentic Indian dinner at Karim's, a restaurant near the Jama Masjid, in one of Delhi's oldest markets; the ambience was as exotic as the food.

As the day progressed, Jennifer's attempts to get closer to him became obvious. She started with little touches on his hands or shoulders, progressing till she ended up taking his arm as they were strolling through the Red Fort. Though uneasy, Chance made no attempt to free his arm.

The ancient fort with its sprawling, lush gardens had an irresistibly romantic aura. Chance had to feel it even if he hadn't wanted to. But he did. It had been a while since he'd been with a beautiful woman. Still, he felt confused responding to Jennifer's flirtations. Unsure where he stood with Ruby made him uncomfortable.

"Would you like to come in for a nightcap?" Jennifer asked as they halted outside her room.

The hint of desire in her eyes tugged at him. But conflicted, Chance hesitated. "Not tonight, Jennifer." He saw her disappointment, realized he'd been too abrupt, and added, "I am very tired. It has been a long day. Maybe tomorrow."

"Maybe." Jennifer gave him a light peck on his cheeks and went inside.

Chance stood in the corridor, not sure why he had turned her down. After a moment, he raised his hand to knock and tell her he'd changed his mind, but then could not bring himself to do it.

On the other side of the door, Jennifer heard him walk away.

Ravinder was feeling drained by the time they managed to extricate themselves from the clutch of relatives who throng every family wedding and related function.

Jasmine too was feeling the pressure; these days, weddings were not high on her list of favorites, especially not with Simran using every occasion to have one or the other of her sisters and cousins try to talk sense into her: marriage sense. Several times Ravinder had seen her surrounded by a gaggle of aunts, looking hurricane-hit. More than once he'd even worked up the courage to wade in and rescue her.

Simran, of course, was thriving. She loved the hustle and bustle of these functions.

By the time they finally got free and hit the road home, it was near the witching hour.

Ravinder was almost asleep when he remembered: He'd forgotten to tell Simran and Jasmine to exercise more caution. And he'd also forgotten to check on the latest with Mohite, about the hunt for Javed Khan and Aslam, the Jaish-e-Mohammed terrorists. The APB that had been put out yesterday and the request to int had yielded several leads that Mohite was following up on. He thought of waking up Simran and telling her, but it had been a long day.

Tomorrow. First thing tomorrow. Ravinder promised himself. *We have to find those bastards before . . .*

DAY THREE

Ruby woke up as their plane began its descent toward Delhi's Indira Gandhi International Airport.

She checked her watch, a Cartier Tank with an ivory dial, blue metallic hands, and black Roman numerals encased in brushed stainless steel, with a steel bracelet with yellow gold links. The sight of it made her smile; Rehana had saved up for it for a long time. Ruby had found it waiting for her when she finished her MI6 training. It had been a part of her life since then.

Well beyond my pay grade, Ruby thought with a wry smile.

Her smile faded as the aircraft hit the ground with a thud, bounced once, and then, settling down, roared down the runway.

Seven days left till the summit.

The ops clock in her head started ticking louder; it happened before every mission. Her spine stiffened and shoulders squared off as she emerged from the plane.

Battle mode was on.

The massive, recently commissioned airport was bustling with energy, flights landing and taking off every few minutes. Mark and she cleared immigration without any hassles and caught separate cabs. Mark would be checking into the Radisson, a short hop from the airport and within striking distance of the target. Ruby headed for the Hyatt Regency, on the Ring Road, also a short run from the Ashoka.

By the time Ruby finished checking in, she knew Mark would

have had time to do his first task here. With the missing Glocks weighing on her, she reached for the phone.

When the phone suddenly rang, Ravinder was getting ready to leave for the office. He paused, one hand still trying to push the links through his shirt cuff, deliberating if he should take the call. Realizing that was not an option, he reached for it.

"Good morning, sir." Ravinder winced as Mohite's voice crackled through, not an auspicious start to the day. "The man from Mossad is here. He wants to know when he can brief us."

Ravinder threw a glance at his wristwatch and a mental prod at his calendar; it would be another chockablock day. But this briefing could be important. "Can he make it at twelve?"

"Of course he can. What else is he here for?" Mohite declared with his usual tact. "I will tell him to be here at noon."

Ravinder shook his head. For a moment he thought of telling Mohite that this was not the way to go around making friends and influencing people, then decided not to bother. He didn't have the energy, not after yet another hour-long session with Simran and Jasmine on marriage. And, knowing Mohite, it would be futile.

"And, Govind, please call up Chance and Jennifer and tell them to be there."

"Why?"

"Because they are going to help us secure the summit, my friend. They need to be in the loop. . . . That's why," Ravinder replied patiently.

"But—"

Ravinder cut him off. "Because I'm saying so, Mohite. And just in case they are not in their rooms, leave a message *and* send them a text." He added, knowing that Mohite was capable of giving that as an excuse for not passing on his message. He was about to end the call when he remembered. "Oh yes, what's the latest on Javed and Aslam? Any progress?"

"Nothing so far, sir," Mohite replied. "We drew a blank on seven of the leads. False alarms."

"How many leads are there?"

"Nine so far. Three from int and six public sightings. I'm having the remaining two public sightings followed up today."

"Yes, do that today, Govind. Keep me posted. And no matter what happens, keep up the publicity on these buggers. That will force them to go underground and keep them on the run . . . not give them time to sit and plan their strikes."

Ruby tapped her feet impatiently, waiting for the phone to be picked up. Her first five calls, made at intervals of ten to fifteen minutes, had gone unanswered. The sixth call finally was.

"Damnit, Mark, where the hell have you been?" Ruby realized she had spoken more sharply that she intended. She added, a lot more gently, "I need you to confirm about that guy for the remaining equipment."

"I had gone down for breakfast and then I was just taking a shower, Ruby. It's been a long flight. Then I had to go out to call our man. . . . I didn't want to do it from the hotel, so I had to look for a public phone."

"And?" Ruby knew he was right with taking these precautions, but she was itching to find out what had happened about the Glocks.

"Anyway, he is out of Delhi and can only meet us the day after."

"No way he can make it earlier?"

"I tried to get him to, but he says that's the fastest he can get back."

"Damn! Well, in that case, let's focus on the reconnaissance for now."

"Where do you want me?"

"Not with me. Not yet. The less we're seen together, the better. Take down the places I want you to check out on your own."

———

Chance and Jennifer were already there when Ravinder walked into the Police HQ conference room. So was Mohite. He sat beside a well-built, fair, taciturn-looking man at the other end of the table.

"Good afternoon." The Mossad man held out a large hand. "I am Ido Peled." His English was only slightly accented.

With time at a premium, Ravinder brought the meeting to order and Peled began his briefing.

"My government has asked me to give you all a detailed account of the Jerusalem attack and the people responsible, since we believe that they will try to disrupt this peace summit too. I will also give you details of all delegates and try to answer any questions you may have." He looked around, but except for nods to go ahead, there was no comment.

"Our investigations confirm that fifteen people were involved in planning and executing the terror strike on Jerusalem. However, twelve women carried out the actual strike. They had four things in common."

Peled, clearly a fluent communicator, had practiced his presentation. He raised one finger in the air.

"Firstly, none conformed to the profiling systems of most security agencies post 9/11. They were ideal, undetectable recruits, selected from among apparently well-integrated members of society."

A second finger came up now.

"Secondly, all identifying dental work and body marks had been removed, and every stitch of clothing on them had been procured locally. Barring false passports, they carried nothing that could reveal their identities or show to which group they owed allegiance."

Finger three rose.

"Thirdly, all twelve were ready to die as readily as they were to kill."

He then took a theatrical pause.

"Lastly, they had all been trained thoroughly, especially the six women who arrived last. The first six entered Israel from various points in Europe. The other six, also of European origin, came from Pakistan. However, since passengers from Pakistan are subjected to extra-stringent checking by most countries, this lot too was routed in through European cities. They had been handpicked from among one hundred eighty-five women trained for the past two years at two special Lashkar-e-Taiba camps at Bhimber and Kotli in Pakistan-Occupied Kashmir." Peled paused for a sip of water. "This was done so that the planners could pass off this attack as a Zionist conspiracy."

Mohite interrupted. "Considering the efforts taken to prevent all this from coming out, you guys seem to know an awful lot."

"Yes, because we pieced the whole thing together from camera footage at the airport, from the targets, eyewitness accounts, and forensics." After a pause he added softly. "Also because we captured one of them alive."

"You did?" Jennifer couldn't contain her surprise. "But that was not in the news."

"We don't want the people behind the strike to know we are on to them."

"Good thinking." Ravinder gave an approving nod. "So you guys know exactly how the raid was executed?"

"Yes, we do."

"Please share it with us. I am sure there can be major lessons in it for all of us."

Peled gave Ravinder a long look. When he resumed, his voice had dropped a few decibels. "The strike on Jerusalem began at precisely ten fifty that morning."

As he spoke, he flicked a wireless controller in his hand. Powered by his laptop, footage from a security camera began to beam onto a screen at the far end. It showed a plethora of tourists milling around. Also visible were some security men. Like a sophisticated voice-over, Peled spoke.

"The attack started innocuously enough, but escalated so rapidly that our security was initially swamped. By the time we recovered and started a counterattack, the raiders had gained a foothold, a tenuous one, but enough to ensure that the damage inflicted was substantial."

His four-person audience were riveted.

A security camera zoomed in to show three women walking up toward the Al-Aqsa Mosque. All seemed to be in their mid-twenties and could not have looked more touristy. They held travel books in their hands, big SLR cameras slung around their necks, and water bottles sticking out of knapsacks on their backs. Their hair was covered with scarves and their full-sleeved shirts and trousers ensured no indecent display of skin.

In retrospect, it was easy to see that their eyes were not still; they constantly darted around, like the advancing scouts of a rifle section. They had divided the area into zones; so between the three they maintained a total view of the surroundings. This heightened awareness was mostly due to benzphetamine pills they had taken a few minutes ago. So they blended well with the throng of visitors at the Al-Aqsa.

It was here that the Holy Prophet was given the commandment to pray five times a day and for the following sixteen and a half months, Jerusalem was the Qibla (direction of prayers), though today Muslims face Mecca while praying.

The Dome of the Chain marked the exact central point of the mosque, which like most mosques had four minarets—three square ones and a cylindrical one from the Mamluk period. Recognizable by its lead dome, which replaced the aluminum covering done in 1964 in order to restore it to its original cover, Al-Aqsa comprised three distinct parts; narrow arcades running along one end, a huge atrium, and a covered area to the south.

Still visible were signs of the damage done to the mosque in 1969, when a fanatic Jew set fire to the covered area. Among the numerous sad losses was the beautiful handmade pulpit from Aleppo. Made of over ten thousand interlocking pieces of wood, ivory, and mother-of-pearl held together without a drop of glue or a single nail, and considered one of the most beautiful in the world.

Today, if the plan developed for these terrorists had succeeded, the damage would have been much more severe.

As the trio approached the main entrance, they were engrossed in animated conversation.

They were fifty feet away when a motorcycle sped past on the road in front. It was clearly visible on the security footage. About twenty meters from the main security post, it lost control. Since the camera feed was not backed by an audio track, none of his listeners could hear the loud thud as the motorcycle slammed onto the road. It would have been followed by a nerve-grating, screeching sound as metal impacted on hard tarmac. The rider's helmet had broken loose. When the bike finally shuddered to a halt, she lay still. Blood masked her face.

Two of the six security men at the monument gates ran forward to help. And the attention of the other four also focused on the fallen rider.

Sitting on the edge of his seat, Ravinder could tell that the security men had been lured into a trap.

Converging on the motorcyclist along with the security men were another nine or ten passersby. The soldiers were among those who reached the crash victim first. This lot was killed by the forty kilograms of high explosive strapped on the motorcycle. Its fuel tank added to the carnage.

"The explosion was so powerful, it was heard miles away, which is what it was supposed to do, since it not only created the diversion for the main assault force, it also triggered the next phase."

While the cloud of motorcycle parts, blood, and gore was still billowing upward, the security camera caught the three *tourists* suddenly pull weapons out of their knapsacks and run forward.

All three were wielding Micro Tavor assault rifles. Of Israeli design, with a length of just twenty-three inches, the MTAR-21 is possibly the shortest 5.56mm assault rifle, shorter even than the Uzi and more accurate due to its relatively longer barrel.

The trio headed straight for the main gate.

People became aware of them only when the terrorist lead-ing the charge hurled a grenade at the security post at the main gate.

"It landed behind the sandbags, which ensured the attackers were safe from the shrapnel." Peled's tone stayed dispassionate. Almost. "None of the security personnel survived."

Charging through the smoke-ridden carnage, Raiders One and Two could be seen racing toward the solitary door on the west-ern side that led into the covered area of the mosque. Meanwhile, the third continued toward the security post on the west, her role to prevent the guards from interdicting her teammates.

It was happening so fast that the security men on that side were caught unawares. All three died. Confirming they were down, Raider Three whipped around and headed for the sentries at the next gate on the west.

The camera footage was grainy, but Ravinder could see her expertly flip her magazine as she ran. Two more security men died next, but not before one of them managed to put a bullet in her, high on her left shoulder.

Ravinder saw her falter. Then she spun around and headed for the next security post. However, by now the guards were ready to engage. She fell to a hail of bullets. For one brief moment every-one involved froze. Then, on the conference room screen a sound-less explosion billowed out darkly as she triggered the explosive in the camera around her neck. Parts of her body were hurled up and outward. The amount of explosive was enough to batter her upper body beyond recognition, which was the aim, since the terror maestros meant to keep the identities of the attackers obscure.

"Her objective was the same as the woman who had crashed her motorcycle, to provide the primary pair of raiders an oppor-tunity to get into the main mosque."

The camera feed switched to show Raiders One and Two rac-ing into the mosque, firing in short, two- or three-round bursts, gunning down everyone who got in their way: tourists, people coming or going from prayers, and security guards.

The camera feed switched again; two more women, Raiders Five and Six, emerged from the crowd of tourists going between the Al-Aqsa Mosque and the Temple Mount. They ran toward the solitary door on the east, which led into the covered area of the mosque, gunning down everyone in their path.

The security forces here, however, were now on full alert.

Caught in Technicolor, Raider Six fell to a hail of bullets halfway to the mosque. Her final act also was to trigger the bomb in the camera slung around her neck. Two more bystanders were blown apart with her. And the explosion created more confusion, allowing Raider Five to slip into the mosque.

"Now three terrorists had penetrated the inner sanctum of the mosque."

The screen went black as Peled switched to the feed from the security cameras inside the mosque.

Raiders One, Two, and Five could now be seen rounding up hostages. The majority they chose were Muslims—again deliberate and part of the plan. Only two of the fourteen they took were non-Muslims, both men in their late forties, from their dress and demeanor both Jewish. One a meek-looking schoolteacher. The second, his American cousin on a sightseeing tour. It now seemed unlikely that he'd be utilizing his return ticket.

Raider One stood guard while Raider Two secured the hands and feet of the hostages. All this while Raider Five could be seen moving from window to window. Every so often, she would raise her weapon and fire.

Peled's commentary filled in the gaps.

"A few hundred meters to the north, the next pair of terrorists, who we now know were called Raiders Seven and Eight, opened fire with their assault rifles at the tourists milling around the Dome of the Rock. Here again, either the terrorists were lucky or the guards not alert, or taken by surprise. Most fell to the initial onslaught. The two who survived managed to put bullets into the attackers, but failed to prevent them from entering the monument. So, with Raiders Seven and Eight inside, both monuments were now in control of the terrorists."

Ravinder threw a quick glance around. The others were as caught up in this as he was.

"As you will note from the proximity of these two buildings"—Peled tapped them out on the screen with a laser pointer—"it would now be extremely hard for the security forces to undertake cleansing operations from the area between them, since they'd be in range from one or both of the buildings."

His audience nodded; the predicament of the security forces was obvious.

"Despite the speed with which the attack developed," Peled continued, "the IDF reaction was fast."

Having studied the lessons of the Mumbai *ghazwa,* Ravinder knew it was imperative to dislodge the terrorists before they got firmly entrenched. Given time, they would not only be able to secure more hostages or kill more people, but also take up good defensive positions and lay booby traps.

"By now our counterterrorism units were racing in," Peled resumed. "Our biggest problem was that no operation could be carried out without damage to the monuments. Considering their religious significance, any damage would incite massive anger in Muslims the world over."

It was clear to this audience that this was what the terrorists' had been banking on. Ravinder could see the others trying to figure how *they* would have reacted.

"The counterterror units were en route. Meanwhile the remaining terrorists swung into action. They had also learned the lessons of the Mumbai attack and planned on multiple targets."

Once again, the screen sprang to life and the footage of another set of cameras began to beam.

Raiders Nine and Ten, another pair of pretty girls in their early twenties, could be seen hauling out Micro Tavors from their knapsacks and opening fire on the tourists at the Tower of David.

Raider Nine was running toward the security post as she fired. She got two of the guards before the others gunned her down. She too disappeared in an explosive thunderclap as Raider Ten raced into the monument.

"The one who had got inside gunned down everyone she came across." Peled's tone hardened; it was impossible not to feel his anger. "Her job was not to secure the monument; it was to inflict maximum casualties and also force our men to come in and get her, thus diverting forces from their primary objective, the Al-Aqsa."

Though everyone in this audience had studied the operation and knew what was coming next, they hung on to Peled's words.

"As soon as information about this latest attack reached HQ, a section of the IDF response team rushing to Al-Aqsa split away and headed for the Tower of David. Post Mumbai and the changing nature of urban jihad, we were now geared to handle simultaneous, multiple threats.

"At the same time as the Tower of David was attacked, one-point-eight kilometers to the north, the final pair, Raiders Eleven and Twelve—two more touristy-looking girls—whipped out Micro Tavor assault rifles and headed for the security post guarding the Chapel of the Ascension."

Peled clicked the controller, and the feed from yet another set of cameras showed two girls racing forward, firing. They gunned down guards then ran toward the chapel.

"Here also they simply gunned down everyone in sight." Peled now was having trouble keeping his emotions in check. Ravinder knew how he felt; in his place, he too would have been livid. Though Peled had started with a well-rehearsed presentation, now it was coming from his heart.

"As soon as we got word of this attack, another section of the anti-terror units converging on Al-Aqsa bled away and headed for the Chapel. Also, as the threat had enlarged, headquarters began to scramble more forces."

On the screen, the footage again returned to Al-Aqsa and the Dome of the Rock. IDF commandos could be seen rushing in and deploying to secure the perimeter.

The camera feed changed and commando detachments could now be seen arriving at the Tower of David and the Chapel of Ascension.

"Within minutes of getting there, we began the operation to retake the monuments," Peled resumed, again using his laser pointer. The units could now be seen deploying sensors and sending in probes.

Ravinder knew their first step would be to gather maximum intelligence. The security forces would already know the layout. Also, in most such buildings there were always cameras and security sensors. The security forces used these for real-time combat intelligence, which was vital to ensure the building could be retaken with minimal loss of life. Ravinder was glad he was not in their shoes.

"There is no doubt that the planners of this strike were veterans of such dark ops. They had planned to enhance the psychological impact of their strikes." Peled's voice stayed low and intense. "They left all audio surveillance, motion or heat sensors alone. Pinpointing and destroying them would have taken too much time. However, they destroyed all surveillance cameras they could find. These would not only give away their strength but also their weapons, location, and condition. However, they left the cameras covering the inner sanctums of the mosque intact. The terrorists needed these to ensure maximum coverage and eyeballs for their gory finale."

Ravinder could see that everyone in the room was still riveted.

The footage changed again, to the inside of the mosque.

The raiders could now be seen moving rapidly from one firing position to another; keeping up a barrage; doing everything to deny operational intel to the security forces and to keep them at bay.

At the Tomb of David, Raider Ten kept firing till she was down to her last magazine. However, her task was complete. As the first commando broke in, she ran forward and detonated her camera bomb. Both she and the commando were annihilated.

"The Tomb of David was back in our hands. Barring the area around the explosion, the damage was within manageable limits. However, eleven people lost their lives."

Peled's words rang bleakly through the room.

"At Ascension, Raiders Eleven and Twelve kept the initial probes of our forces at bay, however they too were running out of ammo. They were setting up explosive charges when IDF commandos raced in and gunned them down. Again, their lives ended explosively. The damage to the chapel was minimal. But our loss here was much higher. Four security men and seventeen tourists gunned down." Peled's voice now carried a hard, brittle edge.

The footage flipped again as it returned to the Dome of the Rock.

Both terrorists had been wounded, Raider Seven so badly that she couldn't move. Raider Eight could move, but slowly.

"That is why their shoot-scoot-shoot strategy did not work. Minutes later, the Dome was back in our hands. However, the death toll here was a shocking twenty-six, including three commandos. The damage to the building was also more severe. But, as you will see now, our problems were far from over."

Once again, the footage changed. The inner sanctum of the mosque hove into view. It showed twelve bound, panic-striken hostages. The three terrorists were moving rapidly from window to window, keeping up a rain of fire on the forces outside. The fourteen arches, twenty-seven marble columns on the eastern side, and the same number of stone piers on the west afforded them cover to switch positions.

Suddenly Raiders One and Two ran back to the hostages. The security camera caught Raider One as she switched on her Black-Berry and began to video record. She was in direct sight of the camera, which revealed tense anticipation on her face.

At Peled's command, the feed now fragmented into two.

On the second half of the screen, Raider Two could be seen lining up the hostages. Starting from one side, she began to gun them down, delivering one shot each to their faces, ensuring that each screamed as she or he saw death coming. Acrid gun smoke furled up in the air.

Ravinder felt a nauseated feeling sweep through him.

As Raider Two proceeded, the killing became more brutal. She shot the sixth hostage first in the lower jaw. His soundless scream rang out. Only then did she put one between his eyes. The eighth was shot twice in the knees before her coup de grâce. The eleventh, the American cousin visiting Israel, was begging for mercy when she put the muzzle against his stomach. There was a soundless click as the firing pin slammed down on an empty chamber.

The kneeling hostage looked up. Amazed. Shocked. Then he vomited. It was so revoltingly real that Ravinder felt as though he could reach out and touch it.

By now Raider Two was directly in front of the security camera overhead. Probably she was aware of it and had positioned the hostages to ensure it caught their slaughter in gory detail. Dropping the now-empty assault rifle, she unsheathed a wicked knife from her ankle holster.

The hostage was still vomiting when she reached down, grabbed his hair, and yanked his head back. The knife moved in a quick diagonal slash across the throat. He gurgled and then slumped forward. His blood rained out in droplets on Raider Two's hands. She licked her lips as she wiped it clean on her pant leg. They all could see the madness in her eyes.

On the second half of the screen, recording all this on a Black-Berry, Raider One had been moving in tandem with Raider Two. They saw an odd expression on her face; as though she wanted it all to end, yet was fascinated by what she was seeing. Her mouth was slightly, almost erotically, open and her chest heaved. And now and then, her tongue forayed out and moistened her lips.

By the time Raider Two moved to the twelfth man, her chest heaved, eyes were blazing, and splatters of blood pockmarked her.

The final hostage did not scream. There was an amazing calm in how he stared at her, perhaps a touch of pity. His lips were moving as though praying . . . for her.

The surge of anger on Raider Two's face at his lack of fear was palpable. Perhaps that he was a Jew fueled her anger. Shifting the knife's angle, she sliced out his right ear. The hostage screamed now. Though no sound emerged, each viewer could hear the animal-like howl of pain.

The scream goaded Raider Two on. She sliced off the second ear now. The scream this time seemed to go on forever. Raider Two reversed her hold on the knife and drove it into the hostage's right eye. The scream ended abruptly as the knife entered the brain and drove life out of him.

Raider Two stood frozen, with the knife buried in the hostage's skull. She seemed depleted. As though it were not just the hostage who had died. As though something inside her had died too.

His mouth dry, suddenly short of oxygen, Ravinder watched; unable to believe the brutality he had witnessed.

Watching it on the BlackBerry's 3.25-inch touch screen, Raider One smiled. She began tapping out something on the keypad.

Yes. She would have needed to get the recording out.

Raider One watched impatiently as the file slowly uploaded, mentally goading it on, aware that time was now desperately short.

The transmission must have completed, because she gave a satisfied nod and was putting the phone away when a stun grenade smashed through the nearby window. It exploded with a mind-numbing roar and blinding flash, so bright that it dazzled Peled's audience.

The two raiders were reeling when IDF commandos raced in and unleashed a hail of bullets into them.

Their mission complete, the two terrorists triggered their camera bombs and death claimed them.

"The BlackBerry handset was also destroyed, so we'll never know to whom she sent that video."

Peled's comment was cut off as Raider Five raced into the central hall. She saw her teammates were down and reached for the trigger of her camera bomb.

A commando had turned when he heard her run in and got off two shots even as her hand was reaching for the camera bomb.

His first bullet missed. The second whipped past her temple. It grazed deeply enough to make her reel and clutch at the wound.

Like a flash, the commando was upon her. His rifle butt bludgeoned her down. She lay still.

The carnage was over.

The silence in the conference room was complete. However, the footage on the screen rolled on.

The task force commander now raced into the mosque. He came to a stunned stop as he surveyed the horrifying bodies.

"The last hostage killed was Ean Gellner, the son of Ziv Gellner, who is one of our delegates for this summit," Peled said softly.

On the screen, the task force commander turned and said something to the commando who had captured Raider Five.

"Keep that fucking bitch alive. We need to find out who was behind this. Whoever it is will pay. By God they will."

Then the screen went blank and the lights brightened. All in the room were avoiding looking at one another. Silence gripped the room.

knew we had to keep her capture from the media." Peled stopped abruptly.

"*You?*" Chance asked, wide-eyed. "You were the task force commander?"

"Yes," Peled replied. "I also did most of the post-event investigation. That is why I was asked to come down and brief you all."

Another long silence. They all remained stunned and revolted.

"Who were the others involved?" Jennifer's voice broke the moment.

"The mastermind was a Qassam Brigade commander."

"Who?" Jennifer again.

"We are still not sure," Peled replied with a straight face. No way Israel would officially admit to Yusuf Sharbati's involvement, not after he had been disposed of in Dubai by a Kidon team barely a week ago. "But we do know that the Qassam commander was funded by someone from the Lashkar-e-Taiba."

"Not surprising," Ravinder remarked. "They've been looking for a way to up their profile in global terror for many years now.

Of late, they've become frantic because their refusal to take up arms against their sponsors, the Pakistani government, has caused them to be tagged as betrayers of Islam."

"True." Mohite added, "That is why they are under huge pressure to redeem themselves in the eyes of the *ummah,* the community. Not to mention that they want to exploit the gap in leadership of Terror Central, with Osama dead and other senior Al-Qaeda leaders having gone underground."

"That could also explain the similarities of the Jerusalem strike to the November 26 Lashkar-e-Taiba *ghazwa* on Mumbai," Chance pointed out. "Mumbai was also their doing."

"True." Peled nodded. "We have certain leads about this man but have yet to ascertain his identity."

"You know we have a very extensive database on all LeT commanders," Ravinder offered. "We have lived with these lunatics for decades now. Let us know if we can help."

"That is very kind of you, sir." Peled gave a grateful smile. "We shall take you up on that."

"Just share your leads with us, and Mohite will help you to dig up possible matches."

"Right." Again, it was Jennifer who brought them back to the present. "So that takes care of fourteen people. You'd said there were fifteen. Who was the fifteenth?"

"There was a thirteenth woman," Peled said quietly.

Hell! Again that bloody number. Ravinder swore under his breath. It had become a recurring theme with this damn summit.

Peled continued. "We do not know much except that she is most probably Caucasian. The terrorist we captured caught a glimpse of her and heard her talking when she'd come to meet the Qassam commander. She says it was a British accent. As of now, that is all we know."

The others were listening, but did not catch the unspoken. Ravinder did. He sensed that Peled knew more than he was telling. Unsure why, Ravinder did not consider it correct to pursue this in public and let it pass for now. He listened as the others let loose a barrage of questions.

It was in a somber mood that the meeting broke up an hour later.

At that moment, barely thirteen miles away, the thirteenth woman, dressed as a tourist, complete with camera, hat, and water bottle, approached Ashoka Hotel. Comfortable jeans, a pale pink T-shirt, and sensible walking shoes completed her attire.

Taking care to ensure she did not become noticeable, Ruby carried out two runs to and through the hotel. The minute she entered it, she knew she had no hope of going past the main lobby or the restaurants. Disappointed but not surprised, she surveyed as best she could.

On her first run, she studied the layout and identified ingress points. On the second, she confirmed the observations she had made, double-checking to ensure she was correct.

By sunset, Ruby had embedded every detail of the venue in her head. Satisfied she had done all she could, she returned to her hotel room and began to work out attack combinations.

It was not going to be easy. She'd seen cops crawling all over the place, as many in plainclothes as in uniform. Most inner areas in the hotel had already been cordoned off. Roadblocks had been set up on all approaches, and security posts at both hotel gates.

It did not take her long to realize that a frontal assault would be doomed. It would have to be a covert attack. But a frontal assault *could* be a useful diversion.

A couple of hours later, her plans tentatively complete, she called it a night. Though she was exhausted, her sleep was hampered by her anxiety about their meeting with Nanda, the arms dealer, in the morning.

I hope that bugger can come up with the Glocks. That was her last thought as she fell asleep.

Dinner in the Gill home was drawing to a close when the phone began to clamor. Simran's exasperation was evident as Ravinder wiped his hands and got up to take the call.

"We have two candidates, sir." Mohite sounded excited. "It took a while, but—"

"Candidates for what, Govind?" Ravinder cut in.

"Oh!" Mohite checked himself, realizing he needed to start at the beginning. "I was helping the Mossad guy, Peled, to sift through our database on the LeT commanders. We have two possible suspects. The first is Pasha."

"Hmm. Give me a moment while I get my laptop out." Ravinder retreated to his study. After booting up the device, he pulled up Pasha's profile. On top were two photos, the only two they had of him.

The first, taken by an Indian intelligence operative, showed a clean-shaven man in a neat and obviously expensive, lightweight, steel gray business suit. He carried the suit well, as though used to it. Short and diminutive; he looked like a jockey. A small but prominent pear-shaped scar was on his right temple.

The second, taken by a Taliban turncoat, showed a different man, heavily bearded with shoulder-length hair, now dressed in typical black Pathani kameez and ankle-high salwar. Almost no resemblance to the man in the first photo.

Ravinder scanned through the man's profile. Born Khalid Abbas Khawaja, he had been a wing commander in the Pakistan Air Force. No one knew if he had retired or was ordered to retire, or if it was made to look as though he had retired. Either way, one fine day, Khalid Abbas Khawaja shed his uniform and vanished.

He appeared to have little in common with the man who surfaced in Afghanistan a year later, the year the Taliban had begun to make its presence felt. The crew cut and sharp pencil-line mustache had been replaced by an unruly beard and shoulder-length hair. The slightly built man, with an AK-74 in one hand and a radio or satellite phone in the other, soon became a fixture in the entourage of the one-eyed leader of the Taliban. He now piloted people, tweaking their destinies and ensuring they served just one purpose: the jihad.

However, as he had been ordered to do, Pasha stuck to the shadows. He feared the powerful generals in Islamabad; he knew they would throw him to the wolves if he dared cross them.

It was Pasha who had planned and executed the November 26 Mumbai terror attack. This much was known . . . at least strongly conjectured.

"Who is the second one?" Ravinder asked when he had finished.

"Well, if it is not Pasha, then the other can only be Saeed Anwar."

Ravinder brought up Anwar's profile. He saw a lot more photos of this portly, skullcap-wearing, bearded, bespectacled Anwar. Clad in white, he was fond of leading public rallies and was a primary fund-raiser for the LeT. He had helped Osama plan and execute the 9/11 strike and was known to have transferred one hundred thousand dollars to the 9/11 hijackers just before the attack.

Yes, he too is a strong possible. In fact, considering the others in the LeT leadership, it seems certain that one of these two must have been behind the Jerusalem attack.

"Good work, Mohite." Ravinder knew the analysis was spot-on. For a change, Mohite had delivered. "What does the Israeli have to say?"

"He said his boss would be talking to you soon."

"Fair enough." Ravinder rang off.

Sure enough, an hour later his phone rang again and he was talking to Meir Dagan.

Though he had met him only once, Ravinder could easily picture Dagan, the current head of the Mossad. Known to be the antithesis of M, the James Bond spymaster, Dagan—an avid student of history, a no-frills man who clocked eighteen hours of work every day—was famous for his bullheaded doggedness, and commanded respect, both within Mossad and outside.

Though Ravinder did not know it, the reason Dagan took an

hour before calling him was because he first needed to get the Israeli PM's sanction; ordering a Kidon hit was not something he had the authority to do on his own.

To have Pasha and Anwar taken out, he had to first ensure their names were added to the "execution list."

Given the severity of the Jerusalem attack, Dagan had little doubt that the sanction to place Pasha and Anwar on this list would be accorded. However, as per protocol, such a request could be confirmed by the PM only after it had been cleared by the designated judicial investigator: a person whose identity was so secret that almost no one had heard of him. He must have been clocking serious overtime that day, since he had sent it back with his approval posthaste.

"Do you agree with the possibility of these two being the most likely candidates?" Dagan came to the point immediately.

"Well, the chances of it being one of them are high. None of the others seem to have the authority to organize something of this magnitude," Ravinder replied. "Also, you can assume that if one is involved, so is the other. These two buggers are thick as thieves."

"In that case, we have a favor to ask of you." Dagan was brutally direct. "We would like to deploy a team to bring them in. We need you to help us with a firm base and some logistical support. I know it is a lot to ask, but given the geography, we have no other options. Not if we want to do this fast . . . and we do."

"Bring them in, or take them out?" Ravinder asked, equally direct.

"Whatever is possible, Mr. Gill." Dagan paused briefly. "We cannot . . . *will not* . . . allow such a heinous attack on our country go unpunished."

"I understand. I really do, but I will need to speak to my boss first."

"If you want, I can request our PM to talk to yours," Dagan offered.

"I will let you know if that's required." Ravinder knew that the

Indian PM would prefer not to know; plausible deniability was much sought after. "Let me clear this with my boss."

"Will you? Please."

"I will do my best to get the clearance right away."

It was with great satisfaction that Ravinder returned Dagan's call an hour later. It had taken him that long to root out the Home Minister and get him to speak to the PM. For once, Thakur had delivered.

"You will ensure our role in this matter remains totally secret?" That had been Thakur's primary concern.

"You can rest assured about that," Dagan confirmed.

Before either of them retired that night, a team from Mossad's Kidon Unit was en route to Delhi.

Like most men in his position, Ravinder too knew a bit about Mossad's elite Kidon Unit. Not much, but enough to know that if anyone could do it, they could.

Mad dogs like Pasha and Anwar deserve to die.

Ravinder had no qualms about how it was done. He was happy that they were going to do it; it was never a bad idea to have someone else eliminate your problems.

He fell asleep content.

It took a long time for Ravinder to realize that it wasn't just a dream . . . the phone was actually ringing. Groggy with sleep, he reached for it.

"Sorry to bother you so late, sir, but I thought you'd like to know." Mohite was sounding shaken. And tired.

"What happened?"

"We just missed them . . . Javed and Aslam."

"What?" Ravinder was wide awake now. "What happened?"

"You remember I'd told you about the remaining two leads? Well, I'd ordered the Station House Officers of the concerned areas to follow them up. The SHO of Friends Colony just called me. They raided the suspected house a while ago and discovered that all three of the bastards had been staying there. Apparently

Javed and Aslam stepped out minutes before the raid. They *just* missed them."

"Missed them or they were warned?"

Mohite was silent, obviously he'd not thought of that. "Let me look into that, sir." Pause. Then he added dubiously, "But Sher Singh, the SHO, is a rock-solid guy."

"That he is, but ask him to double-check his staff . . . the people who knew about the raid." Ravinder ran that thought through again. Maybe he was clutching at straws. "Could be a coincidence, but no harm in checking."

"Wilco, sir. I agree. And they're interrogating the house owner now. . . . He appears to be a supporter. . . . Let's hope they come up with something. . . . I'll rest easy once we have the bastards behind bars . . . or six feet under. . . ." Ravinder could sense his tension. "Damn! To think we almost had the buggers."

"Don't stress about it, Govind. Shit happens. We can only try."

Even to Ravinder the words offered no solace, knowing he was one of the three people the terrorists had been sent in to kill. He knew exactly how Mohite was feeling. Lousy.

Mir Kasab, the suicide bomber he had shot just two days ago, returned to his sleep several times. Whatever little remained of the night passed fitfully.

DAY FOUR

Conditioned by her training, Ruby arrived at the Dilli Haat half an hour before the stipulated time for their meeting with Nanda. She spent it casing the area, watching for anything out of sync. She spotted nothing unusual, no one loitering around surreptitiously, with those giveaway earpieces or bulges under their coats, no hard-looking men . . . or women . . . hanging around aimlessly. Not that she was expecting trouble, but it was not her nature to leave things to chance.

Satisfied, she returned to her hired car and sat down to wait in a cream-colored Toyota Innova, common on Delhi roads. The driver, Kishore, was a slim, polite young man about five and a half feet; his gray Safari suit was well maintained and as clean as his car. He saw she was parking herself in the car, so switching on the engine and air conditioner, he walked away. From behind the darkened window, Ruby could see him leaning against a nearby tree, relaxed yet keeping an eye on her, waiting to be summoned. Over the past two days, she had become fond of him, though she knew that she should often be changing vehicles and drivers. Never a good idea to let others know your routine. Ruby decided then that she would switch to a self-drive, one with a GPS device—she could not spend the rest of her life trying to find her way through this maddeningly large city.

These thoughts were running through her head when she saw Mark emerge from a black Hyundai that pulled up in a slot three cars away. Ruby was pleased that he too had arrived early, and functioning in top form. She wondered if the men he had hired were as good. She hoped they were; her life would also depend on them.

Ruby watched Mark survey the area, sweeping over it quadrant by quadrant.

At ten thirty on a weekday morning, Dilli Haat, the famous crafts market opposite the INA Market in South Delhi, had yet to fill to its potential. A short hop from the Hyatt, the colorful, cheerful market, with its tiny stalls and regional, multicuisine food marts, was popular with Delhi-wallahs and foreigners alike.

Fronted by an elaborately carved stone gate, manned by armed khaki-clad cops and a set of massive doorframe metal detectors, the *haat* had a bright red stone wall encircling it. Ice cream vendors, balloon sellers, and an assortment of ladies in bright ghagra cholis had started setting up shop outside the gates. It was still early, but soon women of all ages would be getting henna applied to their hands and feet by these ladies.

Every so often another car would pull into the parking spaces on either side of the front gate and a crowd of women and children would tumble out, families coming to spend the day at the *haat*. Ruby could tell that it would not be long before it was teeming. That, in fact, was why Mark must have chosen it for meeting Nanda; crowds always offered safety.

"The cream station wagon to your left." Ruby shot off in a text to Mark.

A second later he looked up, gave a slight nod, and went back to scanning the crowds. Things must have passed muster, since he headed over, bought an entry ticket, and walked across to the food stall at the end of the *haat*, the designated meeting point.

When he emerged half an hour later, she saw a portly, slightly balding man with him. Ruby assumed it was Nanda. In the midst of casually dressed holidaymakers, he looked incongruous in his Armani suit. A gold watch and several golden Cross ballpoint pens in his breast pocket lit up his attire. In every way he portrayed a successful businessman. The two parted ways at the entry gates, heading for different parts of the parking lot.

Mark watched Nanda step into a sprightly blue Mercedes 300 as a chauffeur held open the door. The chauffeur was as smartly attired as his boss, his white uniform and cap giving him a regal air. The car pulled out. Only then did Mark make his way to Ruby.

"All taken care of." Mark opened the door and poked his head in. "We will have the weapons on Wednesday."

Three days from now. Three days to D-day.

"All four Glock 17s?"

"All four Glock 17s." Mark nodded. "Ammo and spare clips."

"You think he is reliable?"

"He won't let us down," Mark reassured her with a grin. "Not for the kind of money the bastard is charging us. If he started double-crossing his customers, I don't think he'd last long in this business."

Still parked in the rear of his Mercedes near the parking lot exit, Sanjeev Nanda was watching. He saw Mark walk over to an Innova, lean in, and speak to someone inside, but he was unable to see who. From the faint silhouette, at this distance, it seemed like a woman, but he was not sure. He would have loved to know. Information was money, and to Nanda, money was irresistible.

He felt he had spotted an opportunity. He was not going to let it pass, not if the rewards were lucrative, and in this case the potential was high. A foreign mercenary looking for four deadly, high-capacity weapons, which were hard to detect. The Commonwealth Games about to start. A dozen terror groups had declared that they would not allow them to take place. To Nanda, the numbers looked unbeatable. He *knew* the cops would pay through the nose for this one.

Nanda, lost in his thoughts, did not notice Mark walk away from the Innova, get into the Accent, and drive off. He started when he heard a loud tap on his window. Mark was staring at him, the Accent idling behind him. He noted a strange expression on the man's face and knew Mark's suspicions had been aroused.

Powering down the window, Nanda explained, "I am waiting for my driver." Luckily, a few minutes back, Nanda had sent him to pick up a packet of cigarettes from a shop near the gate. Just then the driver returned, got into the car, and turned to hand over a packet of Davidoff Lights to Nanda.

Grabbing the pack, Nanda snarled at him. "Drive."

Used to his boss's erratic mood swings, the man gunned the engine and they pulled away.

Mark watched Nanda go. The mercenary's survival instincts were sounding an alarm. Right now it wasn't shrill, but loud enough for Mark to take note. He had a feeling; maybe things were not so kosher.

Ruby missed all this. She had stayed on in her car after Mark left. With her reconnaissance complete and most of the preparatory work well in hand, she felt at a loose end. Till the rest of the team arrived, she had only to wait. And going back to the hotel room held no appeal for her.

Deciding to make the most of this unusual venue, she got out and headed for the *haat*. May as well get in some sightseeing; who knew when she'd come to India again?

Will I even survive this mission? That thought halted her. She shrugged. *It does not matter if I don't. My life has no meaning. Not if the delegates survive and the peace summit succeeds. . . . They'd slice up Palestine.*

Pushing away the dire thought, she bought herself an entry ticket. Picking it up and her change, she was looking down to return the money to her wallet and failed to see the man striding up to her. He was closing in fast and approaching her from behind—with excitement on his face and his arms stretched out wide, ready to encircle her.

Ruby felt a shock as arms closed in around her waist. She was so keyed up that her body automatically moved to counter the assault. She was about to raise her hands to break the hold when he spoke.

"Ruby Gill, I presume." The familiar, playful tone shocked her into stillness.

Ruby spun around to find Chance Spillman's smiling face in front of her, just inches away, and he was looking thrilled—the way he had looked at her when they first started dating. God! How she had missed him.

Click!

Something inside her snapped. Leaning forward, she kissed him. For one brief moment, she felt herself in another time as their lips came together. Their breath mingled easily and effortlessly. She could smell that familiar minty taste of his. They were one again. The magic was back.

Then someone passing by laughed, and the moment disintegrated. Reality returned.

"What on earth are you doing in India?" Chance released her. Then that tentativeness, that withholding, so common during the last months of their togetherness, returned. It was again standing between them. Bad. Ugly. But it was there. Both knew they could not wish it away.

Despite that, Ruby could not help smiling. She was thrilled to see Chance. Seeing the feeling mirrored on his face warmed her heart.

Looking at him, in dark blue jeans and white linen shirt, with that cocky Chance smile on his face, Ruby felt her knees go weak. She felt the urge to kiss him again. She might have done it, but just then Chance spoke.

"So? What on earth *are* you doing in India?" he repeated.

She remembered why, and that Chance was also an MI6 agent. *How long has he been here? Did he see me with Mark? That would be disastrous.*

Chance knew Mark well; he'd also know that Mark was now freelancing.

"What are *you* doing here?" She countered, struggling to regain her balance.

"Security for Sir Geoffrey Tang," Chance replied, surprising her with the ease with which he divulged that. The son of a senior SAS officer who had been killed in counterterror operations in Ireland, Chance had a personal ax to grind with terrorists. Ruby knew he tended to be pretty anal about security. Perhaps he was talking as one colleague to another, or perhaps he was as shaken by their meeting as she was.

The name struck a chord in Ruby's head; the name of every summit delegate was embedded in her. "He is here?" she asked innocently. "How is the cranky old bugger?"

Both laughed. Chance knew that Sir Tang had given Ruby one hell of a time when she'd been riding shepherd on him during a state visit to Pakistan. It had happened when they were living together.

"Same old, same old." Chance smiled as he said that. He could never forget how much Ruby had bitched about Tang.

"What's he doing here? A bit far from the House of Lords, is he not?"

"An important meeting he is . . . but mostly for the games." Chance's natural secretiveness had reasserted itself. "So, you didn't tell me. . . . What are you doing here?"

"Also for the games." Ruby eagerly grabbed at the excuse Chance had provided. "And just needed to get away for a bit."

She studied him and decided it had been an innocent question. He stood with his head cocked slightly to the right, a smile dancing on his face, his bright blue eyes taking her in. The sight made her heartbeat ramp up. It was the smile that had first ignited desire in her.

Ruby's mind flipped back to the first time they met.

They had been working on putting down an Iranian spy ring, which Counter-Intelligence had chanced upon during an audit of British nuclear facilities. They'd pinpointed four British scientists at one or the other of the plants. An Iranian-origin but British-bred lawyer who operated out of Kensington had recruited them, obviously the spymaster. Chance and Ruby were part of the MI6 team keeping him under surveillance.

At first, Chance had come across to her as a slick lady-killer type; a breed she detested. And it took her awhile to realize that he was anything but. It was the delicious fajitas he brought for their third stakeout that broke the ice.

"Lovely," Ruby said as she took the first bite. "Where did you pick them up from?"

"I didn't," he replied between mouthfuls, his eyes still fixed on the spymaster's house. "Made them myself."

"Yeah, right?" Ruby laughed, then saw the look on his face and realized he was serious. "You cook very well."

"Thanks." He smiled. "Never had an option, you see. Ma died when I was eight. So just Dad and me." His attention still on the house. Ruby was surprised with his ease in opening up. "And Dad!" Chance laughed. "He had a soldier's palate. He'd eat anything anyone put in front of him. Not me . . . I couldn't handle the tripe he churned out, so I learned to cook. No option." He laughed softly at the memory.

They both focused on the fajitas. The silence was companionable. It lasted longer than the fajitas.

It was during those long stakeouts that they had come to know and like each other. The more time they did together, the more they liked it. Ruby certainly did, and she was woman enough to know that her feelings were reciprocated. But both were also smart enough to know that office romances were not the thing and not how an MI6 agent lived. Things would not have progressed if it hadn't been for the way that assignment ended.

Perhaps one of the agents had slipped up, or perhaps the lawyer-spymaster was smarter than they had given him credit for; either way, he picked up on the surveillance. However, he was not smart enough; he made the mistake of calling up his controller before attempting to leave the country. Alerted that he was going to make a break for it, both MI6 teams on watch were ordered to bring him in.

Chance and Ruby were watching the front of the house, and neither expected the bugger to come out shooting, but he did.

They were approaching the front door; Chance a step in front of her when the spymaster flew out. Ruby saw him first, but by then he was almost upon them. She saw the gun in his hand and knew they were too late; it was up and leveled at Chance.

Ruby shouted and threw herself straight into the line of fire. The bullet hit her bulletproof jacket. The Kevlar stopped the bullet, but fired at point-blank range, its high-velocity impact pummeled her into the ground. Then a thunder of gunfire drowned out everything.

When she opened her eyes, Chance was standing above her, smoke curling out of the pistol in his hand. The lawyer lay dead a few feet away, two neat holes in his head.

It took Ruby a long time to comprehend that she was still alive. Chance could not look away from her. "You jumped into the line of fire?" he said over and over, unable to restrain his gratitude and awe. As he had not been wearing a body vest, it would have been curtains for him if she'd not stopped the bullet.

After hours of tedious paperwork, after-action reports, and debriefing, they were silent as he drove her home. When he stopped outside her apartment, she made no move to get out. They sat in silence for a while.

"May I come up?" Chance finally asked.

She saw a wild look in his eyes. His lips were slightly parted and his eyes shone with desire—an intense desire no doubt fostered by the events of the past few hours. Ruby nodded. A small but definite nod.

Standing side by side in the elevator as it rode up, they did not touch. Their shoulders were touching, but barely so. The silence between them was dense with desire. Almost tangible. Filling up the tiny elevator.

The minute the door to her apartment closed behind them,

Chance's mouth found hers. It was a compelling, urgent, demanding kiss. Warm. Wet. Ruby moaned. Her lips pushed back insistently as her arms enveloped him. She shivered as his hands slid down her back, till they reached her buttocks, seizing them, pulling her closer. Pelvises grinding together.

Buttons and zippers gave way till there were no clothes left between them. Ruby felt his lips and tongue love her body, her neck, and then slide down to her breasts. And then lower still. She pulled him upward.

"No!" Her voice was hoarse. "Take me. Now!"

He did. On the carpet. Just a few feet inside the door. She moaned as he began to move. Almost instantly, her back arched as an orgasm ripped through her. His came a moment later. They just lay there. Then desire returned. But this time they made it to the bedroom. And then, later, in the shower. Each time it lasted longer and became better.

Ruby flushed. Even now the memory of his hard, lean body sent warm wetness flooding through her.

Taboos on office romance be damned, they moved in together a month later. A potent magic flourished between them.

So then why—?

Ruby's foray into the past shattered as Chance spoke again. She had missed something. "Sorry, you were saying?"

"I said I can understand why you needed to get away. I heard about your mother in the office when I got back from Kabul." Chance's smile had vanished and his face had acquired a somber hue. "Terribly sorry for your loss." He reached out and touched her cheeks with his fingertips; it was a very light, tender touch. It overwhelmed Ruby. "How are you coping?"

"Fine." It came out as a choked whisper; Ruby was fighting to stem tears, as much from being reminded as from how Chance had reached out to her. Without warning, the terrorist was overwhelmed by the woman inside.

"Are you sure, Ruby? Is there anything I can do? If there is, you know you just have to ask." His imploring face conveyed his sincerity. Ruby knew he meant every word.

She shook her head, unwilling to trust her voice. She could feel her mind starting to torque away and fought to control it. "I needed to get away," she whispered again. Slowly, the terrorist within regained control. The fragile thread that emotions had begun to weave between them had broken.

"I understand." Chance, at a loss for words, was searching for something to say. "Did you finally meet up with your father? I remember you telling me he was from India."

"No. I haven't met him yet."

"Why on earth not?"

"I know. I have to. That is another reason I chose to come to India. But . . . well . . . I just got in . . . ," Ruby improvised. "I am working up the courage to meet him."

"You? Working up the courage? Since when?" Chance could not hide his amusement. "The Ruby I know would just pick up the phone and call him."

The Ruby you know . . . knew . . . Ruby held that thought at bay. Instead she forced a sheepish smile. "I will. Tomorrow."

"Great!" He smiled. "Talking of phones. This is my hotel number." He scribbled it on the ticket stub in her hand. "We must stay in touch. Don't hesitate if there is anything I can do." She felt a touch of awkwardness as he paused, as though he had run out of words. "There is something I—" Ruby never knew what else Chance was going to say, because a woman walked up to them.

"There you are!" She greeted Chance.

Ruby felt a spasm of irritation. Then surprise. As she took a close look at the newcomer, she got the eerie feeling that she was almost looking into a mirror.

Barring the newcomer's fair complexion and auburn hair, the resemblance to her was startling. Approximately the same age, same height, and similar build. And the woman even wore her hair the same way: straight, shoulder-length hair, right now pulled back in a high pony.

Then Ruby saw the smile on Chance's face, which mirrored the pleasure the woman was displaying. Ruby felt a pang of jealousy. She saw the smile on the newcomer's face slip as the two women assessed each other. The newcomer must have picked up her vibes of shared intimacy with Chance just as Ruby had immediately been able to tell that the other woman was keen on him. And Chance did not appear immune to her charms either. In that second, their instincts confirmed that they were rivals.

"Ruby, this is Jennifer . . . Jennifer Poetzcsh." Immune to the subtle exchange of these womanly vibes, Chance turned to Ruby and introduced her. "Jennifer, this is my friend and colleague, Ruby Gill." The two women shook warily. "Jennifer is with our cousins," Chance added, making it clear she was CIA.

He is smitten. Ruby was now resentful as Chance continued. "She is here with Senator Polk, who has also come for the same meeting as Sir Geoffrey."

"Ruby Gill." Jennifer murmured, giving a small, taut smile. "You are the second Gill I've met since I got here."

"Yes! You are right." Chance laughed. "Funny, isn't it." He turned to Ruby. "The guy from Delhi Police who is helping us with . . . with the conference is also called Gill . . . Ravinder Singh Gill." He spread his hands wide. "Now, is that a coincidence or what?"

Ruby went still. As far as she could remember, just the mention of her father would be enough to agitate Rehana; hence, Ruby had usually avoided the topic. However, on the rare occasions that her mother had spoken about him, Rehana mentioned that her father was in the Indian Police Service, but Ruby had never imagined that he'd be the one to . . . *And there can't be many people with that exact same name . . . can there?*

Then Ruby realized that Chance and Jennifer were staring at her; she must have showed something on her face, or maybe because she had gone silent. "It sure is a funny coincidence," she blurted out.

"Mr. Gill mentioned that he'd been in London in college with Sir Edward, so . . . ," Chance added. "Wonder if you two are related?"

Ruby had recovered enough to laugh it off. "I guess all Gills in India are? That is what my mom used to say." The terrorist was back in control.

An awkward silence now fell upon them. Just minutes ago, Chance had shared an intimate moment with her. Or had she imagined it? *Was it just concern for a colleague? An old flame?* She was no longer sure. Of anything.

"Hey," Chance intruded again, "we were planning to spend some time here. . . . I believe it's a great place. You feel like joining us?"

Ruby almost laughed as she saw the expression on Jennifer's face; it was a fleeting one, which the woman checked instantly, but it was as clear as though she had spoken it out. Ruby bit back a smile. He still had a lot to learn about women. Just to spite Jennifer, she felt the urge to agree, but realizing the danger of prolonged contact, she checked the impulse. "Thank you, but no. You guys please go ahead."

This sudden encounter had shaken Ruby. Now she knew she needed time to think and process her feelings: the woman in her had been challenged; she wanted to step forth and fight for her man. Maybe. And the terrorist in her had been warned. Chance's mention of her father—it was too much, both Chance and Ravinder securing the same peace summit that she was here to destroy. Everything was coming together too suddenly, too fast. She had to be alone, to wrap her head around this.

"Why don't I get the tickets while you two . . ." Jennifer walked off toward the ticket counter.

"She is a very nice person." Chance watched her go, his puppy smile on display.

"Is she, now?" Ruby murmured, her jealousy getting the better of her. "Trying Pepsi instead of Coke, are we?"

He gave her a puzzled look. But before he could say anything, Ruby reached up, pecked him on the cheek, and walked away, half regretting the remark.

Even if he is annoyed, damned if I care, Ruby muttered silently, her head reeling. She was still grappling with the fact that Chance had walked away from her . . . just as Ravinder had left Mom . . . *and me.*

"Men!" she growled as she got into her car and told the driver to take her back to the hotel. It never occurred to her that she had always held Ravinder's leaving her mother as her reason for never committing to Chance.

Chance watched her walk away; he had never been able to figure Ruby out, to understand why she had always held a part of herself aloof from him . . . from them.

He felt angry—*she has no right to throw these verbal darts.* He toyed with the idea of going after her to confront her. Then he remembered what he'd heard on the agency grapevine, about her nervous breakdown when her mother had died, and felt contrite, realizing that he should cut her some slack. He knew she'd been close to her mother. Even when they'd been living together, she and her mother would talk, if not meet, almost every day. Then Jennifer returned.

"I got them." She was holding up two tickets. "Let's go." She reached out and took his arm. Jennifer had been taken aback by Ruby; she so hoped that whatever had been between them was over. She felt glad to have Chance back to herself; she sensed Ruby could be a formidable foe.

Chance was more than a bit distracted as he took Jennifer's arm and they entered the *haat.*

Jennifer looked up at him and smiled. Chance, even if he had wanted to, could not then have missed the similarity to Ruby, especially not after the catty remark Ruby had made.

The realization struck home. Hard.

"It's hot." Jennifer fanned herself. "And I'm thirsty. Would you like some Coke?"

Chance was unable to enjoy the afternoon. Something gnawed away inside of him, constantly reminding him that there was unfinished, unresolved business with Ruby; something that needed to be put to rest. A part of him hoped she would call. Another part hoped he would never meet her again.

Ruby was fuming as she drove away. Chance's interest in Jennifer had hit her hard. She had no idea how confused Chance was in the months they had been together, trying to figure out why there was this part of her he could never touch, no matter how hard he tried to reach out. Once their initial burst of lust subsided and the Monday-morning reality of sustaining a relationship had fallen upon them, Chance came to realize that Ruby was always holding a part of herself back. However, he was not canny enough to know that she was fluctuating wildly between *Yes, I want him* and *But can I trust him?*

But the fact that she had saved his life kept him from walking away. Which was why he had been so relieved when the agency sent him to Afghanistan. Then they slowly but steadily had drifted apart. They had been out of touch for several months now, but there was no closure.

And Chance had been on the verge of bringing it up when Jennifer walked up to them.

Ruby paced her hotel room, the cabal of conflicting emotions churning through her. Finally tired, she sat by the window, the mess of thoughts in her head as chaotic as the traffic on the Ring Road running past her window.

THINK DIFFERENT! The massive billboard with an Apple advertisement across the road caught her eye.

JUST DO IT! The equally massive Nike advertisement next to it exhorted her.

Out of the blue, things clicked together.

Ruby now knew that to get at the summit delegates, she would have to fight her way past her father and the man she thought she loved . . . had loved.

But they abandoned me, after all.

That thought renewed the fire in her belly.

But if push came to shove and one of them stood between the targets and me, would I be able to pull the trigger?

The question petrified the woman. Not knowing the answer confused the terrorist.

Would I have taken on this mission if I had known that my father was the one . . . or did I accept and come to India subconsciously hoping I'd run into him?

She realized she didn't know. Ruby moaned; the pain inside almost physical. A low, petrified cry for help. But no one was listening. She knew.

THINK DIFFERENT! Her eyes would not abandon the Apple billboard. But thoughts continued to clash unchecked.

By late afternoon, these worrisome questions had coalesced into a pounding headache. Then pangs of nausea began to wrack her. She was exhausted by the time she lay down. Sleep came almost instantly. However, it was a restless, dream-infested sleep.

The man who had been haunting her dreams was still faceless. She tried but could not make out who it was—just that he had blood all over his face. Suddenly, Chance emerged from behind him. He too had blood on his face, oozing out from a neat, round, black hole between his eyes.

"Why haven't you spoken to your father yet? Just pick up the phone and call him," he was saying, over and over, his voice a broken whisper. "Why are you hesitating? Don't you want to know how he is . . . what kind of a man he is . . . why he left your mother . . . and you?" His tone became sharp and insistent.

Ruby awoke with a start. Her heart was pounding and she was bathed in sweat, even though the air-conditioning was going full blast. After reaching for the mineral water on her bedside table, she took a long swig, draining the bottle. Still thirsty, she got up and pulled another bottle out of the mini-bar and drank that too. It made her feel better. Marginally.

She lay down again, but this time sleep was driven away by a new need to find out about her father. To understand who he really was. For so many years, confused by his abandonment, she had taught herself to avoid thinking about him . . . *convinced* herself to hate him . . . almost . . . but . . . *I need to find out.* . . . She knew she could not live without knowing any longer.

Why? Why did you leave? What did I do to grow up without a father?

Now the room was pitch dark. Though the curtains were drawn back, not even a speck of light filtered in. The darkness outside felt as deep as the darkness within her.

Now I have no one to call my own.

That thought hammered at her. She longed to reach out and talk to someone. Anyone.

Who?

There was *no one.*

Chance?

Her hand reached out for the phone. But she stayed it. *No.* She did not need the aggravation of feeling her way through whatever still existed between them . . . *if* anything still did.

What about Father? He *was* her father, after all. Ruby dwelt on that for a long time.

Which father? The one who abandoned us? Who did not, even once, over all these years, bother to check on me . . . to come looking for me . . . to hug me . . . hold me . . . talk to me . . . to find out if I was alive.

Ruby felt confusion, hurt, and resentment building up. She fought them; damned if she would allow herself to cry over a father who did not even care whether she was alive or dead.

Did he? Her mind again was playing tag with her, as it often did when she was upset. *Did he really not care?*

She gave up trying to sleep. It was futile. She *needed* to talk to someone. Scrabbling through her bag, she retrieved the ticket stub with Chance's number.

He's met my father; he'll know what kind of person he is.

She also hoped Chance would be happy to hear from her.

The phone at the other end began to ring.

Chance had just entered the bathroom and unzipped when the phone began to ring. He called out to Jennifer, who had joined him for a nightcap after another exhausting day of sightseeing. "Could you get that, please?"

"Sure," Jennifer called back, reaching for the phone.

Hello." Ruby had heard it only once before, but she recognized the nasal American accent. "Hello," Jennifer said again.

Ruby almost spoke. She would have, but her eye fell upon her wristwatch. The glowing dial showed a tad past midnight. She knew she did not need to speak to Chance to get an answer; it was staring her in the face.

Chance has moved on.

She put down the phone and returned to her lonely, restless vigil by the window.

He also has left me.

Wetness began crowding her eyes. With an effort, she pushed it away.

"So what's new? Men do that all the time." Ruby said it out loud, as though she needed to hear it to believe it. A long moment of suspended thought followed. Her father too had done that to her mother. *To me. He was no different.*

Then she cried. And cried. Till she could cry no more.

A sharp spike of anger at Rehana jabbed her. *Why did you have to go and die? Why did you never tell me about my father?* Why had she always shied away from talking about him . . . about what had happened between them? *Why?*

Ruby remembered asking her often when she'd been young. "Where is Daddy? How come he never comes home . . . and to my school like other fathers?"

"How do I explain to you, my darling? You're too young to understand."

But Ruby was always old enough to know that her father was

not there for her. She remembered the nights she had cried herself to sleep; a physical ache as she longed for that huge bearded man who held her close, who made her feel loved, wanted, and safe. The pain had been so intense, so hurtful, that she had tried to stop thinking about him.

That pain now returned. Even after all these years, it was still sharp. Perhaps sharper, since it had been ignored and suppressed so long.

And now Mom has left me too.

But no. As Ruby hit the end of her tether, Rehana reached out from beyond and pulled her out of the abyss.

"Did I not always tell you, my child?" Ruby heard the constant rejoinder echo in her head. "Chance will never understand. Just as your father never did. *No one will.* . . . Our cause is our own. . . . That is the way it has always been. Nothing will ever get better, not unless we fight for it. *They* will not allow it to." She would thumb toward Chance's photo on Ruby's bedside table. "Men like him. They are the ones who killed our family . . . who have been killing our people all these years. It was these bloody Brits who started it all. . . . If not for their support, the fucking Jews would never have had the guts. . . . I am telling you—Chance will use you and dump you . . . just as your father did. Remember that."

The words seemed prophetic now.

A clap of thunder boomed out. Lightning lacerated the sky, intermittently lighting up the road outside.

JUST DO IT! the Nike advertisement tugged at her.

I will show you . . . all of you . . . bastards. . . . Hardening her heart, she got up and threw herself on the bed. The transition from confused woman to committed terrorist was swift.

Drops of rain began to hammer on the windowpanes. The drumming sound eventually dulled her into a deep sleep.

Why didn't you tell me, sir?" Mohite's tone teetered on the edge of insolence.

"About what, Mohite?" Though it was past midnight, Ravinder held his peace.

"About the Israeli commando team that has reached Delhi and is now on the way to Amritsar."

"Who told you about it?" Ravinder asked even though he knew; it had to be Thakur.

"I had gone to meet Thakur sahib when he mentioned it."

"Need to know, Mohite." Ravinder hardened his tone, just enough to let Mohite know who was in charge. "You didn't need to know. That's why."

"Foreign agents are running around all over our country with guns, and I don't need to know? Thakur sahib thought it fit to let me know."

"Then from now on, you can just ask him only to keep you informed!" Ravinder slammed down the phone.

DAY FIVE

Dawn was lighting the horizon when Ruby woke up. The rain had stopped but it was overcast. A stubborn sun struggled to make its presence felt.

Her eye strayed to her wristwatch.

Five days left for the summit.

Ruby suddenly felt she was bursting with energy, as though the night's rain had washed away her confusions.

She thrust herself out of bed. She knew what she needed to do.

The foul aftertaste of last night's call from Mohite was still in his mouth when Ravinder heard his mobile. He checked the calling number. He was not ready to talk with that asshole again . . . not the first thing in the morning, at least. But it was an unknown number. He depressed the green button, hoping it would not be more bad news.

"Good morning, Mr. Gill." It was Ido Peled. He sounded excited. "We have heard from one of our sources in Pakistan that Saeed Anwar is going to be at a safe house near Lahore. Our director asked me to let you know that we would like to send our team in now."

"Be my guest, Ido. I'll put out the word." Ravinder suddenly felt lighter. This was the kind of news he needed to hear. "And all the best."

"Thank you, sir." Peled rang off.

I hope they get the bastard . . . dead or alive . . . one less prob-lem for us to deal with. He was dwelling on this happy thought when the phone rang again. This time he picked up eagerly.

The conversation with Sanjeev Nanda was brief. Ravinder knew that if Nanda said it was important and they needed to meet, it would be.

"Delhi Gymkhana," he told the driver as he settled into the of-ficial Scorpio SUV. The red light on top of the car whirled as it slid through the traffic. Ravinder was not fond of it, nor of the siren his driver tended to use far too often. He winced as the driver gave another long hooting blast, trying to burn a corridor though the dense traffic. But the short drive to the gymkhana still took thirty minutes.

"Whatever this creep has to offer, it better be good," Ravinder muttered as he entered the club.

Nanda was at the corner table in the gymkhana bar, where they usually met. Ravinder had to smile as he took in Nanda's snazzy Armani suit, the gold Rolex, and his diamond-embedded tie clip. *He has definitely changed,* Ravinder reflected. *Who says crime doesn't pay?*

He remembered the first time they'd met.

Ravinder had been in Narcotics. All of five weeks in the de-partment, totally green behind the ears, but full of energy. Nanda was the first crook he had ever turned.

They'd nabbed a Nigerian drug peddler with two kilos of co-caine. Taking a gamble, Ravinder had let him go. In the subse-quent weeks, the Nigerian led them to ten others selling the awful stuff. Rather than round them all up immediately, and more eager to take down the kingpins, Ravinder had put them all un-der surveillance. That had led them up the food chain to Nanda, caught with enough coke to lock him up for a very, very long time. Ravinder then took another gamble, knowing that Nanda was not *the* big man, but someone who knew who the big man was. And Nanda was, of course, weasel enough to shop him to save his own hide.

"You will not peddle again," Ravinder warned as they cut the deal. "If I ever come to know that you are, all bets are off."

"Never, sir." Nanda had crossed his heart theatrically. "I swear it on my mother's soul."

Nanda's patently false sincerity made Ravinder feel sorry for his mother's soul. *Oh well!*

"What else do you have to offer?" Though a greenhorn, Ravinder was savvy enough to know when to bargain.

"You tell me, sir," Nanda said smugly, assuming the cop would ask for a bribe. How else could the man have stayed out of jail for so long?

"I want you to keep your eyes open and an ear to the ground." Ravinder surprised him; a clean cop was something one rarely came across. And honesty was certainly not a career-enhancing attribute, not in this profession. *Perhaps that is why he gets shunted from one lousy assignment to another,* Nanda must have rationalized, tuning in to what Ravinder was saying. "Whenever you come across something big, I want to know."

Nanda felt uncertain; if his brethren ever learned he was a snitch, he'd have a short life and a most unpleasant end.

Ravinder sensed his fear. "This will remain strictly between you and me. . . . No one else needs to know . . . ever." Some of Nanda's fear seemed to recede. "And you will be paid. I will ensure that."

That had sealed the deal; Nanda worshipped money. Thereafter, every now and then, Nanda called Ravinder. Each time proved worthwhile, for both. Nanda enhanced his riches and Ravinder acquired the reputation of a ferocious crime-buster.

"You are looking well, sir." Nanda rose and offered his hand.

"Not as well as you, my friend." Throwing a quick look around, Ravinder sat down opposite him. Layered with rich mahogany, the ornate bar had the colonial feel of an exclusive men's club: large crystal chandeliers; deep, plush armchairs; and carved, round tables laid out at discreet distances. At this hour, it was empty. "So, what do you have for me today?"

"Straight to business as usual, sir. You haven't changed a bit. A cup of tea or coffee first?"

"Not today, Sanjeev. Too much is happening. Tell me . . . what's up?"

Ravinder's face grew somber at Nanda's narrative. And his excitement escalated; this could be a big attack on the games . . . or the peace summit? "There are two of them?"

"Yes, sir—Mark, the Irish guy who got in touch with me, and then the second one he went and met with right after that . . . a woman, I think, but I cannot be sure."

"Why do you think it's a woman?"

"Not sure, sir." Nanda looked away, trying to reconstruct the scene. "Most probably because of the profile I saw . . . but the car windows had dark film on them . . . so I cannot be sure."

"Hmm." Ravinder tried to ferret out more. "Anything else you remember . . . which make of car she was in, the registration number?"

"Sorry, sir." Nanda give a sheepish smile. "I was too far away, but it was a cream-colored Toyota Innova."

Ravinder couldn't mask his disappointment. There were thousands of those in Delhi.

"This guy . . . Mark? What's his full name? Where is he staying?"

"I don't know, sir." Another sheepish smile. "I've dealt with him just once . . . a while ago. . . . It was a small cash-and-carry deal . . . so . . ." He petered off with a shrug.

Damnit! Mark is a bloody common name . . . else we could hunt down the hotel he is at and take him in.

"Call me if you remember anything else." Nanda nodded. "When are you handing over the guns?"

"Day after. Wednesday."

"Where?"

"He said he'd call and tell me."

"You have the number he calls you from?"

"I did check on that. He used a public phone both times."

"The same one?"

"No. Different both times . . . from different parts of the city."

Ravinder nodded, disappointed but not surprised; it had been a long shot; this was a precaution every professional would take. "Fine! Call me as soon as you know?"

"Definitely." Nanda hesitated. "Sir, I am going to be there personally. . . . I hope your people will be careful when they . . ." He trailed off.

"Don't worry. I will be there myself." Ravinder was feeling elated as he headed back to his office. Yes, even good guys caught a lucky break sometimes, though he wished he knew which target they were going for.

Oh well. Ravinder shrugged. Even this was heaven sent. He knew Thakur, keen to show the PM that he was doing well at his new assignment, would be thrilled when they caught the terrorists. *Yes, this could be a big one.* He called Mohite and brought him up to speed.

"Could they be the same ones that the CIA woman . . . Jennifer . . . had mentioned? Remember? She'd said the Lashkar has hired British mercs to strike Delhi."

"Yes, I remember, Govind. They may well be the same . . . though she'd said British, and this Mark guy is Irish."

"Yeah, yeah. British, Irish, what's the difference? These *firangis* are all the same."

"Never mind, Govind." Ravinder sighed.

"This is fantastic!" Mohite was excited. "Thakur sahib will be very pleased."

"Yeah, but keep this under your hat for now. Let's talk to him about it only once we have them in our hands."

"Sure, sure. I agree. Like a surprise gift."

"Yeah right!" Ravinder kept the sarcasm to himself. "Have a team standing by from tomorrow night. They should be ready to move at short notice. . . . What? No! I will go with them. What? Of course . . . you're welcome to come along."

As he put down the phone, he wondered why Mohite always assumed he was being deliberately sidelined. *I guess we see our own identity in others. Anyway . . .* He shrugged, knowing he had to be careful; Mohite had the Home Minister's ear.

Sighing, he got out of the car as it halted outside his office.

The sun had vanished again. The sky was like concrete. Growls of thunder were making their presence felt. Gusts of wind tugged at him. A storm seemed about to break.

Gyan met Ravinder at his office door.

"There is someone here to meet you, sir." Gyan sounded sheepish. "I tried to tell her that she could not meet you without an appointment, but she was insistent. She said she is . . ."

"Who is it?" Ravinder frowned as he pushed open the door. Then he came to a dead stop.

"Oh my God! *Ruby.*" The stunned whisper was half-question. "You look just like your mother."

"Yes, Father, that is what everyone says."

There was a tense silence; the two strangers stood looking at each other.

"You used to call me Daddy . . . always." Ravinder's voice was a strangled whisper.

"I know. And you used to call me princess." Ruby couldn't conceal her bitterness. "But then you left us."

Her words stabbed into him like a hot knife.

He took a couple of steps toward Ruby; he was aching to hug her. "No! I didn't." He halted, uncertain.

"All these years . . ." Her voice broke. "I waited for you to come looking." She started to cry. Ruby did not want to; she was angry with herself for allowing it. The terrorist who'd planned this visit was furious. "Every morning I would wake up and hope you were back. Every day I would come out from school and hope to see you there. Every night I used to pray—"

"I did look for you, but . . ." Ravinder could not go on; nor could he stem the tears that began to trickle down. He realized that Gyan was still standing behind him. Without turning, he said, "Gyan get some tea and . . ." He stopped and looked at the stranger who was his daughter; he did not even know what she liked to drink. There was a time when he would have known when she was hungry, when tired, when she needed to burp, when she was sleepy, when she . . . "What would you like?"

"Tea is fine."

"Get some tea for us, Gyan." He walked up to her, but instead of taking her in his arms and hugging her, as he was aching to do, he took her arm tentatively. "Come . . . please sit down."

Ruby's head was whirling as he drew a chair for her. She had no idea what she expected when she met Ravinder, but she had not expected this. The rush of emotions had caught her totally off guard.

Her eyes fell upon the two photo frames on either side of his computer, simple, mahogany frames. On the left it had Ravinder and a regal-looking woman, with a pretty teenager between them. But it was the one on the right that caught Ruby's attention.

A little girl standing on a chair, reaching out to cut a huge cake in front of her. Wearing a pink frock, the girl had a large beaming smile. The cake was a huge, three-tiered one with a princess on top; the princess too was in a pink frock.

Yes, it is the same . . . the one I forced my mother to have enlarged. And the only one Ruby had ever put up on her bedroom wall.

Ravinder followed her glance. "That was your third birthday." His voice was mellow with emotion.

"I know. I remember. That was the last one all three of us . . ." She looked away. "Then you left. Just two weeks before my fourth . . ." Her voice broke.

"No, princess, I did not leave." Ravinder's throat felt as though something were stuck in it. "I don't know what your mother told you, but it was not me who left."

"No one told me anything. And today you can say anything you want, there is no one left to contradict you."

"But you must believe . . ." Ravinder broke off as he realized what Ruby had said. "*What?* What did you say?" He paused, afraid. Eventually, a reluctant whisper. "Where is Rehana?"

"She is not with us anymore."

"What happened?" Dreading the answer, he could hardly speak.

"Does it matter?"

"Yes, it does." Ravinder was shocked, but he could see how she was hurting. He wanted to take her in his arms and hold her tight . . . the way he had always done when she was small. "Ruby, I really, really loved her."

His words struck Ruby like hammer blows. *Not* what Rehana had told her.

"Rehana meant the world to me," he repeated.

Just then, Gyan entered, bearing a tray. They sat in silence as he poured and placed a plate of biscuits between them. The fragrance of freshly brewed tea filled the room. Ravinder waited till he left.

"I hunted everywhere for both of you when Rehana left, but . . ." The phone rang. Ravinder felt a surge of irritation, and then remembered they were in his office. Giving Ruby an apologetic look, he took the call.

"We cannot talk here," he said to Ruby when he'd finished. "There will always be something or the other interrupting us." He thought for a moment. "Tell me, where are you staying?"

"At the Hyatt Regency."

"Not any longer." Ravinder had made up his mind. "You're coming home to stay with me . . . with us."

"Are you sure?" Ruby asked with a pointed look at the family photograph on his table.

He got the drift and nodded. "That is my wife, Simran, and my daughter, Jasmine." He paused. "I got married again a couple of years after Rehana sent me the divorce documents and . . . that was the last I heard from your mother." The pause this time was longer and more awkward. "It will be okay with them." He sounded more reassuring than he felt.

"If you say so." Ruby felt a triumphant flush run through her; *I'm in*. Being in there could win the day for her.

"Take my car, please go to the hotel and check out. The driver will get you home."

"I have a car."

"Okay, then." Ravinder scribbled his address and handed it to her. "When should I expect you?"

Ruby looked at her watch. "Would it be okay if I got there by about five?"

"That will be perfect." He would have to get home before that, and talk to Simran and Jasmine. He also knew it would not be an easy conversation. He followed Ruby to the door. She was almost out when his voice stopped her.

"Ruby, there is a lot unsaid between us." He began hesitantly. "I do not know what Rehana told you . . . about what happened between us. No matter what you believe, I want you to know this . . . I loved you then, Ruby, more than you can imagine . . . and I love you now. I am grateful God has given us this chance to be together again. I do not want this opportunity to pass . . . not without giving it my best shot." He broke eye contact, feeling wetness creep into his eyes. "But I don't know where to start . . . how to start . . . will you help me? Please."

Ruby could not speak. Her throat was too full. She knew that this man standing before her, the father she had once loved and doted upon, meant every word he was saying. Yes, because she had loved him so much and been so dependent on him was why it had hurt so much when he left . . . why the hurt and the anger ran so deep even now. She replied slowly, "I don't know either, Father. . . . I am not sure you understand what I went through when you left. . . . I am not sure if I am big enough to forget . . . or forgive." She sucked in a large dose of oxygen. "But I will try." The terrorist had no idea when the girl within slipped those words past her.

Then Ruby was gone. Leaving Ravinder happy but also uncertain.

He took a couple of minutes to gather himself before heading for his car. He was opening the door to get in when Gyan came running out. "Sir, there's an urgent call for you. Minister sahib wants to talk to you immediately."

Cursing, he headed back.

"What is this I am hearing, Gill?" Thakur sounded in a foul mood. "The American and British agents are complaining that they are not getting enough cooperation from your people."

"I am afraid I have heard nothing about this, sir, but I will look into it right away."

"How come you don't know what's going on in your department? Mohite knows. He was just telling me about it."

Damn that son of a bitch. "Don't worry, sir. I will take care of the problem."

"How can I not worry? You don't seem to understand how important this peace summit is for India. The whole world will be watching. This is our chance to . . ." Ravinder tuned out as Thakur launched off on his spiel. He was waiting patiently for the call to end when something Thakur was saying caught his attention.

". . . it is very important that we capture these terrorists alive. Mohite was telling me they could be the key to a much larger operation. Have we found out anything else about them?"

Realizing that Mohite had talked about the tip Nanda had given, despite his having cautioned him to keep it under wraps, Ravinder decided it was time to put Mohite on the firing line. He'd keep him so busy that the idiot would have no time for squealing to the minister behind his back. "Not yet, sir, but we are working on it. In fact, since we all know how critical it is, I am putting Mohite in charge of this operation."

"Good idea, Gill. We should allow Govind to live up to his potential." Thakur sounded pleased. "That man has promise. He will be going places one day."

Yeah sure! Ravinder grimaced. *Especially with you watching out for him.* With this clueless interfering minister and a silly second-in-command, he knew there was huge potential for a disaster that could damage India and destroy his career.

Sighing, Ravinder headed back for his car; he needed to talk to Simran before Ruby got back. And that would be a difficult conversation. Somewhere inside, he wished all this were not happening right now . . . not when he needed to focus on the summit and the games. He shrugged fatalistically. *But things happen when they are meant to.*

There was a loud thunderclap and it began to rain. Soon a thick curtain of rain enveloped the car.

When Ravinder walked in, the house was in an uproar. The maids, the gardener, and the driver were running around with buckets and mops. Standing in the center of the living room, Simran was running oversight.

"What happened?"

"What else?" Simran replied with an exasperated cluck. "These awful government houses!" She paused to instruct a maid before turning to him. "The bathroom drain has choked. We have water seeping into the kitchen from every possible corner."

Ravinder opened his mouth to suggest something when he realized he was out of his depth with this one. "Should I have someone from my office look into it?" he finally asked lamely.

"What for? They'll take forever to respond, and by then my kitchen will be a total mess." Simran was so miffed. Ravinder sensed that something else had to be bothering her too. "And by the time they fix it, something else will break down. Why can't we stay at our own house instead of this dump?" She was referring to the luxurious farmhouse in the Chhatarpur area that Ravinder had inherited. "It is lying empty as it is . . . such a waste."

"Simran, we have had this discussion." They of course had. Several times. But despite his best efforts, he had been unable to make her understand that it would not sit well with the powers-that-be for him to be living in such an ostentatious place. Corruption charges were something top cops were always facing. No. No cannon fodder for the media. He chose to live a *regular* life. Not to mention that the remote farmhouse would be much harder to secure . . . something he needed to worry about with those two Jaish-e-Mohammed lunatics still on the loose.

"The Sharmas don't have any such problem?" Simran sniffed,

referring to his colleague who headed up Traffic. "*They* are happily staying in his wife's family home, and that is positively *huge*."

"What they do is their call." He patiently pointed out, "In any case, their house is in Model Town, literally a stone's throw from his office."

"Yeah, yeah! I know!" She sniffed. "*We* are always the special ones. . . . We can never do normal things." They paused, like weary prizefighters. Ravinder had no more to say. Simran's anger was simmering. "I can never understand"—she found her voice again—"why you had to opt for the police? Not when you had the option to join the Foreign Service."

Ravinder sighed. He had no response that would mollify her. Anything he said would only prolong the argument. Even after twenty-four years of marriage, she had not stopped griping about his career choice.

But he did understand her. Born in a Punjab royal family, one not very different from Ravinder's, she must have expected to go on living as she had been used to in her father's house. She'd never thought it through before saying yes to the marriage proposal his mother had taken to hers. In those days, it was considered prestigious to marry a civil servant. He remembered her fury when he, despite being a topper in his course, had chosen to opt for the police rather than the more glamorous Foreign Service. He knew that Simran would have called off the marriage if not for the ignominy that would have led to. There was, of course, also the fact that there were not too many royal males available.

The irony of it almost made Ravinder laugh. He would have too, but that would only further infuriate her and result in another tirade.

She was a good person at heart. And he *did* love her, but he couldn't relate with her on any intellectual level. Also, though he never acknowledged it consciously, somewhere, somehow, Rehana had always strayed between them.

Why the hell did we ever get married? As it had dozens of time in the years gone by, the thought hit him again. A futile question. He already knew the answer.

It was when he had returned from London that his parents, especially his mother, got after him. They freaked out when he'd called up to tell them that he was marrying a Palestinian girl.

He would never have returned to India if Rehana had not vanished, taking his darling Ruby with him.

Ravinder had gone berserk. He had run around like a madman through the streets of first Birmingham and then London, chasing down every possible lead, but Rehana had vanished, as though the earth swallowed her up. He finally had had to give up. Then he had turned and ran to the only place he hoped he would be safe, home to India.

Even today, Ravinder was not sure what had hurt more, the fact that Rehana had left him or the fact that she had left without explaining why. Later, when he reflected on it, he realized that in the weeks before she left, she had been moody and withdrawn.

No. Right from the beginning, Rehana always withheld a part of herself from me . . . from our marriage.

Ravinder had never doubted her love for him, but there *had* been something that she always held back.

"Even if you had to join the police, why couldn't you also manage your postings the way others do?" Simran's voice broke his foray into the past. "Four years in the mosquito-ridden hills of Nagaland . . . with not one decent shop for miles around . . . and . . . and . . ." Spluttering, she waved an angry hand. "Now finally we get to Delhi, and you agree to take over the Anti-Terrorist Task Force. Couldn't you have tried for an easier job? With a normal life?"

"I didn't ask for it, Simran, you know that. When Menon, the previous ATTF chief, died suddenly, they had to move fast . . . with the games and . . . all happening, there was no time to waste."

"And of course you were the only one they could find? No one else was good enough . . . or silly enough . . ."

"Simran." Choking off a retort, Ravinder waved his hand placatingly, trying to calm her. "Could you please stop this? I need to talk to you about something urgent. Could you please listen to me for a moment? Alone."

"What can be more important than this?" She looked at him. And must have caught something on his face, because she dismissed the servants and turned to him. "What is it?"

Ravinder did not know where to start; he had tried to think of an approach while driving down, but hadn't found one. "Do you remember my telling you about Ruby? My daughter from—"

"From *that* woman." Simran always referred to Rehana as "that woman." She hated for that topic to be brought up even after all these years. "Yes. What about her?"

"*That* woman is dead," Ravinder said softly.

"Oh." Her face inscrutable.

"Ruby is here in India."

Simran blanched. "Why has she come here?" She suddenly sat down. But ramrod straight, on the sofa's edge, as though on guard. Ravinder sensed her conjuring up images of a fortune-hunting girl out to stake her claim on her father's property.

"To see me, I guess."

"To see you or to lay a claim on your property?"

"Simran." Ravinder was irritated, but he had to retain his cool or this would be blown all out of proportion. "The girl has just lost her mother. Is it not logical for her to try to meet up with her other surviving parent? Please . . . let us give her a break."

"How do you know?" Simran pushed back an errant hair, which had shaken loose and fallen across her face. A very un-Simran-like gesture. Ravinder could tell she was nervous. "You are so gullible. You believe everything everyone tells you."

"She has not said anything to me about property. She just came to the office to see me; that is all. I invited her to come and stay with us."

"You invited her to come and stay with us?" Simran enunciated each word bitingly. "Here? At *our* home?" Her tone spiraled upward almost out of control. "*Are you crazy?* Do you know what will happen to our chances of getting a decent match for Jasmine if people come to know . . ."

Ravinder had to let her vent for a while, to get her initial furious outburst out of the way. When she halted momentarily he spoke again, his tone even and nonconfrontational yet firm. "You must understand that she is also my daughter. I cannot. . . . I *will not* ignore her."

Simran could hear the steel in his voice; it emerged rarely. She knew enough about him to know that he would not back down now; that resistance would only harden his stance. "How long will she stay?" she now asked in a resigned tone.

"For a few days, I think." Ravinder saw her collapse back into the sofa. He sensed the hardest part of the battle was over, but felt no satisfaction. Her anguish saddened him. "I did not get much of a chance to speak to her, but I guess it will be for a few days only."

"What will we tell Jasmine?"

"Simran, Jasmine knows I was married earlier."

"Yes, but knowing something and having it shoved in your face are two different things." Simran was on the edge of tears, as her carefully constructed world had begun to crumble. But she held herself together.

Ravinder's heart went out to her. Whatever her shortcomings, she *had* stood by him all these years, and he cared for her, for her and the family she represented. When he spoke again, it was gently. "I agree, but I trust her enough to know that Jasmine will not take it badly." He reached out and took Simran's hand.

"So you say." Simran freed her hand and put it back in her lap, along with the other one. She kept looking at them in her lap, as though something precious had trickled out from between her splayed fingers. A moment later, her fingers closed into tightly clenched fists. The knuckles white with tension.

Ravinder did not reply. There was nothing else he could say to make it easier for her.

"When is *that* girl coming here?"

"Ruby will be here"—Ravinder checked his watch—"in another hour."

"Today?"

Ravinder nodded.

Simran gave him a long look. "Fine. So be it." She muttered through clenched teeth, "But promise me that you will not mention this to anyone else."

He nodded again, knowing that the views of society, especially of their relatives, mattered a lot to Simran.

"Let me get the guest bedroom ready." Simran got up. "But . . . I am not going to sit around chatting with her . . . be clear on that. Keep that girl out of my way." She was again on the verge of tears as she left.

Ravinder shrugged.

Now Jasmine.

He steeled himself. Knowing that she was due to return from college soon, he got up and went out into the garden, hoping that she would come before Ruby did. He also hoped she would respond more positively than Simran.

Throwing another look at his watch, he began to pace the garden. His body needed to be in motion. His mind needed rest.

The rain had stopped. A late-afternoon sun was trying to push its way past the still overcast sky. Not quite succeeding.

Ruby went to work the minute she got back to her hotel room. First she called Mark. She had been dying to get cracking on her mobile in the car, but could not have the driver listen in.

"How is it going?" Mark sounded upbeat; India seemed to be working well for him.

"It's going well." Ruby felt in a tearing hurry. "Listen carefully now. I am checking out of here in a couple of hours. I will be staying with . . . at a friend's place . . . not far from here. Make sure that you don't call me. I will call you."

"What if I need you for an emergency?"

"Send me a text . . . something personal . . . like asking for a date or something."

"That's a nice thought." Mark laughed.

"Yeah right, but don't get excited." Despite the stress, Ruby could not help chuckling. "I'm only a woman, remember?"

"Pity. What a man you'd have made." He laughed. "But I get the drift."

"Have you gotten hold of the team?"

"Yep. All three will be here by tomorrow night. The Aussies at Maurya Sheraton and the German at Taj Mansingh. All booked."

"That's perfect." She noted down the room numbers. "They'll have enough time for a thorough recon, then."

"Yes, they will." Pause. "They asked about the payment. All three of them."

"It will be waiting when they get here," Ruby replied, making a mental note to call one of the financiers Pasha had provided; in all the turmoil, that had slipped her mind.

"When is the stuff from Chennai due to reach?"

"I spoke to the transport guy. He said it's en route . . . by tomorrow, for sure."

"Fine, then we're on schedule." Ruby felt satisfied. "Now you have to let me know when and where we meet your man."

"I'm still thinking about the venue." Mark hesitated, unsure whether he should share his misgivings about Nanda.

But Ruby picked up on them. "What is it?" She probed and then listened as Mark told her what had happened after the meeting with Nanda.

"I don't know what exactly he was up to, but I have a bad feeling about—" He broke off. "Well, maybe not bad, but I don't have a good feeling about this bugger now."

Ruby understood the feeling; something all operatives encountered every so often in the field. She had found it was always a good idea to trust this feeling. "I hear you, Mark," Ruby said softly. "And I agree . . . we need to be careful."

"That's why I've got to ensure it's a safe place."

"What do you have in mind?"

"Nothing yet, but I am going to recon a couple of places today. Public parks, monuments . . . that kind of thing."

"Good idea. Let me know." She was about to end the call when it hit her. "Does he know where you're staying?"

"Are you kidding me? He doesn't even know my full name. Just Mark."

"Well, as long as he doesn't treat you like one we're good."

Even so, she was not feeling good when she rang off.

With worry about Nanda and now in a hurry to pack and move, she again forgot to call the financier.

It was almost four by the time she checked out and headed for Ravinder's house. The stress of how Ravinder's family would react to her mounted as the car nosed its way through the crazy Delhi traffic.

She saw colorful banners festooned all along the roads, and huge billboards displayed some Bollywood star or the other; the city was in a frenzy preparing for the games this coming Monday. But Ruby hardly noticed any of it.

Ravinder was pacing the garden when a Toyota Innova halted outside the black metal gates. One of the security guards went out to check on it while the other two covered him, their weapons at the ready. Ravinder was happy to note they were alert; Mohite was obviously ensuring the duty officer was briefing them daily.

The rear window of the Innova slid down, and Ravinder saw Ruby's head emerge. She was about to say something to the guard when Ravinder called out, waving at the guards to allow her in.

The gates swung back, and Ruby's car drove in.

She immediately spotted the harried look he seemed enveloped in and felt a wave of morbid satisfaction. She had no intention of being taken in by his tall tales now, with Rehana no longer around to tell the other side of the story. Yet a part of her did feel his pain. And Ruby again regretted that Rehana had never spoken to her about what had happened between them.

The servant must have heard him calling out to the guards to let the car in; he reached the Innova as it halted, almost at the same time as Ravinder.

"Take the luggage to the guest room and then get some tea for us," Ravinder told him as he held the door open for Ruby. "Come, let us sit in the garden for a bit. . . . It's a lovely day."

Ruby looked around; it certainly was. The rain had melted away and the sun, now on its way down, bathed the garden, imparting a reddish tinge to it. She noted rows of color-coordinated flowers in the beds that bordered the neatly tonsured interior grass, separating the grass from the high, yellow-colored, brick boundary wall that ringed the house. The grass was still wet with rain.

On one side of the garden was an old banyan tree, its leafy branches providing an umbrella-like shade. Under it was a wrought-iron garden table, with an ornate garden swing to one side and matching iron chairs with bright cushions on the other sides. At the far end, she could see an aluminum ladder with a pair of garden shears balanced on the top step.

Despite the road running only a few meters away, the bungalow was bathed in a peaceful silence, broken only by the occasional car driving past. A tranquil picture, in contrast with the turmoil gripping most people here.

Ruby followed Ravinder to the garden table. Then skirting past it, she went to the garden swing and sat facing him.

Before either could speak, a servant came out bearing a laden tray. They sat in silence as the tea was laid out.

An elaborate silver service; and along with it were some delicately cut cheese and cucumber sandwiches, an assortment of biscuits and some walnut cake. Ravinder saw that Simran had ensured everything was just right. He could see her peering out from the dining room window, curious to see Ruby, but too proud—or was it insecure?—to come out.

Ruby was slowly rocking the swing back and forth. She

appeared at peace yet was probably seething with questions. Even as he thought that, she spoke.

"Will you tell me what happened, Father? Back then?"

"It's a long story."

"I have waited a long time." Her bitterness reached out to him.

Ravinder wanted to take her in his arms. Deciding he had to try despite his fears and her anger, he mustered the courage, went across, and sat down in the swing beside her. A world of gentleness was in the hand that stroked her hair.

A wetness came to Ruby's eyes. The woman craved the contact. The terrorist resented it. She blinked, trying to fight it off, but not quite managing. The woman fought back harder; the woman who wanted to know more about her past, her parents, the life she should have had, the incomplete childhood, those untold bedtime stories, birthday parties, family picnics, and all those dreams that had been snatched away. The little girl who just wanted to bury her face in her father's chest. Yes, she wanted him back. But she didn't move. Confusion stilled her.

"Mom never spoke to me about all this . . . about what happened between you two. I think I need to know. . . . I *deserve* to know."

From inside the house, the hissing whistle of a pressure cooker letting off steam sounded, clear as a bell in the silence between them. It subsided abruptly.

"Yes." Ravinder looked away. Nodded. "Yes, you do."

"So, what happened between you two? Why did you leave?"

The pressure cooker whistle exploded again.

"Is that what Rehana told you?"

Ruby pondered before she said, slowly, "No, she never actually said that." Ruby searched for the right words. "But that is what she always implied."

"I did not leave, Ruby." His voice went soft; he felt bad having to discredit Rehana, especially now that she was dead. "Your mother did." He also sensed that the truth would go down badly with Ruby. He was right.

She cringed away. But she knew he was telling the truth.

This had to be why Rehana had always been reluctant to talk about it.

"Why?" she whispered. "What happened between you two? And whatever it was, why did I have to pay the price?"

"You should not have had to pay the price."

"So what did happen?"

"I think the rift between us began when I came home one day and found her hosting a meeting of Palestinian activists, an unsavory bunch. I knew that, sooner or later, they would get Rehana into trouble. She got worked up when I forbade her to have such people in our house again."

Ravinder paused, feeling his way through the fog and trying to recall that day.

"She did not say anything to me, but from that day, her attitude changed. She began to shut me out more and more. And then"—he was having trouble talking—"one day I came home and found she was gone, taking you with her. She had left a short note for me, which really said nothing."

Ruby's tears came as memories of that horrible day trickled back to her.

Rehana had bundled her out of the house right after Ravinder went out that morning. Two suitcases were already packed. Brushing aside her questions, they had gone straight to the airport. Ruby was excited by the surprise adventure, but later she began to tire. She wanted to go home; she wanted her father.

"Why is Daddy not with us?" The first few times she asked, Rehana had fobbed her off. Eventually, when Ruby did not stop, she lost her patience.

"He is not."

"But why not? I cannot sleep unless he tells me a story."

"I will tell you a story if you stop crying."

"No! Daddy always does that."

"Well, he will not do that anymore."

Then she'd let off loud tearful sobs. By time they subsided, the drone of the aircraft engines and her ears getting blocked made her cry again.

Ruby felt relieved when Ravinder's words intruded on her memory. "Though Rehana had been uneasy for some weeks . . . I had no idea she was so upset. I never actually came to know what had happened."

They both lapsed into silence. Neither knew where the conversation was headed, but both did know whatever it was, it now needed to be out in the open.

Ravinder mused. "Do you have any idea what happened? Where did you guys go?"

Ruby was about to reply when she realized that she could not tell him that Rehana had taken her to Palestine. She sensed that it must have been the cause of her people that made Rehana leave; she'd always placed that far above everything else . . . *even me*.

"We moved so often . . . before we finally settled down in London," Ruby recovered, needing to move away from this dangerous question. Rehana's love for her cause and the manner of her death were two facts that might well make Ravinder sit up and take notice. Even question her sudden arrival here.

"Yes, I thought so," he said, "since the divorce papers were from a London lawyer. I asked him several times where you two were, but he refused. And all the letters and messages I sent came back unopened."

"You did not contest the divorce?" Ruby challenged. But even as she spoke, the realization that Rehana had lied about all this hit her hard.

Would Mom really have done that? What else did she lie to me about?

"How do I explain to you what things were like for me in those days, Ruby? With you two gone, I was . . . devastated. And my parents were giving me hell. In fact, it was my mother who first received the divorce documents. I was not at home, and she only told me about them after the court dates were over and the divorce was a done deal."

Ruby, relieved that the conversation had moved away from problematic territory, changed the subject. "How did the two of you meet?"

A slow smile lit up Ravinder's face. "You sound just like Rehana." His mind fled back thirty years.

Ruby sat still, eager for answers to the questions that had always plagued her.

"It started as one of those regular evenings." Ravinder was now hardly aware of his solitary audience. "I was coming back from college and decided to go to the pub with some friends. We came out after a couple of beers and were strolling down the street when we heard a loud scream."

Rehana was walking a couple of steps behind her aunt Zahira, more to avoid conversation than anything else; an arrangement that suited the aunt just fine since she had yet to figure out a way to handle the highly strung Rehana and was still uneasy in her company.

Two muggers erupted out of an alley as Zahira and Rehana came abreast. The one who had a knife landed plumb in front of Rehana, slashed the air menacingly with his knife. "Your money, bitch," he hissed.

The second gave Zahira a hard shove, dropping her on the pavement, then threw himself on her and bit her gold ear bobs off. Zahira screamed. Blood spurted. The mugger was making a beeline for her other ear when a volley of shouts rang out.

"Hey! What's going on here?"

They all looked and saw three young men rushing toward them. The muggers fled, vanishing into the gloom.

A few windows had opened across the road and people were peering out. One must have called the cops because a patrol car pulled up just as the men who had chased after the muggers returned to the shocked women.

By now Rehana had recovered her wits. She was trying to staunch the bleeding from her aunt's ears when the cops arrived.

"We need to get you to a hospital, ma'am," the copper said after one look at Zahira's torn-off earlobe.

He was helping her to the patrol car when Rehana noticed

one of the rescuers. In his twenties, dressed in jeans and a light wool jacket that set off his broad shoulders and contrasted with his navy blue turban. He was staring at her as though struck by lightning. Flustered, she gave a tentative, grateful smile.

That was all it took.

Ravinder gave a happy laugh. "She was standing there with flushed cheeks and long, lush hair blown all over her face, still shaken. Then she looked at me . . . and smiled."

Ruby could almost see the story playing in his head as he narrated it to her.

"How can I explain to you what Rehana was like in those days, Ruby?" He gave her a long look. "She was just like you. The same look . . . the same smile . . . the same . . . One look and I was gone. I fell for her hopelessly." He laughed again. It was infectious. Ruby could not help smiling back.

She could tell from the faraway look in his eyes that the story was not yet over.

"I soon found myself in the hospital with Rehana and her aunt." Ravinder's voice was soft now.

Perhaps he still misses Mom.

How could it be? Mom could not have lied to me about all this . . . could she?

"I realized I had not even introduced myself."

I am Ravinder." It was only at the hospital that I said that to her. Zahira was off being tended to by the doctor. "Ravinder Singh Gill," he expanded, his tone soft. He spoke the clean, pristine Queen's English, a hallmark of most top-notch Indian public schools. His gaze fixed unblinkingly on Rehana, as if looking away would be unthinkable.

"Rehana," she replied, taking his proffered hand.

Ravinder was happily oblivious of his having latched on to it, like a Crusader who had chanced upon the Holy Grail.

She gave him a sharp look, which softened into an amused glance as she realized there was no malice in the man hanging on to her hand. The adoring look Ravinder bestowed upon her was starting to unsettle her, but in a *good* way. Rehana realized that she . . . yes, she liked it.

"My hand," Rehana pointed out softly with a smile.

Puzzled, he looked at down at it. "Oh!" he said feeling embarrassed. "I did not . . ." Then he ran out of words. After a few false starts, he repeated, "I am Ravinder Singh Gill."

"Yes, you told me." She smiled back, mischievously now. She was beginning to enjoy the moment. "I am Rehana."

"Rehana," he repeated. "It is a lovely name. I like it." He again realized what he had said and turned red. "What does it mean?"

"You should know. You're an Indian."

"How did you know?" He realized it was a dumb question and turned redder.

Rehana smiled, giving his turban a pointed look. "You guys are everywhere."

"Yes." He laughed. "I guess we do get around."

"And how. I don't think the Brits had any idea when they quit India that you guys planned to follow them home . . . and take their jobs."

This time both laughed.

"So? What does 'Rehana' mean?"

"It means a handful of sweet basil."

"Basil? Hmm . . . I like basil."

"Do you, now?"

Of course, Rehana did not know it then, but in the coming days he'd latched on to her, making no bones about his intention to woo her.

Rehana *loved* it. For once, there was a person who had no agenda but to pivot his existence around her. Walks in the park, trips to the theater, lunches and dinners and, of course, soon stolen kisses and long, fevered hugs. He swept her off her feet.

Anyone who met Ravinder in those days would not have believed that just days ago he had been a dedicated and hardworking law student. His parents, who with heavy heart had sent their firstborn to London, would have been aghast.

For him too, it was a new emotion he was experiencing. He'd had his crushes before, but nothing close to this.

For both of them, everything was perfect. Even the London weather was behaving.

To the chagrin of her uncle and confusion of her aunt, Ravinder became a fixture in their lives. They were irritated by the unabashed attention he was giving to their niece. That he was not a Muslim bothered them, but not overly. And that he was a well-brought-up young man from a family of means did not escape their attention either. But what was most confusing was that their niece became an absolutely new person. Usually withdrawn and taciturn, Rehana was now unable to stop smiling. Zahira was blown away to find her helping with the housework and being pleasant about it too.

But the uncle worried. "Don't you realize what a responsibility it is for us?"

"But what can we do?" Zahira retreated. "She is adamant."

At his wit's end, the uncle threw the ball at Yusuf in Ramallah. "He is her older brother. Let *him* decide."

Yusuf's decision came hard and fast. "There is no way in hell you are going to continue seeing him!" he screamed at Rehana on the phone.

He should have known better.

When his parents came to know, the reaction was equally predictable.

"She is not a Sikh?" His grandmother, who held sway over family matters, raised an aristocratic eyebrow. Despite her age, it took a brave man to stand up to her. Those raised eyebrows and her cold, derisive smile were generally enough to send people scooting for cover. She had *that* aura.

"She is Arab," Ravinder's father, the head of a small princedom in India's northern state of Punjab, who had just spent an hour reciting the sordid tale, reiterated patiently. "From Palestine."

"A Muslim?" Ravinder's mother, whose hot Punjabi blood would often surge past the wall of royal snobbery, wrung her hands in despair. "How *could* he do this to us? What will people say?"

An expression of disgust crossed his grandmother's face. That was about as far as she would go to respond to her daughter-in-law's plebian display of emotions. Till this day, she had never forgiven her late husband for having picked her as a bride for their eldest son.

"Maybe he is just sowing his wild oats." The grandmother sounded more hopeful than convinced. She had sensed the steel in the polite, well-mannered Ravinder.

But they were all shocked out of their wits when they learned that Ravinder was not just sowing wild oats; he was planting royal seeds as well.

I think it was the resistance we met from both families which decided things for us. No, don't get me wrong, Ruby. We *did* love each other. I am . . . was . . . madly in love with her. For me, the sun rose when she did and set when she slept."

Ruby saw his face and voice go soft again; she had seen that happen every time he mentioned Rehana.

Could it be that even now he is still in love? . . . The thought was uncomfortable. Ruby pushed it away. That would rock the foundations of her mission. *Unthinkable.* Ruby could not allow it to even come close to her. Ruby could not remember a single day, not since she was a teenager, when Rehana had not reminded her of her purpose in life. *You will be the one to avenge us . . . to avenge all these years of injustice we Palestinians have suffered.*

"You see, the family resistance simply crystallized things." Unaware of her turmoil, Ravinder continued. "We ran away to Birmingham and got married."

"Why Birmingham, of all places?"

"I had friends and relatives there." He gave a sheepish smile. "You see, when I told my parents I was going to marry Rehana, they cut me off without a dime and I still was studying." He shrugged, somewhat sheepishly.

"You did not think about getting a job?"

"Nope. I was too used to the royal thing back then." They both laughed. "Yes, those were mad, mad days. But I would go through it all over again if—" He broke off, and it was a while before he resumed. "Rehana looked so gorgeous that day, bedecked in bridal finery. I tell you, Ruby, it felt as though we were living in a fairy tale."

"Dad!" a sharp cry intruded on them. *"Da—ad!"* A second one sounded more exasperated.

Ruby looked up to see a young woman come toward them. She was about five feet four, with a figure that might have compelled a priest to kick holes in church windows. Dressed in black pants and a white shirt, the typical attire of law students in many Indian colleges. She had clear skin unblemished by makeup. *She doesn't need it*, Ruby thought enviously.

Ravinder spotted apprehension writ large on the girl's face. He knew that Simran must have briefed Jasmine on the phone. He felt a chasm opening up between them and moved forward to close it. "Jasmine, how are you, kid?"

She did not reply, but sailed into his arms and buried her face in his chest. Ravinder held her close, willing her turmoil to seep into him.

"Mom called me," Jasmine whispered. "I want you to know it is okay with me. . . . I understand."

Ravinder felt a pulse of love throb through him. He held her shoulders and pulled her away, wanting to look at her, wanting her to look at him, *needing* her to know that nothing had changed between them. He became aware that Ruby was watching them closely . . . cautiously.

"Jasmine, I would like you to meet Ruby. Your half . . . your elder sister."

Jasmine stayed close, clutching his hand. Turning to Ruby,

she smiled; a tentative smile. Suddenly Ruby realized, for some reason she could not yet fathom, that it was important for Jasmine to accept . . . no, to *like* her. Ruby gave her warmest, most reassuring smile and extended her right hand.

"Hi, Jasmine." She paused. "I hope we can be friends." She heard a nervous plea in her voice.

Jasmine's smile broadened. Brushing aside Ruby's extended hand, she reached out with open arms. Ruby felt a lump in her throat as the younger girl hugged her.

"Of course we can," Jasmine said. "We share our father . . . the same family name. . . . *Nothing* can take that away from either of us."

Ruby now could not trust herself to speak. She felt overwhelmed.

Watching them from across the table, Ravinder too was shaken. He was about to speak when his mobile trilled to life. Reluctantly, he reached for it.

"Sir." Mohite sounded excited, really excited. "It is me . . . Govind."

"Go on, Mohite. What is it?"

"I think you'd better get here . . . to the office . . . right away. I think we have just had a major breakthrough."

"Tell me what happened, Mohite."

"I just got a call from Thakur sahib. Apparently, the Israeli team managed to get hold of Saeed Anwar."

"That's fantastic. Where is he now?" Ravinder masked his dismay, that Thakur was again bypassing him. He stepped away, moving out of earshot.

"Dead as far as I know, but the important thing is that Anwar confirmed that it was Pasha who financed the strike on Jerusalem. He also confirmed that Pasha has hired a British mercenary . . . a woman to carry out a strike in Delhi."

"How do we know that?"

"Easy, because Pasha had asked Anwar to alert one of their money men here to be ready to hand over cash to the mercenary when she contacted him."

"What is the target?"

"Anwar did not know that. I assume it's the summit." Mohite's voice now lost some of its shine. "Could be the games too, though," he added, playing it safe.

"I see. Excellent. Put a surveillance team on this financier immediately."

"I am doing that right away. I messaged Peled and he has e-mailed the name and details of this guy to both of us."

"Fantastic. Good work, Govind. I have yet to check my mail."

"Well, I have done so and activated a team to watch the guy. We may be able to catch them both red-handed."

"Not *may*, Govind. We *have* to. We have to catch the mercenary when she meets him."

"I agree, sir. That is why I was asking if you want to come down and brief the team. Though I am going to personally supervise this operation."

Ravinder realized that Mohite wanted him involved so that he could pass on the blame if things fell apart. Well, so be it. He sighed. "Hang on. I am coming right away."

"Good. I also wanted to know if we should preemptively start rounding up single British women in the capital."

"Are you nuts, Mohite? Do you know how many there would be, with the games about to start?" Ravinder couldn't believe him. "The Brits will blow a bloody gasket if we pull stunts like this."

"Well—"

"Hang on, Mohite. I will be right over. Brief the surveillance team, but don't start anything else."

Pressing the red END CALL button, Ravinder threw a quick look at the girls. "I have to go to the office. . . . Something important has come up." He paused, concerned how Ruby would feel about being left alone. And there still was so much that he had to tell her. . . . They had a lifetime to catch up on.

"Don't worry about Ruby, Dad." Jasmine sensed his worry and jumped right in. "I will take good care of her."

Ravinder blew her a proud kiss and rushed toward his car.

Perhaps they would blunt this terror attack before it got off the ground.

As his car nosed out of the bungalow and into the cacophonic Delhi traffic, he was pondering the impact of what Mohite had reported . . . on the Commonwealth Games and the peace summit.

What is the British woman's target? The games or the summit? And from where will the strike come? When? How? Is she alone? Or are there others with her? Is she the one Nanda mentioned? Where is she right now?

There was silence between the two girls for a while after Ravinder left. Ruby was perplexed by this family that she suddenly found herself immersed in.

"Would you like to go out for dinner with me?" Jasmine was giving her an expectant smile.

"Sure. That would be wonderful." She smiled back. "It is very sweet of you to—"

"Nonsense." Jasmine cut her off. "I have never had a sister to go out with . . . till now." She broke off, suddenly embarrassed. Ruby reached out and gave her hand a squeeze. Jasmine asked, "Would you like to settle down first? Come, let me show you to your room." Still hanging on to Ruby's hand, Jasmine led her inside.

Neither noticed Simran watching from the kitchen door as they crossed the living room and went up the stairs. She was still holding the kitchen knife she was using to slice sausages when she had heard the girls come in and stepped up to watch them. Her fingers were wrapped so tightly around the hilt that they had begun to hurt. But she was oblivious of the pain.

Ruby was ready when Jasmine walked into the guest bedroom. The younger woman was wearing a mauve silk sari with a black border and a black blouse. The sari was slung low, low enough to display a slim, fetching waist. Her tiny sleeveless blouse made the best of her small breasts. She also had a diamond pendant held close to her long neck by an almost invisible golden chain. Matching diamond earrings sparkled in her ears.

"My! You are certainly dressed to kill." Ruby gave an approving smile. She felt her own black and red dress looked dowdy in comparison.

"I don't usually wear saris . . . in fact I just learned to wear one," Jasmine giggled, "but I thought tonight should be special. After all, how often does one go out with a sister one has never met before?"

"Very true. Not often." Both smiled.

"Say! Why don't you wear a sari too?" Jasmine cocked her head to one side and studied Ruby. "That dress is lovely, but won't it be fun for both of us to wear saris?"

Ruby laughed, shaking her head. "I wouldn't be able to put one on or hold it up for—"

"Don't worry. I will tie it for you." She said excitedly, "What fun! Come, let's do that." Grabbing Ruby's hand, she led the way to her bedroom, down the corridor. Her excitement attracting Ruby, pushing everything else aside. Suddenly they were just two young girls . . . sisters . . . out to have fun.

Half an hour later, Jasmine stood back and surveyed the result of her effort. "You look gorgeous."

And Ruby did. The deep blue Kanjivaram sari with a black border set off her dusky complexion. With straight black hair framing her face, she looked stunning. Jasmine's blouse was small for her; making her breasts seem fuller. Looking in the full-length mirror, Ruby could not believe it was her. She looked so different.

I even feel different, Ruby thought with surprise.

"I feel nervous." Ruby swiveled around slowly, clutching the folds of the silk sari. "What if it falls off?"

"The men there will be in for a treat, then." Jasmine chuckled. "You don't do that." She removed Ruby's hands from the folds of the sari. "Just let it fall free. Don't worry. It won't fall off. Now try to walk."

Ruby took a few tentative steps. Then realizing it was not flimsily tied, she walked more confidently. Jasmine watched her go up and down. "Better? Think you can manage?"

"Much better." Ruby nodded. "I think I can."

"Then shall we, Ms. Gill?" Jasmine gestured at the door with a big smile. Ruby nodded and, picking up her clutch, got ready to follow. Then Jasmine frowned. "Wait. What's missing?" Ruby gave her a perplexed look. "Now I see it. You need something to set it off." Returning to her dressing table, Jasmine scrabbled in the jewelry box and pulled out a pearl necklace and earrings.

"There is no need for that, Jasmine."

"Nonsense. We are going to paint the town red." Jasmine cut her off and helped her put them on. "Let Delhi know that the Gill sisters are out tonight."

Ruby tossed her hair back coquettishly. "Yes! Let's go get them, girl."

She was turning away from the dressing table when she spotted a pistol in the open jewelry box.

"You keep a gun?" Surprised, she asked, "Why?"

"Oh no, I hate guns." Jasmine gave a shudder. "That's not mine. Daddy put it there. He even made me learn how to fire it."

"What on earth for?"

"Ever since we moved here and he was put in charge of the ATTF, there have been threats against him. He says it is not a problem, but just in case . . . He even makes me carry pepper spray when I go out."

Silence fell upon the two women.

"Well, it's not so bad." Jasmine giggled. "You should have seen Mom's face when he made *her* go for firing practice. . . . She was fuming."

Her giggle broke the somber mood. They were laughing again when they headed down. Jasmine caught hold of Ruby's hand as they descended. Ruby found the gesture strangely natural. It made her feel sad. She realized that this was what life would have been like if Ravinder and Rehana had . . . Ruby fought an unexpected surge of tears. Stopping, she turned and gave the surprised Jasmine a big hug.

"Thank you, Jasmine. Thank you very much." The words came out hushed.

Jasmine's eyes were moist too. Then she forced a laugh as they headed out. They were at the door when Jasmine stopped. "Wait. I need to tell my mother when we will be back." Leaving Ruby, she went to the base of the stairs and called out. "Mom! Mom!" There was no response. Jasmine headed up.

When she returned, her smile had vanished.

"She is upset?" Ruby murmured, lightly touching her arm. Jasmine looked away. "I can understand. Anyone would be."

Jasmine looked at her; a long, close look. She realized Ruby was sincere and nodded.

They did not exchange another word as they got into Jasmine's car, a silver Tata Vista hatchback, and drove out. Their silence was awkward. Suddenly the car alongside swerved and cut them off, diving in front of them.

"Screw you! Moron!" Jasmine flipped her middle finger at the errant driver. She saw Ruby watching her with a smile and giggled. "That's Delhi traffic for you."

They both laughed, and their awkwardness vanished.

"What kind of food do you like?" Jasmine asked as they hit the roundabout near India Gate.

"All kinds. Tonight, you decide."

"Fine. Chinese it is, then." Jasmine giggled. "I can never get enough of it."

"So be it. I like Chinese a lot too."

"Strange, isn't it?" Jasmine said. "How similar people can be? Despite being so different. Look at us. I'm an Indian, born and bred here. You are half Indian–half Palestinian, brought up in London. And yet, we both love Chinese food."

Yes. We both laugh when we are happy. We cry when we are hurt, or sad. We bleed when we are cut. Ruby did not say that out loud, of course. *Then why so many differences?*

Then Jasmine turned the car into the Oberoi Hotel on Dr. Zakir Hussain Marg. The two young women, so similar, yet so different, walked into Taipan, the Chinese restaurant.

The large, well-lit room had tables placed comfortably apart, all sparkling with crystal ware. Snow-white linen lent a pristine touch to the ambience. Soft oriental music was playing in the background, loud enough to be audible, yet soft enough to allow the guests to converse easily. Despite being a weekday, it was almost full.

Ruby was touched; she could tell that Jasmine was going out of her way to make this evening memorable.

"I love Chinese food, but am not very good at ordering it," Jasmine said as they sat at a table in the corner. "Would you like to do the ordering?"

"Not at all." Ruby smiled. "Just go ahead and order what you like. I am sure it will be perfect."

"At least help me with the wine, please. You see I rarely get to have a drink. Mom doesn't like me drinking any alcohol."

"We need not have wine, then. . . . No point upsetting your mother, is there?"

"Nonsense! Of course we will have wine." She consulted the waiter and ordered a Maotai, a fiery 106-proof concoction.

This was the second time Ruby had heard Jasmine talk about her mother. She noted with surprise that she also called her mother "Mom."

Genes?

Ruby watched the younger girl as she placed the order. She seemed childlike. Innocent. Guileless. Secure.

"Didn't you get a bit carried away?" Ruby asked as the waiter walked off. "Are you sure we can eat all that?"

"Of course we can. Just you wait. . . . The food here is excellent. It's not the usual Chindian stuff you get in Delhi."

"Chindian?"

"Chinese Indian. Like Chilly Chicken Manchurian. I bet most Chinese never heard of it, till we invented it for them." Jasmine grinned. "Sometimes I think they'd wage war on us if they realized what we've done to their food." They both laughed.

That was when Jasmine noticed two young men at an adjacent table throwing glances at Ruby. Her hackles rose. Getting up, Jasmine exchanged places with Ruby, much to her amusement, so that she was the one facing them now. Her angry glares soon turned the men off.

"I *can* take care of myself, you know." Ruby chuckled; and yet moved that Jasmine felt so protective about her.

"I'm sure you can, but you should not *need* to . . . not here . . . not on *my* watch."

Ruby laughed again, touched by Jasmine's indignation. And then the waiter arrived.

Soon they were biting into pan-fried scallops with XO sauce. Seared in hot oil for a short while, their crusts were thin and crisp and yet tender.

"So," Jasmine asked when the waiter had served them. "Tell me about yourself."

"What would you like to know?"

"Whatever you feel like telling me." Jasmine smiled. "Seeing that I know nothing about you, whatever you tell me will be new."

Ruby was stricken by the reality of who she was and why she was here, but she kept a smile on her face and gave a bland synopsis of her life, steering clear of her profession and of Rehana.

If the scallops were good, the shark fin soup was unlike anything Ruby had ever tasted; ingeniously wrapped in a thin layer of egg white, it left an exquisite aftertaste in her mouth.

"Your mother never pestered you to marry?"

"No. Not really." Ruby shrugged. "I needed to devote myself to my career first."

"See." Jasmine sat back with a sigh. "That's exactly what I keep telling my mom."

"She wants you to marry now? But you are still so young."

"S*he* says it's our family tradition."

Ruby held her peace, sensing Jasmine might not take it well if Ruby commented on her mother.

"I keep telling her that I need to finish my law degree first, but . . . it's this silly royal blood thing—" She stopped when she saw Ruby's puzzled expression. "Didn't you know? Both Dad and Mom are from royal families."

"No, I didn't know that. I thought all that went out with the British."

"Yes, but you wouldn't know it to hear Mom go on and on . . . that I'll die an old maid. And my aunts are even worse. . . . They pump Mom up every time they meet her. Luckily, Dad is supporting me or I don't know how . . ." She trailed off.

"Do girls marry young in India?"

But again the waiter arrived. The braised bean curd with crab claw was of medium-firm consistency, smooth-textured, and had a slightly sweet, pleasant flavor. It was followed by a steamed codfish with garlic and preserved vegetables. Ruby felt she was in culinary heaven.

Jasmine resumed, "They don't marry so young anymore. At least not the ones who are educated." As she picked her way through the codfish, she said, "If they're career-minded, they study as much as they want and work on their professional lives. It is just like in your part of the world. I know. I have so many friends—" She broke off again. "There I go, rambling on about myself." Jasmine gave a shy laugh, suddenly embarrassed. "Tell me about yourself." She giggled. "Do you have a boyfriend?"

Ruby felt reality tug at her again. "I am not sure right now." She was surprised to find herself answering truthfully, as though happy that she was actually able to share her thoughts.

"What does that mean? You either do or you don't?"

"Is it that simple?"

"Isn't it? You have one or you don't. He is either there or not there."

Ruby pondered her beautiful simplicity. "Then I guess I don't."

"What happened? You two had a fight?"

"No. Not really." Ruby gave a wistful laugh. Almost wishing they had. "I don't know. . . . Somewhere something just went off track." She fell silent.

Jasmine asked. "Your mother did not like him?"

"No! Mom never liked him."

"Fortune hunter?"

"What?" Ruby laughed. "No. No fortune to hunt. Not in my case, at least."

"As per my mom, there are only three kinds of men. Fortune hunters, sex maniacs, and the right ones."

Ruby asked, after she finished laughing, "Okay, the first two I get, but who are the right ones?"

"In my mom's viewpoint, firstly, he has to be from a royal family . . . with more than just a dollop of blue blood. Secondly, he has to be as rich . . . if not richer than us."

"I see. Fair enough."

"Oh, but the list is not over yet."

"Go on, please." Ruby smiled.

"Thirdly, he has to be as educated, if not more. And lastly, he must be a Sikh. Trust me, Ruby. *That* is a heavy-duty checklist. It seriously trims the field down. In fact, sometimes I wonder if there is anyone still left in the world."

They both laughed.

"By the way, I did want to ask you, do you go to the mosque or the gurudwara sahib to pray?" Jasmine asked. Realizing she may have strayed into sensitive territory, she quickly added, "I mean, because Dad is Sikh and your mother is . . . was . . . sorry . . . Muslim."

Ruby almost chuckled, but controlled herself, realizing that Jasmine might have been crushed. "Neither, actually. You see, Mom was a devout Muslim, but she never compelled me to follow suit." Suddenly somber, Ruby looked away, her mind in a tailspin; suddenly aware that she could allow Jasmine to enter only so far into her mind; her . . . *their* father *was* the enemy. She could not allow herself to forget that. "Also, I guess I was too busy trying to fit in with the others . . . at school and in the neighborhood, I mean." She saw Jasmine's puzzled expression and explained, "Most were Christians, you see. Though we also had a lot of Jews . . . and some Buddhists and Hindus . . . and of course, a number of freethinkers."

Jasmine gave an understanding smile.

"So I kind of grew up freewheeling. I mean, I do believe there is a god, but to my mind religion, well . . . most preach love and brotherhood, but in reality they're the cause for so much hate and destruction."

"I agree with you." Jasmine gave a grave nod. "But you have to have some religion . . . or what will they do when it is time to deliver the last rites?"

That got them both laughing.

"I guess I'll cross that bridge when I come to it." Ruby grinned. "Though, of course, I'll have much less control over what they do to me once I am gone." They both laughed again. "I just hope they select the most eco-friendly option." The laughter increased.

"Okay, maybe last rites was a lousy example," Jasmine resumed, "how about this: What rites will you get married by?"

"I guess I'll worry about that when I find the man I want to marry." Chance returned to her head unbidden and she fell silent.

"Me," Jasmine said between mouthfuls, "I wish I could find someone like Daddy. He is so amazing. You know, he is my very best friend." Jasmine could not imagine the impact her words were having on Ruby and continued unchecked. "I feel so lucky. . . . He is the best father a girl could want. He is such a caring man."

Ruby felt a pang that drove through her. The dried hasma that she was eating; a delicious Chinese dessert, turned to ashes in her mouth.

"I don't know anything about him." Then neither spoke for a while. "I just remember that he used to call me princess when I was small."

Jasmine nodded animatedly. "That is exactly what he has always called me."

Ruby's pain now turned into bitter jealousy. Somehow that felt right.

Unaware of Ruby's turmoil Jasmine rambled on. "You know once I was very ill. . . . I think when I was four . . . or five, I don't remember, but I was very ill and Daddy never left my side even for a moment. He would hug me and sleep with me. In fact, whenever I've been ill or gotten hurt, he would do that. Mom got upset that I would always cling to him, but he was cool about it. He always said that whenever his princess is ill or hurting, he'll always be by her side."

Ruby burned with resentment.

By now the level in the wine bottle had fallen and the alcohol had risen to their heads.

The dinner bill arrived and Ruby reached out for it.

"No." Jasmine plucked it out of her hands. "Please allow me." She threw a look at it and gave a low whistle as she pulled out a credit card. "Wow! That wine was expensive."

"I can afford it, Jasmine." Ruby held out her hand.

"Dad can too, Ruby."

"I didn't know that Indian cops are so well paid."

"They are not." Jasmine shook her head. "But dad's family is loaded. So is Mom's, for that matter." She signed the charge slip with a flourish. "Might as well make the most of it, is what I say." Jasmine laughed. "Otherwise, what's the point of having a rich dad?"

"I wouldn't know." Ruby hated the grim tone of her voice. *Why did I say that?* She looked away, suddenly teary-eyed. Shame assailed her . . . or was it a feeling of inadequacy? Betrayal? Guilt? She felt a surge of anger. W*hat did I do to be so deprived?*

This time Jasmine noticed it and fell silent.

The uneasiness between them held as they left. It remained as they waited for the valets to fetch Jasmine's car.

The valet must have switched the car radio on, because it crackled to life when Jasmine started the engine.

We lose direction / No stone unturned . . . Elton John's song "Sacrifice" burst out from the local FM station. His voice filled the car. And seeped into their heads.

Neither wanted the song to go on, but both were grateful for the sound filling the void between them. The song ended. An enthsiastic RJ came on, brimming with energy. Followed by Doris Day. *When I was just a little girl, I asked my mother . . . Que sera sera / Whatever will be, will be. . . .*

All the way back, Jasmine was silent, and hurt at the change in Ruby, but not mature enough to know how to deal with it. Ruby made no attempt. On the contrary, something inside her made Ruby want to nurture her yet-to-be-defined but decidedly ugly feeling.

They bade each other a muted good night at the top of the stairs, and Ruby retreated to her room. Her resentment stayed with her as she lay down in the cold, strange bed.

Of course, I have *been cheated*, she snarled in the dark, *of a complete childhood . . . a childhood that can never be returned to me.*

Outside, it began to rain again. No thunder, no lightning. Just sheets of rain.

Ruby was crying when sleep finally claimed her.

Somewhere in the darkness of that long night, Ruby eventually laid her demons to rest. Or so she thought. Because a bit later, the dream came again, bringing with it the same faceless man who kept beckoning to her.

Suddenly, the face became clear. It was Ravinder. He was years younger in the dream, the way he had been when Ruby last saw him. She knew that face so well; it was embedded in her heart. He had a loving smile and was searching through the house. Every once in a while she could hear him call out in a singsong tone, "Ruby, my princess, come out, come out . . . wherever you are. . . ." They were playing hide-and-seek.

Suddenly he vanished . . . or to be precise . . . the face became dim again. Then clearer. Now it was Uncle Yusuf. He was calling out to her, pleading for help. . . . The gaping cut in his throat was like a hideous smile. He was desperately waving to attract Ruby's attention, but his dismembered arms lay helplessly beside him.

Ruby knew where he was telling her to go. She did *not* want to go, but followed helplessly . . . down the long, dimly lit passage . . . into that cold, oh-so-cold room. Suddenly he also vanished. Now Ruby was alone, totally alone. Lying before her were the charred remains of Rehana. They too were pleading to her. Crying. Tugging at her.

Ruby did not realize she had cried out in her sleep. It was a pain-ridden cry. Then again. And yet again.

The cries would not stop. They reverberated through her on and on. The thick walls of the guest bedroom contained them.

No one heard her mewing cries for help.

Ruby was soaked in sweat when she awoke. Shaking off that horrid feeling she reached for the water on her bedside table. The jug was empty. She remembered she had finished it off before lying down. Grabbing the jug, she got up and went down to the kitchen.

Barring trickles of light from the windows, the house was dark and silent, though she could hear the faint rustle of security guards moving near the gate. Then, the clang of metal against metal as the turning guard's rifle butt collided with the gate. Then a murmur of voices.

Her eyes gradually adjusting to the dim light, she finally located the refrigerator in the corner and took a long drink before she refilled the jug. She was on her way back when she saw a flicker of light from the room across the living room. It was casting shadows on the opposite wall. Ruby felt an eerie sensation that someone was hiding there, watching her. Her grip on the jug tightened; the filled jug was heavy, it would make a potent weapon.

Could it be an intruder? Or . . .

Jasmine's warning echoed in her head: "Ever since we moved here and he was put in charge of the ATTF, there have been several threats against him."

She considered raising an alarm.

"Who is it?" she called softly. There was no response. Hefting the jug, Ruby ghost-footed forward, ensuring she was clear of the door as she circled to bring the inner room into view.

The culprit was a laptop. It lay open on the study table, facing away from the door. The screen saver flickered. That was what had been causing the fluctuating light and shadows.

Ruby was not sure why she went up to it. Possibly only to close the lid and put it in sleep mode. But when she touched it, the screen came to life. Displayed on it was Ravinder's Outlook. He must have been working on it and forgotten to shut it down. Ruby hesitated only briefly before she put down the jug and leaned forward to read his e-mails.

On top was one from a Govind Mohite. It confirmed that Mr. Thakur, the Home Minister, had been informed about the LeT financier identified by the Mossad agent named Ido Peled. It went on to say that the financier Rizwan Khan had been placed under surveillance to enable ATTF to identify everyone who came to meet him, including the British woman terrorist they had been warned about.

Ruby's blood ran cold as the name of the money guy hit her. Rizwan Khan was one of the two names Pasha had provided her, of people to tap for money to run the operation. He was the one she had meant to call earlier that day.

Fuck! What a close call! Ruby gave a sigh of relief. For a moment she wondered if Pasha knew that the Mossad was on to his financier. Then a second realization: *British woman . . .* so they knew a hit was coming.

She had just clicked open the next mail when the clapping patter of slippers hit her ears; someone was coming down the stairs. After swiftly shutting the lid of the laptop, she snatched up the jug and returned to the living room. She was halfway across when Ravinder entered. She saw a pistol in his right hand; it was level, ready for action. He gave a start when he saw her and thrust the pistol into his gown pocket.

"Oh! It's you. I thought I heard something and—"

"I came down for some water and was going back to my room." Ruby held up the jug, almost dizzy from the rush of blood pounding in her head. Luckily it was dark so Ravinder could not see the shock on her face.

"Okay." He half turned away to go back. "Did you girls have a nice time?"

"Yes, we did, thank you." Ruby smiled. In the dim light he did not notice that only her lips had moved; her eyes were cold and still. A part of her wanted to lash out at him. Another part wanted to ask him again what she had done to grow up without a father.

"I'm glad." He looked happy too. "Jasmine was telling me that you enjoy different types of cuisine. So I was thinking, why don't I take you for lunch to this really nice northwestern frontier place? It has been a while since I ate there, but it is supposed to be very good."

"I would like that, thank you, Father."

"You're welcome, princess." Now that once-precious word did nothing for her. "Tomorrow is bad because—" He broke off, not wanting to talk about his work. "No, actually, it would be perfect since I have to go to the same hotel for work in the morning. I will finish by one. Is that okay with you?"

"That would be nice."

"Great. So be ready by noon. I'll send the driver back to take you to Ashoka Hotel; they have this lovely restaurant called Frontier. Okay?"

Ashoka Hotel! Ruby was thrilled. She now would get in there again; she knew Ravinder would be going to check on the security arrangements.

"No worries about the car. I'll get to the hotel on my own."

"If that works better for you." He half turned. Stopped, hesitated, then decided to speak. "We never got a chance to talk properly. . . . There is so much we have to catch up on." He paused, hesitant. "What did happen to Rehana? When and how—?"

"It's a long story, Father."

"It feels strange . . . your calling me Father. You always called me Daddy. Don't you remember?"

"Sorry. I will try to remember that."

"No worries." He gave another tiny smile. "I understand. It's been a long time."

"Yes, Fath—Daddy. It has. I was hardly four when you left." Ruby's tone was brittle. She could not smother her resentment.

The mood turned somber.

"You still don't believe that it was not I who left, do you?"

"I don't know," Ruby replied bluntly. Perhaps she did not *want* Rehana's story to be a lie. "You told me your story. Mom told me something else. I am not sure whom to believe."

"I understand."

"Do you?" Ruby asked bitterly. "And does it matter whether you left or she did? . . . You did not come looking for me . . . never . . . not once in all these years."

"I did, Ruby." Ravinder struggled with the reply. "In the beginning I really did, but then I thought . . . maybe . . . that Rehana wanted me to leave you two alone . . . and . . . then . . ." He trailed off.

"You're a cop, how difficult would it have been for you to find us?"

"Not very," Ravinder admitted reluctantly. "But I didn't want to intrude. Rehana's lawyer made it very clear that she wanted no further communcation. And then, as time passed, I thought maybe you guys had started a new life. . . . I didn't think it was right to . . ." He ran out of words again.

"Because you had." Ruby's anger and bitterness were palpable.

The ensuing pause was growing unbearable. Ravinder felt compelled to fill it. "So what happened to Rehana?" he asked.

"Like I was saying, Dad, it is a long story and it has been a long day. I have to get up early for my morning run. Some other time?" There was no way she would tell him where and how Rehana had died. It would only make him suspicious about the timing of her arrival . . . *especially now that they are looking for a female mercenary from England.*

"You are right. I didn't realize. . . . Seeing you has brought back so many memories . . . so many questions. It's been an emotional roller coaster. For you too, I'm sure. Sleep well, then, princess."

The words sounded hollow to Ruby.

He gave her a hug as they parted ways at her bedroom door. It was a tentative one. And she felt in a hurry to get away.

As she returned to bed, something kept nagging at her. It was something to do with the second mail she had opened just when Ravinder had come down. She tried hard, but nothing coherent emerged.

DAY SIX

Ravinder woke early the next morning, raring to leave for the office. Ruby's arrival had energized him. And feeling guilt at Simran's stress also pushed him.

When he entered his study to pick up his laptop, he immediately noticed the round water mark left on the table by Ruby's jug.

He was looking at it perplexed when he heard the gate grate open. Looking out the window, he saw Ruby come jogging down the drive, her maroon tracksuit soaked in sweat. He smiled. Rehana too used to go jogging every morning. How clearly he could still see Rehana come thundering down the road just like that . . . ponytail flailing the air behind. . . . *Like mother, like daughter.*

Ravinder was going out to talk to her when his phone rang. Returning to the table, he took the call. It was some anal-retentive type at PMO asking for clarifications about the summit security plan.

"I will need to get to the office and send them to you," Ravinder told him.

"Fair enough, Mr. Gill, but we need them urgently."

He forgot about the water mark and, pushing the laptop into its bag, headed for the waiting car. His mind was whirling with so many conflicting thoughts and worries that, for the first time in years, he did not return the salute of the men standing guard at his bungalow gates. The two new, additional security guards did not notice it; the regular one did—he'd been with Ravinder's security detail a while and knew the IG was a stickler for protocol.

The rain, which had taken a short breather at about daybreak, began again. Drumming down on the car roof with a metallic beat.

By time Ruby got ready and came down, Jasmine had left for college. Simran was sitting alone at the dining table when Ruby entered.

Ruby nodded: a tentative, hesitant good morning.

Simran nodded back as she rose, but it was a cold look. "Ravinder left early." Simran said in a monotone; a weather forecaster would have shown more emotion. It sent an eerie feeling through Ruby, arousing the little girl inside her to seek some emotion, the little girl who had craved her father. Before Ruby could think of anything to say, Simran added, "Please sit down, I will tell the servant to serve you breakfast." Doing her duty as a host and making it clear that Ruby was only a visitor to this house . . . would always be one.

Ruby felt a compelling need to gain her approval—well, if not approval, at least the simple acknowledgment that she existed, that she was there, in the same room, even if with hostility and anger, hatred, *anything* rather than the hurt of being dismissed, brushed aside.

"I am sorry," Ruby called out when Simran was at the door. Simran half turned and looked at her; another expressionless stare. "I know I have disrupted your lives by coming here like this, but—"

"You have." Just that, a flat statement, with no hint of an accusation. Even that might have mitigated the wanting churning inside Ruby.

"I just wanted to meet my father," Ruby plunged on. "I just wanted to know what he is like. That is all." Simran did not respond. "He is a good man, Mrs. Gill."

"I know."

A distasteful silence rose between them.

"I am glad I came and met him . . . and you all."

Still no response from Simran. Again, not even an angry look. Ruby felt her urge to be acknowledged rise. She could no longer rein it in.

"I know how you are feeling."

Simran's left eyebrow went up slightly, as though to ask, *You do?*

"I promise I will not disrupt your lives much longer." No response. "I will go away." Again no response. By now, Ruby was almost shaking; aching to be acknowledged. "Soon." This last word trembled out.

"Good." Simran was out the door.

That parting word echoed painfully in Ruby's head. Her resentment escalated. Soon the terrorist was back in control; she was emotionless. Almost.

Though no longer hungry, Ruby knew she needed energy and plowed through a silent breakfast before returning to her room. There was work to be done. Pushing away the emotions, she picked up the phone. After retrieving the number of the second financier Pasha had provided her, she called.

"Ahmed Siddiqui, please."

"This is Ahmed." Though with a distinctly Indian accent, the voice was cultured.

"A mutual friend gave me your number. He asked me to tell you that Sabiha's wedding is on Friday and the arrangements need to be made."

"Ah!" Ahmed replied, perking up. "I have been expecting your call for a couple of days now."

"I was busy."

"I understand. When would you like to collect the items?"

"Two hours from now? Is that okay?"

"Of course. I have it ready."

"How big is the package?"

"A small briefcase." Sensing her concern, he said. "Barring some for local use, I have kept most of it in its original form so that—"

"That's perfect." Ruby felt relieved; handling large denominations would be so much easier. And also more convenient for her team. "My man will come to collect. He will use the same contact procedure."

"I was told you would come yourself."

"I would have too, but your security sucks."

"What do you mean?" Ahmed was clearly irritated.

"Do you know Rizwan Khan?"

Silence. "Of course I do. Why?"

"Well, so do the police."

A sharp intake of breath at the other end. "What are you saying? Are you sure? How do you know?"

"Go visit him if you want to check? And they may well be at your door before the sun sets." Ruby was reluctant to continue, even though she knew chances of the ATTF chief's home phone being bugged were negligible. After confirming the place and time, she called Mark. Although concerned that exposing him to so much cash was not a good idea, in light of the e-mail she had seen last night, she chose that rather than risk exposing herself.

Then she called Kishore and told him to bring the car. *Tomorrow*, she told herself, *as of tomorrow I will use a self-drive. No more Kishore . . . or at least hire another cab.*

By the time Kishore arrived, thirty minutes had elapsed and Ruby knew she'd have to move fast if she did not want to be late, first for the cash pickup and then for the lunch with Ravinder. No way was she willing to pass up an opportunity to case the target venue.

By the time she linked up with Mark and they arrived at Khan Market, they were already a couple of minutes late. They lost another fifteen in the traffic and then in finding the obscure bookstore Ahmed had told her to come to.

Ahmed was waiting outside the shop, holding a big black umbrella to ward off the rain, now a light but irritating drizzle.

Ruby picked him out from across the parking lot and indicated him to Mark.

"I just go up to him and collect the briefcase?"

"No, you repeat the contact procedure, then take the case and walk away."

"That's it?"

"Yep."

"What's in the case?"

"Nothing that explodes." Ruby chuckled. Then she handed him the zippered cloth bag from her handbag and briefed him.

"Right." He nodded; satisfied that she was being cautious.

Ruby tensed as she saw him walk away. Mark paused near the car he had arrived in and dumped the bag in the rear seat, then continued toward the bookshop.

Ahmed appeared to be behaving strangely, shifting uneasily from one foot to the other, constantly peering at something inside the bookstore. Perhaps Ruby's news that Rizwan had been blown had spooked him.

Or perhaps he too has been turned . . . or blown.

Ruby felt her breathing even out, as though she were going into combat. Her hand instinctively reached for the gun that should have been on her waist. Nothing. A horrid, naked feeling. Her fingers clenched in frustration.

Mark stopped near Ahmed. Ruby saw them exchange words. Her tension ratcheted up. She felt so acutely alive, she could feel the blood pulsing through the veins in her temples. If the cops were on to Ahmed also, this was when they would make their play.

Apparently, they were not.

Ruby felt her adrenaline recede as Mark collected the briefcase and walked away. However he was not returning to her. Instead he angled across the parking lot. Ruby watched to see if anyone was keeping tabs on him. Her trained eyes swept the area methodically, one sector at a time.

A beggar standing by the dustbin outside a tea stall caught her eye; he seemed to be watching Mark. Then his attention wandered back to the dustbin and he began rooting inside it.

False alarm.

Her eyes kept sweeping ahead and then looping back, stopping whenever they spotted anything out of sync. They rechecked the beggar again. Nothing. They tried to spot people moving in tandem behind Mark. Again, nothing. So far, so good.

Now the next step.

Mark returned to his car and ducked inside. She could not see him, but knew he would be transferring the contents of the briefcase into the cloth bag. He was out of sight for barely a minute. When he rose, the bag was on his shoulder and he was moving swiftly, the now-empty briefcase in his hand. Without stopping, he dropped the case into a dustbin. If a tracking device had been placed in it, someone would soon be following a dustbin, or a ragpicker.

Ruby watched as Mark walked to the end of the parking lot. Without any change in speed, he came on to the road, hailed a passing auto rickshaw, and left the market. Fifty meters behind, Ruby followed, keeping a sharp lookout. Satisfied that he was not wearing a tail, even so, she stayed behind him as he skirted out of the market, drove down toward India Gate and then around it, before returning to Khan Market.

By the time they got back, Ruby was sure there was no tail on him. Also sure that the auto rickshaw driver Mark had hired would be amused with his foreign passenger's antics.

"That's a lot of money," Mark said softly as she came up to him, an inexplicable bland expression on his face.

"Yeah." She examined him closely, knowing that if greed overcame him, he could be dangerous. Ruby wished she were carrying a weapon, but she kept a smooth face, allowing nothing to show. "You said the guys wanted to be paid."

"That they did."

"So pay them now."

He gave her a long, level look. "I do that?"

"Sure, Mark. You hired them. Besides," she added casually, "I trust you." Her eyes were riveted on his. "I can, can't I?"

He did not look away. "Of course you can." A soft laugh. "I know better than to kill the golden goose."

"Good." Ruby smiled back, a cursory smile; her eyes were hard. "And don't you go forgetting, bro—this is one hard goose to kill."

"I know." When she extended her hand, he held out the bag. Using the cars on either side as cover, Ruby transferred some of the money to her handbag and handed the rest back to him. "That will take care of the Glocks, the stuff from Chennai, and the team. The rest we pay to them only when we finish the job."

"I got it." Mark slung the bag back on his shoulder. "What next?"

"The Glocks."

"I've picked the place for our meeting with Nanda. Scouted it out last evening. Want me to show you?"

"Yes, good idea. We have the time, if we move fast."

"Let's go, then, boss."

When Ahmed reached his office, he headed for the phone and called a New York number.

"I have handed over the items for Sahiba's wedding," he confirmed.

"Good." The man at the other end was about to hang up when Ahmed spoke again.

"There is something else. The other party told me that Rizwan *bhai* is sick . . . *very* sick. He could go any time."

At the other end there was silence. "I will take care of it," he said brusquely, and punched off the line. Two minutes later, he was on Skype passing on the message to Pasha in Muridke, Pakistan.

Pasha spent a few minutes trying to figure out how that could have happened. Realizing it made no difference. It had happened, and now needed to be fixed. He made another Skype call; this one to Aligarh, a small city an hour's drive from Delhi. The man at the other end heard Pasha out carefully. Ten minutes later, he was in his car headed for Delhi.

His car left Aligarh just as Ruby and Mark were reaching the venue for the weapons pickup from Nanda.

It was pushing noon by the time they finished checking out the venue Mark had selected. Then Mark proceeded to the warehouse to check on the items sent by Chanderan while Ruby headed for Ashoka Hotel. She had a lunch date to keep. On the way, she swung by the house and left the money she had taken from Mark in her suitcase, taking care to lock it. She quickly showered and changed before heading out.

When the man from Aligarh reached the outskirts of Delhi, there was a long line of cars at the security checkpoint. Due to the security for the Commonwealth Games, they were checking everyone's identity. The man held out a voter's identity card.

The cop took the card. "What are you going to Delhi for?"

"Going back home, sahib. What else?"

"Where do you live?"

The troubleshooter pointed at the card in the cop's hand; it had a Delhi address. The card was not a forgery, so the man was not worried; it would take more than a cursory check to ascertain that the man it had once belonged to was now playing with his ancestors. And it was no coincidence that the dead man resembled the man now using the card.

It had been a long, fourteen-hour stint for the cop on duty, the norm. After all, there were only so many men available for duty. The rain, which seemed to have made up Delhi's annual quota of water in a week, was not helping. He handed the card back with a nod. The man from Aligarh waited till the other two cops had checked the engine compartment and trunk. When both slammed shut, he engaged gears and drove off. His heartbeat returned to normal as the checkpoint vanished in the rear-view. Hardened though he was, such encounters always took their toll.

He now headed for Saket, a residential colony in South Delhi.

Ruby sat back as Kishore navigated through the traffic. The road was covered with large puddles. Every once in a while brownish water sprayed into the air as a vehicle sped past. Ruby watched with unseeing eyes.

Aware that rest was an imperative, she was using the time to unwind. She now felt a bit relaxed. Now the secret agent was in control; she had pushed the weak woman with her emotional baggage into the background.

Ruby reviewed the situation, ticking off the action points on her checklist. The money had been collected. The strike team would be in Delhi in a few hours. The munitions from Sri Lanka had clocked into the warehouse. In fact, she checked her watch; Mark should have picked them up by now. He would divide them up between the two Maruti vans they had hired, which the teams would be using, and park them safely. The venue Mark had selected for the Glock pickup was nice and public. As safe as it could get.

Then that unseeing, uncaring look on Simran's face returned to her, stabbing at her. And again her anger began to smolder. By the time the car pulled up outside Ashoka Hotel, it felt simmering inside her, as if waiting to explode.

The troubleshooter sent by Pasha approached Rizwan Khan's house in Saket. Just before reaching it, on a lonely stretch, he pulled over to the side of the road, retrieved his weapons from the hidden compartment in the rear seat, and checked them. Both pistols were loaded. He most probably would not need them, but out of habit he checked the spare magazines and ensured they were ready.

Having parked at the entrance of the Saket residential complex, he made his way down the road on foot. Due to the rain, there were not many people about. He maintained an even, steady pace and stayed on the side opposite Rizwan's house. It took him just one pass to spot the first cop car. Parked across the small colony lot, opposite the target's house, it was an off-white Tata Safari SUV. He saw three men inside, two in front and one in back. The one in the back had a headset on and two directional mikes pointing out, facing the house. The mikes were well placed, not visible to a casual observer.

The second car, a sky blue Tata Indigo sedan was harder to spot. It had been deployed in the drive of the adjacent house. He would not have spotted it if one of the watchers had not stepped out for a smoke.

Still not satisfied, the troubleshooter waited half an hour before making another pass. He needed to be sure there were no more watchers. His life depended on it. Only when absolutely certain did he return to his car.

He could have done the job right away, but Pasha's instructions were clear; an example had to be made. He hated such complications, but there was no choice; Pasha demanded his orders be obeyed.

Pulling out his mobile, he sent off a text. Three minutes later he received the reply. Deleting both messages, he settled himself behind the wheel and began to wait.

It would be a long wait, but he was patient. Waiting was not just an essential tool of his trade, it was also his forte.

At Ashoka Hotel, Ravinder was almost at the tail end of his security review when his mobile rang.

"Yes, Sanjeev?"

"Sir, me . . . Nanda. How are you?"

"I am well. Tell me."

"The guy is collecting the items at four tomorrow."

"Where?"

"The Garden of Five Senses."

"Damn!" Ravinder grimaced as he pictured the venue; it would be a pain to put down a team discreetly. "Why did you select—?"

"I didn't. He did."

Smart guy, Ravinder reflected. A pro. He'd picked a place and time where the crowds would be heavy. "Okay, we'll be there."

"Sir," Nanda asked hesitantly, "you are going to be there . . . right? Yourself?"

"Of course I will."

"Thank you, sir." Nanda sounded relieved. "I was worried. Sometimes your people can get trigger-happy."

"Don't worry about it, Sanjeev. I'll be there." Ravinder saw Chance and Jennifer coming up to him as he ended the call. "Is everything okay?" From the look on Chance's face, Ravinder sensed it was not.

"Well, Mr. Gill, I don't want to seem critical, but we are having a problem with the guards holding on to their posts every time we run an emergency security-breach drill."

"Really?" Ravinder was perplexed; the drill was simple and clear. He had just been through it with Mohite; the minute an alert was sounded, everyone stuck to their posts and ensured nothing moved in or out. "Why is that? Any specific problem you could identify?"

Chance hesitated, aware he was on shaky ground. However, over the past few days he had established a good rapport with the Indian ATTF chief. Also he knew the issue had to be sorted out; if something happened to the British MP, his arse was grass. "I think it is because Mr. Mohite keeps countermanding orders from the control room and issuing fresh ones based on what he feels the threat is."

"I see." Ravinder ensured his curses were not audible. This had to be solved by him ASAP; Mohite had no business doing that. "Let me take care of it."

Chance saw Ravinder check his watch and realized they should be moving on; he trusted Gill. Jennifer and he exchanged glances and took their leave.

Ravinder wanted to return to the eighth floor and deal with Mohite, but realizing that Ruby was about to arrive, he headed for the Frontier Restaurant.

The maître d' was escorting him to a table in the center, right below an exquisite glass chandelier, when Ruby entered. Ravinder's heart skipped a beat as she spotted him, smiled, and began to approach; so striking was the similarity, he could have sworn it was Rehana.

Ruby was wearing a pale pink dress and had a matching leather clutch in her hand. Her high heels gave her a sexy, leggy look, and her black hair framed her face in a perfect oval. Ravinder noticed every male eye in the restaurant swivel toward her. She looked beautiful and poised; his heart swelled. Then he noted the aloof expression on her face, and his heart fell. Somehow she seemed to have moved away . . . far away from him. As though the closeness they achieved yesterday had been lost during the night. He sensed an awkwardness hanging heavily between them.

Ravinder could not let it pass. He felt a need to reach out to his firstborn. He waited till the maître d' had seated her.

"What has happened, Ruby? There is something different about you today."

"No. Nothing in particular." Ruby shrugged. "Just one of those days, I guess."

"But you're okay, otherwise?"

"Don't worry about it, Dad. I will be fine."

Ravinder knew it was more than that, but he did not know how to deal with it.

The maître d' returned. "Here are the menus, sir."

They were about to pick up the menus when Ravinder, who was facing the door, saw Chance and Jennifer enter.

Maybe some company would do both of us some good. Ravinder seized the opportunity.

Rising, he waved to them. "Come and meet my daughter." Ravinder gestured proudly toward Ruby as Chance and Jennifer walked up to them.

Chance's eyes widened. "So you two *are* related." He grinned. "Now, isn't it a small world?"

"You two know each other?" Ravinder was surprised.

Stunned, Ruby struggled to regain her composure.

"I should say we do," Chance answered before Ruby could. "We work together."

"Really?" Ravinder gave Ruby a long look. *Why did she not mention that she worked with MI6?*

Maybe because I never asked her . . . but I did. He remembered asking her categorically. Now, when he replayed their conversation in his head, he thought she had been evasive. *Oh well, it is not as though MI6 agents would go around advertising the fact. But I am her father and—*

Chance's voice interrupted. "We have been working together for almost three years now."

"Fantastic." That was when Ravinder noticed Jennifer's expression: a polite smile plastered on, which did not conceal the guarded look she was giving Ruby. He sensed something was afoot.

Are they both vying for this fellow? A mischievous impulse ran through him.

"Why don't the two of you join us for lunch? I would love to hear more about my daughter, since"—he threw Ruby an affectionate look—"she does not talk about herself at all."

The lack of enthusiasm on Jennifer's face was clear. And it was mirrored by Ruby.

Chance began, "We would not like to intrude on a family—"

"Nonsense. I absolutely insist. Please—" He rose and pulled up the chair facing him for Jennifer, ensuring that Chance had to sit opposite Ruby. They were all sitting when their similarity struck Ravinder. "My God! You two look so alike." He gave Jennifer and Ruby a fond smile. The fact that neither smiled in return did not escape his attention. Chance too looked uneasy.

Ruby cursed silently as Chance and Jennifer sat down. She would have to ensure the conversation stayed away from dangerous terrain. All three were already on the lookout for a female British mercenary.

To Ruby's relief, the maître d' arrived to take their orders.

"It is as much fun watching the chefs prepare the dishes as it is eating here." Ravinder gestured toward the men working the barbecue a few meters away. "Would you like me to help you with ordering?" he asked.

All three nodded.

"That would be great." Chance smiled.

"Easy on the spices for me," Ruby added.

"That's funny." Ravinder bestowed a loving smile on her. "Your mother loved spicy food."

"But I am not able to handle them."

"Me neither," Jennifer chimed in.

Ruby, Jennifer, and Chance watched the chefs working expertly with a multitude of barbecued dishes as Ravinder conferred with the maître d' and ordered. Reminding him to keep the spices low, he ordered tandoori tiger prawns and a mixed kebab and vegetables platter. For the main course, he ordered Peshawari daal, burrah kebab, murg malai kebab, Peshawari kebabs, karahi gosht, tandoori gobhi, subzi seekh, pulao, and raan.

The service was fast, and soon their table was laden with fragrant dishes.

Luck was still with Ruby. The conversation remained either on the food or on related trivia. Perhaps, she reasoned, they were reluctant to talk about work in front of her, as it would have to be about the peace summit.

It was the murgh malai kebabs that caused a problem; despite Ravinder's caution, it was too spicy for the two ladies. Jennifer's hiccups increased as the table was cleared and the phirni arrived. Giving the dessert a pass, she excused herself and made her way to the ladies' room. Ruby lasted a moment longer and then she too headed there.

"I am really happy that you two managed to get together," Chance said as Ruby walked away. "Ruby had been apprehensive about calling you."

"Really?"

"Yes, she was. I met her the other day and she—"

Ravinder could not help interrupting. "You two seem to know each other well."

"Well . . ." Chance was unsure of how to proceed. "Well, we have worked together for three years now."

Ravinder immediately sensed there was more to it. Unwilling to put his guest on the spot, he was about to change the topic when Chance spoke again.

"I have been worried about Ruby. We all are. You know . . . considering the horrible way in which her mother was killed. It broke her apart. So much so that the agency psychologists recommended she be sent on extended medical leave." Chance was feeling awkward about saying all this behind Ruby's back. But he thought telling her father might help her, so he continued. "There's no way she'll be taken back on duty till the shrinks clear her . . . it was that bad." Another pause. "I am happy to see her looking so much more relaxed."

Ravinder could not hide his shock. Chance spotted it. "You know about that, don't you?"

"I know that my . . . that Ruby's mother has passed away, but"—Ravinder shook his head—"but that's it. Ruby did not say any more. I guess she does not like to talk about it."

"That's understandable."

"What happened to her mother?"

"No one knows for sure. Just after the recent terror strikes on Jerusalem, she went to Palestine and was taking part in a peace march. The Israelis say that Qassam Brigade terrorists bombed the march. The Palestinians say that the IDF carried out an artillery attack, and shells landed on the marchers."

Ravinder felt a faint alarm begin to hiss in his head. Something was amiss; Ruby should have told him about this, even if she did not want to talk about her job as an MI6 agent. There had to be a reason. He began to ponder that.

The more Chance told him, the louder the alarm in his cop's head became. Even the father was unable to wish it away. A part of his brain had already begun to relive everything that had transpired since Ruby moved in. He realized that Ruby *had* been evasive about her life; she had not avoided any questions, but her answers had always been vague and sketchy. Though hating himself for the thought, Ravinder sensed that Ruby was not just physically similar to Rehana; she possibly had the same hard streak too.

Could Rehana have passed on her obsession for the Palestinian cause to her? The thought dropped into Ravinder's head. *Could she be the woman Nanda had mentioned . . . the one he thought he had seen with Mark?* Ravinder couldn't push it away.

Could she be the thirteenth woman that the man from Mossad had talked about? Could she be the woman from England Anwar had mentioned . . . who is expected to meet the LeT financier? And could the man sitting opposite him have some of the answers?

"What do you—?" Ravinder leaned forward to question Chance when he spotted the two girls returning. He pulled back, breaking off in midsentence.

Chance sensed the sudden shift, looked around and saw Ruby and Jennifer threading their way back. Jennifer looked pale and washed out; the spices had hit her hard.

Ruby noticed Ravinder pull away from Chance. She also noted the sudden shift in conversation. She sensed they had been talking about her. Instantly she went on red alert. Chance had said something, which had put her father on guard.

So much for all the I-want-to-make-up-for-it bullshit he was giving me. Ruby felt a stab of anger. She had to stay focused on her mission. This father stuff was too much for her to handle.

The rest of the lunch passed with only sporadic attempts at polite conversation.

The troubleshooter from Aligarh watched as the shift changed; a new set of cops came by, in ones and twos, and relieved the old set. He did nothing while they settled down.

Then, when he felt things appeared as normal as they could get, he rechecked his weapons and got ready.

Everything was in place for him to set the example Pasha had ordered. The jihad allowed for no mistakes.

Ravinder had signed the charge slip and was returning his credit card to his wallet when his mobile rang. He grimaced when he saw the number.

"Good afternoon, sir. How are you?"

"I am fine, Mr. Gill." Thakur's unmistakable nasal tone came through loud and clear. "Where are you?"

"I am at the Ashoka Hotel, sir."

"Good. I am reaching there in a few minutes. I would like to review the security arrangements."

"There is no need for you to bother, sir. I have just finished doing that."

"It is no bother, Mr Gill. This is my duty. I am here in the neighborhood, so why waste the opportunity."

"Right, sir." Ravinder sighed. It was going to be a sheer waste of time, but he *was* the Home Minister and had to be pandered to. "I will meet you in the lobby." Ending the call, he turned to the others. "Duty calls. I have to go."

Chance and Jennifer thanked him for the lunch and left.

"Come, Ruby, let me walk you to the car." Ravinder wanted to restart the conversation they had started before lunch, but now suspicion had joined with the anger he felt between them.

They were halfway through the lobby, when Ravinder heard Thakur's voice. "Ah! There you are, Gill?"

He turned to see Thakur saunter up to them, with his complement of Black Cat commandos around him. Thakur's Gandhian white kurta and pajamas contrasted sharply with the black combat dress of his PSOs. The thick gold chain around his neck and the gold-plated Rolex on his wrist were not Gandhian, though. And Ravinder was not surprised to see a nattily dressed Mohite walking beside him. What he had been planning to say to Ruby went unsaid.

Then Thakur spotted Ruby, and his politician's smile switched on. "And who is this lovely young lady with you? Is she the one from the CIA?"

"No, sir. This is my daughter, Ruby." Ravinder introduced them. "Ruby, this is Mr. Thakur, our Home Minister."

Thakur was beaming as he shook Ruby's hand. "You are beautiful, my dear. How come I have not seen you before?"

"She has just returned from London, sir." Ravinder kept the explanation brief. "We were having lunch. I was just dropping her off to the car."

"What is this, Mr. Gill?" Thakur's smile was now in full flow. "If you had told me you were busy with your family, I would never have bothered you. Anyway, don't let me disrupt anything. Just show me the security arrangements, and then you two can go ahead." He turned to Ruby. "Come, my dear, stay with us. I shall only take a few minutes of your father's time."

"I don't think that is a good idea, sir," Ravinder protested. "That is a restricted area."

"Come, come, Mr. Gill. You must stop being a policeman all the time. . . . She is family, after all. Isn't that right, Govind?"

"Of course, sir." Govind did his Yes-Minister bit.

Ravinder had to struggle to keep his exasperation in check. Before he could respond, Thakur had taken Ruby's arm and was heading for the elevator, talking to her about London. Mohite, fawning over them, led the way.

Ravinder had to follow. They were getting into the elevator when an idea struck him. He chewed on it. *Why not? If I can't avoid it . . . and if Ruby is somehow involved with disrupting the summit . . . I can use this opportunity to pass on some disinformation. That will . . .*

Mohite's voice intruded. "Let me explain the security plan to you, sir." Ravinder's heart sank; Govind, in an attempt to impress Thakur, was going to spill the entire plan to him, right in front of Ruby.

He was right. Mohite was leaving no stone unturned. "Every entry point to the secure floors is manned by ATTF personnel, two per post. Similarly, we have a section-sized picket on both the hotel gates and another section at the two roadblocks set up on both sides of the road leading up to the hotel."

The elevator doors now opened on the seventh floor. Leading the way out, Mohite continued. "We have two men securing the staircases on either end of the floor. Likewise, two men at either end of the elevators, so no unauthorized person can enter. This seventh floor will be totally occupied by security and admin staff, and the eighth one is for the delegates . . . and, of course, meetings."

Turning left from the elevators, Mohite led the way to the first room on the outer side of the corridor.

"This room and the adjacent two have been converted into our security control room. We will be monitoring and supervising the complete operation from here."

He held open the door for Thakur. The minister sauntered in with his entire party in tow. Men were busy setting up a bank of monitors, with wires and cables strewn all over.

"They are setting up the closed-circuit television network." Mohite explained, "Both gates, the hotel lobby, the elevators, staircases, and all entries and exits to the seventh and eighth floors will be monitored twenty-four/seven from here. The camera feed is also to be piped into Mr. Gill's room, which is just down the corridor on the other side."

"What are these?" Thakur pointed at an open cardboard carton containing neatly tied bundles of colored plastic cards.

"Security access cards, sir, for issue to all authorized personnel. No one can enter without these cards. The blue cards are for the seventh floor only, and the red for access to the entire secure zone." He eased a red card out and handed it to Thakur. "This one is for you, sir. It allows you complete freedom of movement over the secure zone."

Thakur idly flipped the card around in his hand. He knew he would not need it, but the card had a nice, important feel. He pocketed it with a smile.

Mohite threw the bundle back in the cardboard box and led them out, again holding the door for Thakur.

With one card taken out, the bundle had become loose. When the bundle got tossed into the box, some cards slipped out and scattered, a few falling out of the box. The PSO standing closest to the box bent down to pick them up. Ruby, next to him, stepped forward and helped him before joining the others in the corridor. No one noticed her palm a red card and slip it into her handbag. Ravinder, on the other side of the minister, saw her bend, but was more focused on what Mohite was saying, trying to spot a way to stem his blabbering.

When Ruby joined them all out in the corridor, Mohite was saying, "Also on the other side of the elevators are the rooms for the MI6 and CIA agents." He pointed them out. "Directly opposite is the room we have kept for you, in case you want to rest."

Ravinder was disgusted. *Did the man have no shame?*

Standing a little apart, Ruby was watching this interplay with interest; she picked up on the stress between her father and his second-in-command. But she was taking care not to appear to be paying attention. Her trained mind, however, was recording every detail.

Mohite was continuing. "Next to your room, sir, is mine—and beyond that is Mr. Gill's." He turned to the minister and waved his arms. "The others are for the security personnel traveling with the delegates."

"Very good planning, Govind. Your boys have done an excellent job."

"I am not done yet, sir."

"Oh, but I need to get back to my office now." Thakur threw a look at his watch.

Ruby was dismayed. The opportunity for a visit of the floor where the delegates would be located was slipping away. She hoped Mohite would not be dissuaded. He obliged.

"Certainly, sir, I am sure you have much to do. So I shall just tell you about the rest from here only." He marshaled his thoughts. "The eighth floor, also the hotel's top floor, has been sealed off. Everything coming into it, including food and drink . . . even water . . . is coming from safe, tested sources." Thakur nodded approvingly. "It's only for the delegates and, of course, for meetings. We have four conference rooms; one on every corner of the floor."

"Why four? Will they need more than one?"

"Well, there is one main one on that side"—Mohite pointed to the right—"and three smaller ones in the other three corners, just in case the delegates need to confer in private."

"Good thinking, Govind." Thakur turned to Ravinder and beamed. "You have a good man here, Mr. Gill."

"Most definitely, sir." Ravinder tried to sound enthusiastic but did not quite succeed.

Even Mohite noticed, and his expression altered. Of course, Mohite caught himself immediately; his fleeting frown was replaced by an ingratiating smile.

"Then, sir," Mohite resumed, eager for the limelight, "the roof is secured by snipers."

"Excellent." Thakur was clearly bored by now. "I better get going." He headed for the elevators.

Mohite raced ahead and pressed the elevator button. While they waited for it, he persisted with his briefing. "From day after tomorrow, no one will be able to use these elevators to come up to the two secure floors unless they have the special access cards. Without them, the elevators will not rise beyond the sixth floor."

The elevator arrived with a pinging chime. Led by Thakur, they all trooped in. With the minister's security officers, Mohite, Ravinder, and Ruby, it was a tight fit. An awkward silence set in as Mohite realized that he had run out of things to say. Suddenly he burst out again, "I forgot to mention that the air force is going to enforce a strict no-fly zone around the hotel once the delegates arrive. As a matter of fact, the whole city is a no-fly zone . . . because of the games also. So no chance of any nine/eleven-type of attack."

"Excellent, excellent. I can see that you guys have looked out for everything." Thakur now kept glancing at his watch.

"Of course we have, sir." Mohite became animated again as he remembered something else he had forgotten. "Just as a precaution . . . not that we are expecting any trouble, but just in case of an emergency, we have also secured the top two floors of Hotel Samrat and duplicated the same arrangements there also."

"Samrat? The hotel next door?"

"That's the one, sir. It is a logical choice, since we have an interconnecting, easy-to-secure corridor between the two hotels . . . from the rear side."

The doors opened with another ping as the elevator reached the ground floor.

"All this seems to be very good. I am sure everything will go off well," Thakur announced as they walked through the lobby; one of his PSOs ran forward to summon the car. "In any case, I shall be here every day."

"Every day, sir?" Ravinder kept his tone neutral, but the thought of Thakur messing around, adding to their security hassles, was scary. Mohite pandering to him all the time would be a nightmare.

"Yes, of course. I must give the delegates confidence and let them know that we are taking our precautions very seriously."

"But of course, sir." Mohite again preempted Ravinder. "That will be perfect. I will receive you at the gate every morning."

"I like his enthusiasm," Thakur declared to Ravinder. "I will be here about half an hour early on the first day so that I can spend some time with the delegates, but from the second day onward, I will come just a few minutes before the summit starts." With that, he turned to Ruby again. "Sorry for keeping your father so busy, but this is an important event we are hosting." Thakur beamed as he shook Ruby's hand. "I hope to see more of you, my dear."

"I am sure we will, sir." Ruby watched him get into his car and drive away. An idea had begun to germinate in her head.

"I am sorry you had to be put through all that," Ravinder said to her as Thakur drove off. "You must have been bored stiff."

Ruby noted a watchful look in his eyes. "Not at all. Fascinating stuff."

"Even for you? Don't you see enough of this in your agency?"

So that is what Chance told him. Ruby kept her face expressionless. *What else did he tell him?*

"Each one is different. I had no idea you guys were doing such a massive event."

"Oh well." Ravinder broke off as Mohite came back to them. Whatever he was going to say got lost as a clamor of mobile phones erupted, both Ravinder's and Mohite's. Ruby watched as both took the calls. She saw their expressions turn serious.

"Excuse us for a minute, Ruby." Ravinder pulled Mohite aside.

Ruby watched them converse intensely. Ravinder seemed angry. Mohite looked defiant yet sheepish; she had a feeling it was something to do with her.

How the hell did they get past our men?" Ravinder was yelling at Mohite. "You had assured me that you were looking into this personally."

"I don't know, sir. I had briefed them thoroughly. They must have done something stupid."

Ravinder clenched his teeth; this was not the time to teach the idiot basic leadership lessons.

"Whatever! Let's go and find out what happened." He headed back toward Ruby. "Please go back home in my car; something urgent has come up. I need to go somewhere with Mr. Mohite."

An hour of hectic driving later, they reached Saket and walked into the carnage that had once been Rizwan Khan's house.

Ravinder quickly realized that the killer must have known about the surveillance. One car, a Tata Safari parked across the park, had been bombed into oblivion and the occupants of the second had been gunned down as they ran out to respond.

"It was detonated remotely." The bomb disposal squad man told Ravinder, "Most probably from in front of the subject's house. That allowed him to shoot down the men in the second car when they ran out on the road." Both men lay sprawled in front of the gate. A professional, for sure, Ravinder noted. Both had been classically shot, mob-execution style, once in the head and once in the heart. "Then he ran into the subject's house and took him out."

They entered it. The front door had been shot open. Men from the crime team were scouring the house for evidence. One was walking around with a plastic evidence bag, collecting spent cases. "Nine millimeter." He held up the bag for Ravinder.

"Two weapons . . . both most probably Berettas," the leader explained as he joined Ravinder. "He got Rizwan and both his sons."

The three bodies lay in the living room—one, a sixteen-year-old boy, right at the door; he must have come running in when the firing started. These three had also been dispatched in the same professional manner, one through the head and one in the heart. Chances of survival were nil.

Ravinder felt sick. It was a while since he'd been at a crime scene, especially one as gory as this. The sickening stench of blood was still billowing through the house. Controlling the urge to hold a handkerchief to his nose, he asked, "Where is the wife?"

"Luckily, she and her daughter had gone to her parents' place in Faridabad. They should be here soon."

"Any witnesses?"

"Three—two from the house in front, and one from the house on the right. They all saw a man in his thirties run out. All three said he was clean-shaven, wearing dark trousers and a dark shirt. A gun in each hand. Beyond that, nothing useful." After a pause, he added, "But we are still questioning them. I've already called the artist to sit with them and run out an Identi-Kit of the killer."

"Right." Ravinder dismissed him and turned to Mohite. "I want a detailed report first thing tomorrow. Make no mistake, someone will be held accountable. This is absolutely—" His anger overtook him. "We may have lost all chance of laying our hands on that woman terrorist."

"I have already had the borders sealed and roadblocks set up all over South Delhi," Mohite said.

Fat lot of good that would do. By now the killer would be miles away. But Ravinder did not bother to speak. He was fuming as he walked away. Perhaps they'd made a mistake by not arresting Rizwan immediately when they had learned from Peled that he was a Lashkar financier. But then they would have lost any chance of arresting the British female terrorist who was expected to collect cash from him. The Mossad intel on that had been clear.

Goddamnit! We have blown our chance of catching that British mercenary.

His anger continued to stew as he got into Mohite's car and told the driver to drop him home. It was only miles later that his anger subsided enough for him to think of the more worrying issue.

How did the killer know about Rizwan? We just got the lead and mounted the surveillance. Not more than a handful knew about it. There has *to be a leak. . . . Who is it?*

He was still brooding about it when he lay down. But he was so exhausted that sleep came instantly.

Two bedrooms away, Ruby also lay down to sleep. As she had been doing for the past hour, she again ran through the action checklist in her head. The launchers and rockets had been collected, and were now safely stowed in the two hired vans, one launcher and two rockets per vehicle. All three heavy hitters whom Mark had engaged had reached Delhi. Tomorrow, as soon as they had collected the Glocks, Mark and Ruby would brief them and then give the men time for reconnaissance. Their money was already with Mark. Most important, after today's visit to Ashoka and Mohite's briefing, she now had a better idea of how to penetrate the secure zone. And even had an access card for the complete secure zone. Now just the Glocks remained.

So tomorrow was going to be crucial, they *had* to collect the Glocks from Nanda. That was critical; the final remaining piece.

But the confrontations with Simran that morning and with Ravinder and Chance in the afternoon had left their marks on her. The more she interacted with Ravinder, the more she realized that Rehana had not been honest with her. Ruby could tell that he was a straight-shooter; not a dishonest bone in his body. The bond between his family and him spoke volumes.

Pangs of uncertainty filtered through her as she tried to sleep. She could no longer shy away from the fact that Rehana had lied to her.

But what else did Mom lie to me about? Am I really doing the right thing? Is this truly my destiny?

She felt a headache begin to build. If she allowed it to escalate, it would develop into a crippling pain between her eyes. Hauling herself out of bed she turned on her MacBook and began to play Pac-Man on mute. The mindless game, where only her eyes and fingers moved, usually proved cathartic. But tonight Pac-Man provided no help. With an exasperated sigh, she ended the game and began to root through the MacBook. As though working on their own, her fingers flicked through the Finder till they settled on the video Pasha had sent her from Dubai.

A moment later, the slightly grainy but clear picture, shot obviously by a mobile phone camera, began to throb on the screen. Yusuf's body lay on the hotel bed. Large gashes on his cheeks . . . his throat gaped open . . . Ruby vomited as the video spooled on. She had seen it earlier. Several times. That made no difference. Each time, her reaction had been the same.

When she was sure she would vomit no more, she went to the bathroom and cleaned up, first herself and then the carpet.

By now exhausted. She had reached the end of her tether. She so wished that she had not thrown away the meds the shrink had given her. Collapsing on the bed, she passed out.

The last thought in her head before sleep overwhelmed her was, *I wish I could put a* DO NOT DISTURB *sign on my mind*.

Fifteen seconds later, she began to moan again, as the dead man in the video returned to haunt her.

Yusuf Sharbati, her uncle, had been stripped naked. He was lying flat on the bed. The large slit in his throat was overshadowed by the slashes on his cheeks. Both his hands had been chopped off and were displayed on his chest. The bloody stumps of his outstretched hands gave him a strange, grotesque look. His eyes were still open. Wide open. They were staring straight at Ruby. Beseeching her.

"Take revenge. You must take revenge." They pleaded, "Do not let my death go unpunished."

Once again, her piteous cries went unheard.

She would have been even more horrified if she knew how meticulously Pasha had stage-managed this video for her. The veteran agent provocateur had known it would keep her on track, would reinforce her anger should she begin to falter.

And Ruby *had* begun to falter. But the gory video did propel her back.

At about the same time, miles away, the troubleshooter from Aligarh pulled over to the side of the road. After retrieving both pistols, he wiped them clean and dropped them over the side and into the murky waters of the sewage drain, the flow below swallowed them up. They were good weapons and he was not happy to see them go, but he knew it was the smart thing to do. And he knew Pasha would be pleased. Thinking about the fat bonus that Pasha would dish out, the man with many names and no permanent home walked back to his car and drove into the night.

DAY SEVEN

Ravinder knew something was wrong when Mohite rushed into his office, looking stressed.

"What's happened?" he asked.

"SIGINT just intercepted a phone call from Muzaffarabad. They identified the caller as one of the Jaish-e-Mohammed commanders."

"And?" Ravinder prodded. "Whom was he calling?"

"That's not certain, but it was most probably Javed Khan." Mohite gave Ravinder a quizzical look. "You remember . . . Javed—"

"Of course I do, Govind. So . . . what was the call about?"

"SIGINT couldn't clarify that." Mohite looked uneasy. "They were using some kind of onetime use and discard code. The thing is that they triangulated the mobile on which Javed was talking. . . . It's somewhere in South Delhi . . . in the Lado Sarai area. The call was too short, so they couldn't get an exact fix."

"Hmm." Ravinder realized the implications; Lado Sarai was virtually a jungle of alleys and unsurveyed houses. Trying to find a couple of men in it would be like looking for a needle in a haystack. Even if Javed were still hanging around. The manpower required was not available. But it would have to be done. "Have some more posters of Javed and Aslam plastered at prominent places. And tell the SHO to carry out a cordon and search. Even if they don't find them, at least they will spook them and keep them on the run."

"Right, sir." Mohite turned for the door.

"And Govind," Ravinder called after him. "Tell—"

There was a loud bang. Both men spun around toward it. The window had flown open. The latch had broken loose. The two men exchanged sheepish glances. Ravinder noted that Mohite's gun was out. His own hand was on the butt of his weapon.

Damn! Ravinder realized they were both on the edge. The relentless stress was taking a toll. *Not good!*

Pushing away the tension Ravinder resumed. "Tell the duty officer to again take a round and brief the guards at the office and all three of our residences."

Mohite nodded unhappily and left. Both knew that till such time as Javed and Aslam were captured, the threat to Ravinder, Ashish, and Mohite was acute. Both also knew that the chances of catching the terrorists were slim, unless they got lucky . . . or one of those bastards slipped up.

Pushing away the unease, Ravinder called Gyan to get the window fixed and began to run through the arrangements for Nanda's meeting with the terrorist for the weapons. They *needed* to get that right. With Rizwan Khan knocked out of the picture, it was now their only hope of catching the buggers and stopping the terrorist strike.

Hopefully it will be the same lot—

The phone rang again, disrupting his thoughts. It was Ashish. Before Ravinder could brief him about the latest SIGINT intercept, Ashish told him that Thakur was on his way to the games village and wanted to meet both of them there.

Fuck! This was the last thing he needed now. He checked his watch; there was still time for the weapons pickup. Calling Mohite as he headed for his car, Ravinder briefed him to take care of the deployment for Nanda's meeting.

"I will be there as soon as I can," he assured Mohite. "Just make sure our teams are deployed carefully . . . and in time. And ensure that the weapons being carried by Nanda have been dummied. I don't want live weapons in the hands of a terrorist."

"What's the problem with that, sir? We will take the bastard in as soon as he lays a hand on the weapons."

"Even so, just ensure you brief Nanda."

"Don't worry about it, sir." Mohite perked up, happy at the opportunity to redeem himself after the fiasco at Rizwan Khan's.

But knowing Mohite, Ravinder couldn't help worrying.

Ruby saw Mark cross the road and walk up to the main gate of the Garden of Five Senses. He saw her and gave a discreet nod before heading inside. Ruby continued ahead to the predecided spot, at the end of the garden, from where she could keep an eye on the handover without exposing herself.

Located at the Said-ul-Azab village in Mehrauli, the Garden of Five Senses is spread over twenty acres and is one of Delhi's famous tourist attractions. With geometrically arranged plants, meandering pathways, and beautiful lotus ponds, it was a popular spot, and hundreds of people flocked to it daily—for exercising, de-stressing, or just plain old-fashioned romancing. It was teeming with people.

For the next half hour, the deadly duo scoured the ground: one visually, and the other physically. Between them they raked through every inch, quadrant by quadrant, checking for anything out of the ordinary. They spotted nothing. No hard-looking goons. No flatfoot cops in civvies. No! Nothing out of the ordinary.

For once, Mohite had used his brains. All three teams were couples pretending to use the park for what most couples do, some intimate conversation and a lot of necking. But all three teams had their eyes and ears tuned in; eyes on the garden and ears to the tiny earpieces through which Mohite was controlling them.

None picked up on Ruby, parked at the periphery, but two of them spotted Mark as he entered the park. The third pair was alerted by a hissed communication from Mohite. Six pairs of hands instinctively inched closer to their weapons.

Sitting in the car park near the garden's smaller, side entrance, Mohite nodded as he watched their target heave into the ambush site. He was sure this massive Caucasian was the man they sought.

"I think our man is here." Mohite excitedly called Ravinder on his mobile. "Blond *firangi* . . . huge . . . like a bloody tank."

"Good. That is how Nanda described him . . . Mark." Running late, Ravinder was en route. As usual, Thakur had arrived late and kept them hanging till the last minute. "Make sure everyone is alert. I am almost there . . . the bloody traffic is terrible today."

"No worries, sir. I have everything under control."

But that was what was worrying Ravinder. Cutting the call, he went back to cursing the traffic. Even with his siren and cop light, they were not making much headway; a truck had overturned somewhere ahead, blocking the road for miles. Agonizing minutes later, they passed the upturned truck and speeded up.

Ravinder halted the conspicuous cop car away from the garden and covered the remaining distance on foot. He was across the road, opposite the garden's main gate, when he saw Nanda drive up in his Mercedes, retrieve a blue carry bag from the car, and head into the garden. He halted, unwilling to let Nanda see him. The arms dealer was clearly nervous and might acknowledge his presence; that wouldn't do, since the terrorist named Mark, or his accomplices, were certain to be watching Nanda now . . . to confirm if he was alone or—

Mohite called again. "The weapons dealer is also here."

"I know, I can see him. I am now across the road, Govind. Opposite the main gate. Careful now . . . very careful. Remember, take him down immediately when he hands over the bag."

"Wilco, sir." Mohite appeared overeager to make up for the disaster at Rizwan Khan's.

Mark spotted Nanda as soon as he cleared the main gate. Mark stayed in the lee of a tree trunk he had taken position behind and watched, looking for signs of movement behind Nanda. He saw none. Despite that, he was racked by unease; something did not seem right. He began to examine everyone and everything around.

The three surveillance teams stayed immobile, watching. Their hands now within reach of their weapons. They needed only a word from Mohite to close in and seize the terrorist.

Though still uneasy, Mark waved at Nanda when he felt certain the man was alone. Nanda changed direction and headed for him. Mark spotted the beads of sweat on his brow, unusual, considering the chill in the rain-soaked air. A closer look showed that Nanda was decidedly restive; trying to act casual, he kept furtively looking around.

Mark's already tingling internal alarm began to screech louder. He intensified his scrutiny of the people around. The ambush teams stayed still, so he spotted nothing. But he wished to hell he had a weapon.

Well, I will. Soon. Mark had spotted the bag Nanda was hefting.

"Are you okay?" Mark asked as Nanda came up.

"Sure." Mark's unbroken stare unnerved Nanda. He got the vibes that Mark was suspicious and tried to make up for it. "I am not used to doing such stuff myself, but because it is you—"

"Is that the stuff?" Mark ignored him; he was on edge and just wanted to grab the guns and get the hell out. Reaching out, he snatched the bag from Nanda.

Still across the road, Ravinder saw Mark grab the bag and cursed when he saw that none of the teams had moved in.

"*Now!* Take him down now!" The man clearly identified himself when he'd accosted Nanda and taken the bag. "What the hell are they waiting for?"

Stupid motherfucker! Cursing, Ravinder reached for his mobile and dialed Mohite.

At the other end, the phone rang.

Mohite heard, but his attention stayed focused on the two men in the middle of the garden.

"Wait! No one move." He hissed into his radio set: "I want to see who else is with the *firangi*."

The takedown teams stayed still.

"Nobody move. Give him another minute or two."

Unzipping the bag, Mark saw four Glock 17s in it. They had been unpacked and looked cleaned, as he had asked Nanda to ensure. Lying between them were two boxes of ammo. He unslung the cotton bag from his shoulder and tossed it to Nanda. "Here's your money. Want to count it now?"

"No, no." Nanda shook his head, too emphatically. He was sweating. The handkerchief in his hand looked soaked from his attempts to dry his face. "I am sure it is all right. I trust you."

Mark sure as hell did not. Without another word, he turned and strode away swiftly. The alarm in his head had begun to clamor loudly. The need for the comforting feel of a weapon overwhelmed him. Quickly dipping both hands into the bag, he expertly broke open a box of ammo and loaded a clip. The magazine slid into the weapon with a satisfying click.

Mohite heard his mobile ring again. This time, seeing Ravinder's number, he took the call.

"What the hell are you waiting for, Govind?" Ravinder's fury erupted into his ear.

"I want to see who else is with him, sir. Don't worry, I have it under—"

"Shut the fuck up, Mohite, and tell the teams to take him down. *Now!*"

The last word exploded out like a bullet. Dropping the phone Mohite, reached for the radio and then screamed into it. "Move! *Move!* Take him down now."

———

Once he'd chambered a round, Mark meant to shove the pistol into his waistband when he saw the couple in front of him, about thirty feet away, suddenly spring to their feet. Mark simultaneously spotted the weapons in their hands. He knew he'd been blown. His mind automatically triggered a response.

Instead of pushing the Glock into his waistband, he brought it up and fired at the couple. Once. Twice. Thrice. So rapidly that the sound cascaded into one roar. Despite the distance, his aim was spot-on. Both dropped. Turning, Mark saw Nanda had begun to back off, about to run, panic on his face.

"Son of a bitch!" Two more shots erupted out of the Glock. Nanda took the first in his chest and the second in his neck. He was thrown backward and hit the ground with a thud.

After spinning around again, Mark ran straight toward the cop couple he had dropped with his first burst. He knew the surveillance teams in any such operation would be spread out. With the team in front down, that was now the safest way. Clutching the precious bag, he broke into a sprint. He had to make it to the road. With the office rush hour at its peak, that would give him a fighting chance to melt into the crowds. They'd also prevent the cops from firing at him.

Mark was moving fast, but not fast enough to outrun the bullets that now came at him from two sides. The other two cop couples had seen what happened to the first team. As their guns thundered, the Garden of Five Senses erupted in pandemonium. People scattered and ran in all directions.

From her end of the garden, Ruby saw the flurry of movement and saw Mark go down. Though the gunfire was barely audible, the picture was clear. She felt an acute pain, not just because she had lost her main man, but also because of the Glocks fallen in the grass. She needed those. Her mind screamed at her to get clear of this area before the cops spread a dragnet. Reversing swiftly, she pulled out into the traffic, weaving through the press of cars as fast as she could.

M otherfucker! Stupid bastard!" Ravinder was unable to contain the string of expletives that exploded out of him as he ran across the road toward the garden. But it was useless. The terrorist had to be dead. No way he could have survived that barrage. Still, hoping for a miracle, Ravinder ran; maybe he would get a couple of minutes to question him before he died.

I need to know what the target is . . . and who else is with him. . . . Then he ran into a cream-colored Toyota Innova that came barreling down the road. When he'd angrily waved it to a halt, he skirted around it and headed for the park. He was halfway toward the fallen body when it struck him that the vehicle had seemed familiar. Ravinder *knew* he had seen it before . . . recently. His mind began to strain.

"He is dead, sir." Mohite was feeling the fallen man's neck.

"Damn!" Ravinder slapped a fist into the palm of his hand. "Why the hell did you wait so long? You should have ordered them to take him down the minute he took the guns from Nanda. And why had those guns not been dummied?"

"I wanted to see who else was with him." Mohite avoided the second question completely. "After all, he was not operating alone. Even Thakur sahib agreed that—"

"Fuck Thakur sahib. My orders had been *very* clear." Ravinder checked his urge to slap Mohite. "And why did you not have the guns dummied?"

"I forgot," Mohite whispered sheepishly. "I didn't think it would matter since we were going to catch him—"

"You didn't think it would matter?" Ravinder was having trouble keeping his anger in check. "Tell that to the families of those. . . ." He pointed an angry finger at the bodies of the cop couple that had been gunned down by the terrorist. He saw his finger was quivering with fury.

Ravinder controlled himself. It was pointless, the damage all done. Now he had to ferret out the way ahead, to try to salvage whatever they could out of this fiasco.

There have to be some leads here. There are always leads. . . . One just has to look hard enough . . . and be lucky, of course.

Praying for a break, he brushed Mohite aside and, kneeling beside the dead man, began to search Mark's pockets. He struck gold in the first one, an almost-new iPhone. Its memory was blank; no record of calls received or made or any numbers stored on it; the man was too experienced not to delete the call history after every call. However, there *was* an unread message. Ravinder clicked it open.

Ok. I will meet you at Machan coffee shop at 7 pm. RG

Ravinder checked the time at which it had been received. Only four minutes ago. Around the time he was shot.

Ravinder checked; it was almost five. The bloody hotel was at least an hour's drive away. He would also need time to deploy the takedown teams.

Rapidly making up his mind, he turned on Mohite. "Get a team ready to leave with me right away."

"What happened, sir?"

"This bugger was going to meet someone at Machan, the Taj coffee shop at seven. I'm going to see who it is—"

"Should I go with you?"

"No, just give me four men. You clean up the mess here."

By now, cops of all varieties were all over the garden. They seemed to have spilled down from the trees. And throngs were milling around. And soon the media would land up. "And Govind," he called as he walked away, "I want no impromptu media interviews. Just stay with 'no comment' and 'the matter is under investigation.' Got it?"

Fifteen minutes later, he was off, with four men from the support party in tow. Ravinder briefed them on the way, making

WEAPON OF VENGEANCE | 199

sure he covered all possible contingencies. This time he had to take this man . . . or woman . . . this RG . . . *alive,* he reminded himself.

He wondered if RG would turn out to be the person Nanda had spotted . . . or thought he had spotted with this terrorist, Mark, at the Dilli Haat.

The thought of Nanda saddened him. Ravinder knew he had a wife and a couple of kids.

Oh well . . . at least he is leaving them with plenty of dough. Live by the sword, die by it. He should have chosen a safer profession.

Then he began to focus on the task now confronting them; hopefully no shoot-out.

In the confines of a hotel coffee shop, the damage would be . . . He shuddered and pushed away the horrifying image.

I wonder what RG stands for? That held his attention briefly. It could be anything. *RG.* There was something about . . . Then he remembered Mohite's G-string joke. "Each of the delegates has a name starting with *G* . . . either the first name or the family name . . . even we . . ."

A wry smile creased Ravinder's face; even the bloody terrorists attacking Delhi had names starting with *G.* He marveled at the coincidence.

RG! Ruby Gill? The shock pulverized him. *Could it be Ruby?*

Ruby's head was still pounding when she reached home. After the close call with Ravinder, it was a long time before her heartbeat returned to normal. Ravinder suddenly running in front of her vehicle had shaken her. It had been too close a call. If he had spotted her, the game was up. As it was, he had been guarded with her ever since that lunch with Chance and Jennifer. She wanted to be home well before he returned. Home and safely tucked away in bed; that ought to preclude any conversation and awkward questions.

With the loss of Mark and the Glocks, she would now have to

rework the complete battle plan. Her options had narrowed sharply. And they hadn't been great to begin with.

"Would you like me to get your dinner ready, miss?" the maid called out as Ruby was ascending the stairs. Jasmine had told her that Westerners liked to eat early, much earlier than the Indian dinnertime of nine or ten o'clock.

"No, thank you." Ruby called down. "I have a bad headache. I think I'll lie down for a bit." She tore off her clothes and stood under the steaming shower for a good five minutes, finally regaining some semblance of normalcy. Then she lay down to think.

The soft knock on her door caught her by surprise. She was in no mood to chat and hoped to hell it was not Jasmine.

"May I come in, please?" Simran's voice came through.

Ruby sat up. Shocked. Pulling herself together, she called out, "Please come in."

Simran entered tentatively. "The maid told me you have a headache." She held out a strip of tablets. "So I thought I would get you some aspirin."

"Thank you." Ruby took them, trying to get over her surprise. "Thank you very much."

For a moment the two women stood looking at each other. Ruby sensed that Simran wanted to say something; she seemed to be groping for words. Then, with a shrug, she turned and began to leave.

Simran was at the door when she turned. "It is not you I am angry with." The words hung between them. "Perhaps it is myself." By now Simran's voice had fallen to a faint whisper. "Perhaps it is Ravinder. I do not know." Another pause. "I am just human, you know. I have the same fears that we all do. Of losing the things that mean so much to me." A distinct wetness had crept into her voice.

Ruby could see she was fighting hard to maintain her composure.

"I understand how important you are to Ravinder. He is a good man . . . one who will always do the right thing. He is the kind of man who will give his life for his children." Simran sniffed, still trying to regain control. "He is equally important to me. And Jasmine."

Ruby wanted to respond. She *needed* to respond. She felt the angst in the older woman. But she could not find words. A crush of emotions rendered her speechless.

"I am sorry about what happened to your mother."

Now the silence was deafening.

"And I do want you to remember . . . no matter what happens, he *is* your father. . . . He will always be your father. . . . We will always be there for you. . . . This is your home . . . always. You can stay as long as you want."

Then Simran was gone.

Leaving behind a mass of pain in Ruby's heart.

It was sixteen minutes to seven when Ravinder finally took up position in the coffee shop. He chose a table in the far corner, from where he could see the whole place. His four cops were strung out, two at tables on either side of the entrance and two in the center.

He scanned the restaurant, taking it one section at a time. A large rectangular room with about twenty tables. He saw no single man or woman seated at any of the tables. Not that he could be sure his corpse was to meet just one person.

No Ruby either. He did feel relieved.

Six minutes later, a tall, athletic-looking woman wearing a light cotton dress walked in, about thirty, Caucasian. Ravinder studied her; no, her snug-fitting dress could not hold a concealed weapon . . . not unless a small pistol was taped to her leg.

But . . . she is still a possible. Ravinder took note of her position as she sat down at a table in the center.

Then two men entered separately. It became clear they were together only when they sat at the same table.

Another cluster trooped in. It was hard to tell which of them were together and which on their own. The possibles now escalated.

Ravinder maintained a sharp eye on the door; but scanned the coffee shop periodically.

His cop alarm went off as another man walked in. Hugely built. Broad shoulders, muscled arms, which his light green Lacoste T-shirt displayed. Ravinder saw a colorful eagle tattooed on his right arm, only partly visible. He was slouching, as though to camouflage his sense of purpose. But his eyes gave him away. They were moving across the coffee shop swiftly and expertly; too alert to belong to someone not in the game.

Relying on his intuition, Ravinder rose and began to walk casually toward the exit. The money he had left on the table would cover the coffee he had ordered. The four-man team, seeing him get up, got ready to move.

Willing them all to stay calm, Ravinder withdrew the iPhone he'd recovered from Mark's body and dialed the number from which the text had been received. By now, he was almost level with his suspect, who was halfway into the coffee shop, his eyes still searching the tables.

Ravinder noted a puzzled expression on the man's face, but no alarm. Yet. The suspect glanced at his watch; it was three minutes past seven. Then his mobile rang.

The shrill trilling was nearly drowned out by the hullabaloo of the coffee shop, but Ravinder, passing right by him, heard it clearly. He thumbed the iPhone, terminating the call. The trilling ended too.

Ravinder had his man.

Swiveling around, Ravinder gestured to the nearest cop to move. A sharp head shake. He was hauling out his revolver as he did so. Three strides, and Ravinder was behind the man.

Perhaps Ravinder had made a sound, or perhaps the man's instincts were acute, but it was already too late.

The suspect had begun to turn when the pistol in Ravinder's hand crashed down on his head, a powerful blow, with as much force as Ravinder dared. He did not want to kill the man. Not just yet.

As the man stumbled, two of the cops closed in and pummeled him onto the ground. Despite the suddenness of the assault, he fought back hard.

Ravinder felt a surge of satisfaction as they subdued him. One cop slapped a pair of handcuffs on him. The second ran an expert hand over him, checking for weapons.

The man named RG had been taken alive.

Now we will find out what these buggers are up to. . . . Satisfaction swept through Ravinder. *At last! At long, bloody last, the break we needed.*

Thirty minutes later, they began interrogating RG at Chanakyapuri Police Station. Two hours after that, they were still no closer to any truth.

"He is a tough bastard." The SHO, Inspector Jai Ram, a short, powerfully built man with a large belly, whom Ravinder had tasked to do this, came into his office wiping his hands on a towel. Patches of sweat stained his rumpled uniform. Despite that, he appeared alert. "Name is Rafael Gerber." Jai Ram said the unfamiliar name slowly. "Not a peep out of him. Keeps on insisting he's here on holiday and wants us to call his . . . the German . . . embassy. Do you want us to give him some third degree, sir?"

Ravinder considered that. It was a sticky wicket he was playing on now. If the man turned out to be innocent, there could be hell to pay; his embassy would raise a furor.

If . . . Ravinder knew he wasn't. *There is no way he can be.* He made up his mind. Whether it was the games or the summit, the stakes were just too high. Sometimes one could not play by the rules. The fucking terrorists never did.

"Break the bastard," Ravinder commanded. "Do whatever it takes, but get him to talk. Fast!"

"Leave it to me, sir. He will talk." Jai Ram had a cold grin on his face. "You go home. I will call you." He was twirling the ends of his large Genghis Khan–style mustache. His eyes were pitiless pinpoints. Right now, he was a walking contradiction to the godly name his parents had given him.

Ravinder almost felt sorry for the captive; Jai Ram was going to give him a taste of hell. Then he thought of the stakes, and his heart hardened. *What has to be done has to be done.*

"No, I am staying right here."

"It might be a long wait, sir."

"No worries."

The SHO departed. This was his chance to score points with so senior an officer. Opportunities such as this came but rarely.

Ravinder returned to mulling. Too much was coming together too fast. He could also feel the fatigue wearing him down. Calling for another cup, he tried to caffeine his tiredness away.

He was plowing through his fifth cup when Jai Ram returned, again wiping his hands on another towel. This one was spotted with blood, as were his hands and his shirtfront.

"He is talking." Ravinder saw a satisfied grin on Jai Ram's face. "In fact, he is more than happy to talk now."

"Excellent. Who is he, and what is he here for?"

"He is German . . . a freelancer, a mercenary. The dead guy . . . Gerber says his name was Mark Leahy . . . had called him down to India for an operation."

"What operation?"

"He doesn't know. Says he was to be briefed by Mark when they met today and would be shown the target tomorrow."

"Was it the Commonwealth Games?"

Jai Ram shook his head. "He has no clue."

"Damn! Are you sure he is telling the truth?"

"Right now, sir, the motherfu—" Suddenly realizing to whom he was talking, Jai Ram choked off the profanity. "He wouldn't lie if his mother told him to. He doesn't know what the operation is, but he *does* know that Mark has also called in two more mercenaries for it. He does not know who they are, but he was told they are from South Africa."

That should give us something to work on. Ravinder thanked the man. "Keep the pressure on him, Jai Ram. Set up a relay of interrogators, and make sure he does not get to sleep. I want to know everything he knows."

He was pulling out his mobile as he headed out, when it rang. Prophetically, it was Mohite.

"Govind. Just the man I need." Ravinder could not resist the pleasure of ensuring that Mohite would now have to keep working. It was because of his idiocy that they'd failed to take this Mark alive. "The man we captured at Machan has talked." He brought Mohite up to speed and quickly told him what had to be done. Then he called Ashish and briefed him also. As long as they were not sure what the target was, both Ashish and Mohite had to be kept in the picture.

Minutes later, an APB went out. The instructions were short. Every available beat constable in Delhi was hauled out.

Every hotel and lodge has to be checked. Before sunrise. The two South Africans have to be found. They may be armed. They are dangerous. Exercise precaution and do not approach alone. All sightings to be reported prior to attempting capture.

Ravinder's car had yet to reach home when hundreds of boots hit the ground. The hunt was on.

Unfortunately, neither Rafael nor the interrogator was to be blamed. Rafael Gerber had not lied. Mark *did* tell him that the other two men were coming from South Africa. What he had forgotten to mention was that both Shaun Ontong and Gary Boucher were Australians. They'd been operating in South Africa, but held Australian passports.

Ruby did not stop crying for a long time after Simran left. The strip of tablets lay forgotten in her hands, mangled. Not that it mattered; they would have been useless. Her pain was beyond medication. The raging conflict had started fragmenting her, loosening the already tenuous hold of sanity on her mind.

"Why did you lie to me, Mom?" She cried out, "*Why?* All these years . . . my life has been a lie."

"Your life has not been a lie, Ruby." From the depths of memory, Rehana tugged at her. Just as always. "Don't get taken in by all this sweet talk. Ravinder never understood me . . . us . . . our cause. For him, it had no meaning. He loved the little cocoon he created for himself. You tell me, can the life of one man be greater than the agony that hundreds of thousands of our people have suffered . . . continue to suffer? Can it?"

"No! But why did you—"

"You cannot falter now, Ruby. We have sacrificed everything to get you ready. You are our revenge." The dream of Rehana was piercing her. "I could have had a normal life too, but I chose our cause over that. Have you forgotten, Ruby? Have you forgotten what they did to us . . . to *me*?"

Reluctant though she was, Ruby could not stop these thoughts. They pounded her, hammering her down memory lane again.

Once again, as though it were happening all over again, Ruby found herself back in Palestine. She saw herself get out of the car and walk up to her uncle Yusuf. He was tall, really tall. And gaunt.

Unshaven and red-eyed, he was in nondescript jeans and a maroon T-shirt. A cap pulled down masked most of his face.

"I can never get over it." He stepped forward and took her in his arms. "Do you know how much you look like your mother?"

"Everyone says so." Her words emerged as a whisper. She began to cry as Yusuf folded her in his arms.

"I told her a million times not to come back." Ruby heard him as though from far away. "But she never listened. . . . You know your mother. . . . She would never listen . . . even as a kid."

Yes. I know my mother. Ruby wanted to scream, but she had no energy. *Yes! I* knew *my mother.*

"Rehana was with the peace marchers, at the front . . . with the leaders . . . to hand in a petition. It was a peaceful march . . . even some international participants from peace organizations.

That's when the artillery shell landed . . . right at the head of the column. Those bloody Israelis . . . now they say that one of our people bombed the march . . . but that's a lie . . . the bastards . . . they killed her." Ruby heard him choke. "There was nothing much left of any of them." He was unable to go on. Then he finally whispered, "Come, let us go inside and you can rest for a bit . . . you must be exhausted from the flight."

"No, not yet. I would like to see my mom."

"I don't think that is a good idea, child. There is not much to see."

"Whatever is left, Uncle Yusuf, I want to see her. She is . . . *was* my mother. I want to see her."

"You are so stubborn . . . just like her." Resigned. "Okay. If you are sure."

"I am sure."

Yusuf nodded, then went to the man who had driven her from the airport. For Yusuf, going to the hospital was out of the question. *They* would be watching out for him. He had no illusions what would happen if the Israelis got their hands on him.

An hour later, Ruby was at the hospital morgue, her heart pounding. The painful hammering increased as a white-coated, portly attendant pushed open the door and held it for her.

"I want to be alone with her," Ruby said. Her tone did not leave room for discussion. The attendant nodded as he flicked on the light.

The ghostly darkness dissipated as white light flooded the room. Puffs of icy cold air hung in the freezing room, adding to the chill inside her.

The attendant gestured at the long metal tables in the center. Each had a body, someone who had once been a person with a name, a family, and friends . . . perhaps enemies too. "The third one from the right." He pointed and left.

Ruby felt starkly alone. Never before had she felt so alone.

The silence was total, more unnerving than the screams reverberating in her head.

How can Mom be so small? Her hands felt as frozen as her mind. She willed them to reach out and pull away the white sheet. She saw sickly, yellow-red-black stains on it. Then the body. The tectonic plates of her mind began to slip.

So little was left of Rehana, especially the upper half of the body. Even the lower half was charred, tattered bits of flesh and bone. Surprisingly, the right hand remained untouched, as though the God of Death had wanted it so, to ensure the living would identify her easily. Rehana's favorite blue sapphire ring shone brightly, beckoning at Ruby. That cemented the reality of her death. Ruby now *knew* she would not be coming back.

A huge spurt of vomit surged up, sprayed out, all over the floor, by Rehana's table. Ruby collapsed, right into the vomit. The world around her went black.

Ruby came to in a bed in an unfamiliar room. The light streaming in told her that she had been out the whole night. Yusuf was sitting by her side.

"I told you not to go, child."

Ruby did not reply. *How to explain? I had to. There was no option. . . . There never has been . . . not with Rehana. . . . Mom is . . . was . . . Mom . . .* She kept looking at him. After a while, she began to cry. Quietly. Soon he too was crying.

They were still crying when a man entered. He whispered something in Yusuf's ear and left.

"It is time." Yusuf touched Ruby lightly on the shoulder. "We . . . you need to go. They are waiting."

"You will not come?"

"I cannot, Ruby. They will be looking out for me. Bid her farewell for me."

"I will."

It began to rain as they laid the cloth-covered body into the ground. Surprisingly the lifeless bundle appeared much larger than the . . . than what Ruby remembered had been left of Rehana.

The rain strengthened as they began to throw mud over the body, covering it, burying it. Soon it was as though she had never existed.

By now it was pouring. Claps of thunder boomed out. Slashes of lightning tore up the skies. Everything was gray. And dark.

Long after it was all over and the handful of mourners had left, Ruby stood in the pouring rain, watching the spot where Rehana's body had gone. The torrent of water streaming down her face tasted salty. Ruby was surprised that she had again started crying. But she felt no sense of finality . . . of closure. She *knew* it was not over. She did not know what, but something unfinished remained. She knew.

Finally she turned and started walking back to the waiting car. That was when the thought struck her.

Someone should pay for this.

The thought festered.

Somebody will.

Yusuf too had dried his tears by the time they got back. Neither had anything to say. Words seemed futile.

"Get some rest. You must be tired." His hand caressed her head. "We will talk tomorrow."

Ruby lay helplessly in the now-dark guest room in the Gill house. The darkness outside slowly faded as a new sun rose. The darkness within her stayed. It lay inside her, cold and clammy.

They should pay for this. Her silent promise now reverberated in her head. *I must make them pay.*

"So be it." Ruby did not realize that she had spoken aloud. "I will do my duty, but I will not harm any of the Gills. . . . They are family too."

I am not alone. The thought caught her by surprise. *I never was.*

That was her last thought as she fell asleep. In her still unfamiliar bed.

Unaware that Gerber had been captured and the noose around her was closing.

Ravinder awoke suddenly, his mind crystal clear.

"Sorry, sir," the now-dead Nanda was saying to him with a sheepish smile, "I was too far away to get the number, but the car was a cream-colored Toyota Innova."

In his mind's eye, Ravinder again saw the cream-colored Toyota come barreling down the road, almost running him down as he ran toward the garden gate. He saw his hand come up to stop it and a blur of motion inside the vehicle, as though someone had ducked. He ran the scene in his head a dozen times, but he couldn't put a face to the person; it had been too fast, too sudden. His attention had been elsewhere. But Ravinder knew it had been a woman. He did not know why, but he knew.

So, she had been there for the weapons pickup . . . whoever she is. . . . Damn! I should have thought of it. . . . I should have put more teams down to look out for her. . . . Damn!

Ravinder cursed himself for the lost opportunity. As he fell asleep, he wondered if he would get lucky again . . . or would that damn woman's luck continue to hold.

DAY EIGHT

Ruby wearily cracked open her eyes as the alarm on her mobile buzzed. She felt exhausted and unrested, as though she had just fallen asleep. She had. Barely an hour ago. Yet again, she wished that she had not thrown away the medication from the shrink.

Things were at a disastrous crossroads. The only saving grace was that Mark had not been taken alive; he was the only one who had known her identity *and* the target.

She was about to fall back asleep, when the TV sprang to life; the timer had been set for the morning BBC news.

Much to her disgust, there was no change in the situation in Israel. The IDF blockade of Gaza was still continuing. The turmoil in the Middle East was escalating. Then the local news came on. Her eyes widened as news of Gerber's arrest played out. The arrest of a foreign terrorist in Delhi on the eve of the Commonwealth Games was hot news, and the newscaster milked it for all it was worth.

All vestiges of sleep fled. This news devastated her. She hadn't yet figured out how to proceed without Mark and the Glocks, and now this . . .

Ruby felt another headache begin to build. She forced herself to get up, put on her tracksuit, and head out of the house. Perhaps a run would clear her head.

How is it possible that you have not been able to find those two mercenaries? All foreigners have to register." The early call from Mohite had shaken Ravinder awake. "Did you get the list from the Foreigner Regional Registration Office like I told you? They *have* to be on it."

"We did, sir. And we have been tracking everyone on that FRRO list."

"Then someone has slipped up." Ravinder was furious. "They *have* to be somewhere. Also they cannot check into any hotel without passports."

"But we have rounded up almost everyone from South Africa who even remotely fits the bill," Mohite repeated, sounding desperate. "We have nothing . . . except some very irate South Africans and an even more irate embassy official yelling at us."

"You handle them. And keep the search going. We have to catch those two." *Well, at least Mohite has something to keep him busy and out of trouble.* "There is no time, Mohite. The summit starts day after . . . In twenty-four hours, the delegates start arriving."

Putting down the phone, Ravinder sat up and began to think. *What have I missed?* There had to be something.

He was still brooding when he walked into his study and took his laptop out of its bag. There was a whole day of e-mails to be replied to.

Damn!

The small mark left by water had been wiped clean. Now only a faint ring on the polished tabletop remained. It tugged at Ravinder; irritating him.

He snatched up a paper napkin and scrubbed at it. It faded a bit, but would not go away completely. He was getting up to tell the servant to fetch some wood polish when memory struck.

Ruby was carrying a jug of water when I ran into her that night.

He froze. An alarm jangled in his head.

After clicking open his Outlook, he went to the date on which he had run into Ruby. It was late at night. Ravinder began to sift through the mails. The e-mail about the LeT financier caught his eye immediately. The next one too was relevant; it was about the meeting with Nanda.

If Ruby has seen these . . . Ravinder sat back. That would account for the elimination of Rizwan Khan. *But then why did she still send Mark to pick up the guns? Unless she saw the first mail, but not the second.*

Ravinder leaned forward and checked the time log. The two had come in almost simultaneously. If she had seen one, she would logically have seen the other.

Unless . . .

Straightening up, he raced out. He had to talk to Ruby and get to the bottom of this. Her room was empty. Coming down, he checked with the servant, who said that she had left early.

"Did she say where she was going?"

"Not to me, sahib. But she was wearing a tracksuit. It looked like she was going for a run."

Ravinder returned to his study to think. The stakes were too high. He could not allow anything to happen, to the games or to the summit. Though, knowing the Rehana angle now, if Ruby was somehow involved it would be the summit she was targeting.

The vibrating ring of his mobile tugged at him.

"Yes, Ashish?"

"We have found three improvised explosive devices near the Jawaharlal Nehru Stadium." DIG Ashish sounded grim. "Big ones, sir. Had they gone off, they would have taken out a large chunk of the stadium."

"Where?"

"Behind the ticketing booth, sir. The bombs seem to have been there awhile."

"An inside job. Round up all personnel who have access to that area."

"Already started that, sir."

"Good." Ravinder felt relief that Ashish was handling it, not Govind. "Ensure everyone's predecessors are checked. I want that bastard found . . . whoever he is."

"Don't worry, sir. I am on it. Whoever it is, we will find him. Or her."

"Fine." But that was not how Ravinder was feeling when he put the phone down.

Or her.

Ashish's final words ricocheted in his head. Too many things happening on too many fronts.

Slow down the game.

From his memory, Ravinder heard the voice of their college basketball coach. What he'd always told them to do, especially when playing a better team.

Yes!

He needed to calmly take stock of everything.

The few options still open to her churned through her mind as Ruby pounded down the silent road. At this early hour, not many people were around. Puddles littered the road, leftovers of last night's rain. The sense of isolation, of being alone, filled Ruby's head too. She needed help. Or, at least, someone to talk to.

Should I call Pasha? What would he be able to do from Pakistan? She toyed with the idea. *What other options do I have? Even if he can't help, maybe I can talk it through with him.*

Halting, she pulled out her mobile and her fingers dialed the number of his satellite phone, which was embedded in her memory. She could think of no one else.

The thought depressed her so much that she felt the urge to scream.

Ravinder broke out of his reverie. The father in him could no longer ignore that his own daughter might be a part of this awful threat.

Could she really be part of some conspiracy? An MI6 agent? Is it not possible that she is just a girl hurting from the loss of her mother? Who turned to me because she needs her father to stand by her at this dark hour? Could the sins of her mother . . .

The father begged him to give her the benefit of the doubt. The cop equally firmly urged him to fill in the gaps in his information. To complete the picture and deal with his suspicions. He *needed* to know.

Ravinder got dressed and left for his office. He would gather more information and size up the threat in its totality. The push–pull between father and cop continued as his car navigated through the traffic.

Yes! Time to slow down the game and seize control . . . before it spun out of his hands.

Ruby's finger was about to press the final digit of Pasha's number when she paused.

Do I really need him? What good will his footsloggers be?

She thought.

Do I need poorly trained zealots breathing down my neck?

Her finger stayed, hovering.

And can I trust his security? After all, the cops knew about Rizwan Khan. Who else has been blown?

She made up her mind with a snap. Her finger hit the red button, ending the dialing.

I can do this without him. Without anyone!

Pushing the phone back in her pocket, she began to run again. She had no idea what molecules sweeping through her had caused these abrupt mood and energy shifts. If she had, she might have realized that the medications the shrink had prescribed could have kept her sane.

An hour later, nothing had changed. The reality was stark. She had best to acknowledge it and adapt.

I will have to scale down. She saw no other options. *Hell, even if I manage to take down a couple of the delegates, it would kill the summit.*

But then her truant mind started playing games.

And you? You think you will get out of this alive? Without your primary and diversionary attacks?

Then a wave of sadness overwhelmed her. But, as abruptly, the agent-turned-terrorist took charge, returning to fortify her.

It doesn't matter. Even if I die, it doesn't matter. But they must be made to pay. . . . She stopped running and hailed the first passing cab. Time to get the operation back on track.

Ruby *knew* she was up to it.

Ravinder marshaled all the data. Everything recovered from Mark, along with a photograph of his body was laid out on one side of his office table. The items from Gerber and his hotel room were on the other side, along with a transcript of his interrogation. In the middle, on a paper, he had jotted down all the contradictory facts that he had gleaned about Ruby. He mulled everything and identified the gaps that he still needed to fill. Then he reached for the phone.

The first call was to London, to Sir Edward Kingsley, Director of MI6.

"Does this have anything to do with Sir Tang's visit to Delhi?" Kingsley asked bluntly. The two went a long way back, and the Director knew he could talk freely with Ravinder.

"Maybe . . . maybe not," Ravinder replied. "That is what I am trying to ascertain."

"I see. Give me a couple of minutes." Computers in London whirred into action, but neither Rehana's nor Ruby Gill's names elicited anything useful. However, Sir Edward promised to dig deeper.

Ravinder's second call was to his counterpart in Tel Aviv, the head of their Counter-Terrorism Task Force.

"What did you say the names were?"

Ravinder could hear the tapping of a keyboard as he repeated the names. They appeared to get an instant response.

"Would you mind if we call you back?"

"I am in a bit of a rush."

"It will take only minutes. Someone here would like to speak to you."

Seven minutes later, Meir Dagan called him back on a secure line.

"Firstly, I must thank you for all the help with that problem across the border." Dagan was aware of the risk India had taken; it would have been disastrous if any of the Kidon team had been taken alive. "My government appreciates it."

"A pleasure, Mr. Dagan." But Ravinder couldn't keep the anxiety out of his voice. Dagan picked up on it and asked him why. Ravinder told him.

"Before I answer, I want your assurance this conversation will remain off the books."

"If that is what you want."

"It is."

"So be it. Whatever you say will remain with me. Even if I take action, I will not divulge the reasons or the source."

"Thank you. I must warn you, though . . . this is going to be unusual. I am not sure if my government would approve of it."

"These are unusual times, Mr. Dagan."

"They certainly are, Mr. Gill. Does the name Yusuf Sharbati mean anything to you?"

"Hmmm . . . I have heard it—" Memory kicked in with a snap. "Isn't he the Qassam Brigade commander who was . . . who met his end at Dubai a couple of weeks ago?"

"Perfectly right. The very same. Yusuf was the one who engineered the Jerusalem strike with help from the Lashkar-e-Taiba. His death was our payback."

"I understand."

"I think you do."

"I have no issues with Yusuf's death. He got what he deserved. But I am not able to understand what he has to do with my queries."

"Do you know that Sharbati was not his real name? He took that on as a nom de guerre only when he joined the Qassam Brigade."

Ravinder felt a sense of something evil coming at him.

"His real name was Yusuf al-Moghrabi. Does *that* name mean anything to you, Mr. Gill?"

The sick sensation now turned into a pain. "Moghrabi was my first wife's family name," he whispered, the shock sinking in.

"Yusuf Sharbati was her brother."

"But Rehana said both her brothers had died."

Dagan did not say anything.

"Does Ruby, my daughter, know about Yusuf? Did she know him?"

"We do not know. We think she does. We have reason to believe she met him when she came here for Rehana's funeral. But to be honest, we are not sure."

"Tell me more," Ravinder said, dreading any answer.

"We picked her up the minute Ruby Gill landed in Tel Aviv. The immigration officer kept her engaged as he informed our office. By the time she left the airport, we had a surveillance team on her and a beeper on her suitcase. An hour later, she managed to lose both and simply vanished into the West Bank. Why would she have done that if she had nothing to hide?"

Why, indeed?

"We picked her up again at her mother's funeral, but once again, Ruby lost the surveillance. When she showed up at the airport the next day, we questioned her. Our man specifically asked her if she knew Yusuf. . . . He showed her his picture. She denied meeting him, even denied knowing him. Our man reminded her that as a British government employee, it was her duty to help us track down a known terrorist."

"What did she say?"

"'I would if I could, Officer. I wish I could.'" His words hung between them for a while. "And, since there was no evidence of any wrongdoing, we could not detain her."

Then a silence, before Dagan continued.

"I must also tell you almost the same thing happened when Rehana reached Israel after the Jerusalem strike. Our computers picked up her name and we mounted an electronic and physical surveillance. We managed to track her to the house of one Abdul Bari, who had been the neighbor and lab assistant of her late father. Bari took her to meet Bashshar, the local Hamas man, also a junior Qassam Brigade commander . . . someone we've had our eye on for some time. A couple of hours later, Rehana managed to lose the bugs and the men watching her. The next we heard of her, she had been killed during the Interfaith Freedom March, at the Main Square on Abu Bakr Street."

Dagan allowed Ravinder to assimilate all this before he resumed once more.

"So, though we have no proof that either Rehana or Ruby met Yusuf, their actions were not above suspicion. Why else would they have ditched the bugs or the surveillance?"

"Why else, indeed?"

"So, like I said earlier, no real proof. And yes, there is one more thing. Our people recovered a mobile from Yusuf Sharbati in Dubai. One call was made to it, from a satellite phone, which we traced to Pakistan—"

"Yes. Your man, Ido Peled, told us about that."

"So we put that satellite phone on our monitoring list and then we picked up a call made to it from London."

"When was that?"

Dagan told him. Ravinder did the math; it had been made when Ruby was still in London. *But what does that prove?*

"Was it—?" He hesitated, knowing this could be the key question. If the caller was Ruby, the father could no longer deny the cop; his duty would be clear.

"We have no idea who it was." Dagan second-guessed the question. "The caller didn't say a word. The satellite phone was answered by a man, who said his phone was low on battery and he would call back. That was it. So all we know is that the call originated from a public phone in central London."

Ravinder, deeply troubled when he put the phone down, knew he could not stop. He redialed, and minutes later he was on to London again.

"Like I mentioned earlier, Ruby Gill is currently on medical leave."

"Yes, but I need only to know where she was on these dates." Ravinder gave out the fortnight spanning the weeks on either side of the Jerusalem terror strike. Ravinder again could hear keys clicking.

"Well, she was right here . . . in England. We cannot say where, but she was certainly in the country. . . . We have no record of her having traveled out at that time."

"I see." Ravinder couldn't tell if he was relieved or more troubled.

He was brooding about this when Gyan entered. "Sir, the agent from London is here to see you."

"Send him in." Ravinder wondered what Chance wanted, but he was glad to see him. Perhaps he could help.

They were exchanging pleasantries when Chance spotted the photo of Mark's body on Ravinder's table. With the Congo operation fresh in his memory, he recognized it immediately. "That's Mark Leahy. What's he doing here?"

"You know him?" Ravinder was surprised.

"Yes. He's ex-military, did some work for . . . our government." Chance broke off, realizing this was an area he did not wish to go into. "Ruby also knows him."

"She does?" Somehow Ravinder was not surprised; but it made his heart slump.

"Better than I do. He was her backup for our last operation. Why?"

Ravinder took a long minute to marshal his thoughts. And to decide how much he should take Chance into his confidence. But he took the hard call and brought Chance up to speed, telling him everything except what Dagan had told him in confidence.

"The arms dealer was sure it was a woman?"

"No, but he believed it was."

"What do you think the target is?"

"If Ruby is involved, I'll bet it's the summit."

"What next, then?" Chance, trying to mask his own confusion and distress, was watching Ravinder carefully.

There was a silence.

Inwardly, Ravinder flinched. Outwardly he displayed no sign. Ravinder met Chance's gaze head-on. "Then we take Ruby in."

"Is it that simple, Mr. Gill?" Chance leaned back in his chair, running his hands through his hair.

"What do you mean?"

"With the evidence you have so far . . . such as it is, our government will blow a gasket if you arrest her. Ruby is a British national . . . and an MI6 agent. You will not be able to hold her for long . . . if at all. . . . You can bet on that."

"It'd be only for a few days," Ravinder shrugged. "The delegates start arriving tomorrow. A week at best, and it will all be over."

"Yes, but I don't see that happening. Not unless you are willing to risk a big international incident."

Ravinder closed his eyes, pondering. If he arrested her and could not come up with proof, it would be the end of his career. And *if* he were wrong, it would be the end of any love with his firstborn.

"Also, if she is involved in any strike," Chance pointed out, "how likely is it that she'd be operating alone? How sure can we be that arresting her will stop the strike."

"From what Gerber has told us, we know she's not alone." Ravinder referred to the yet-to-be-traced South African mercenaries.

"Right. And considering the timeframe," Chance asked, "she might have already deployed them and others that we may not even know about . . . right?"

The silence this time was longer.

Ravinder realized that taking Ruby in might not actually stop a strike. But he had to be doubly sure that the father in him was not standing between the cop and his duty. Finally he nodded. "Yes. That makes sense."

"So then, why don't we leave things the way they are. We allow her to believe that we do not suspect her, and maintain status quo. If she continues staying at your house, not only can you keep an eye on her, but she may even lead us to the others."

It took Ravinder time to respond. "Okay. I agree."

Even as he said that, he felt a nagging doubt tug at him. *Am I doing the right thing? Would it not be simpler to just take her in and—*

Then Mohite rushed in, excited and disheveled. "I think we have them, sir."

"Who?"

"The two South African mercenaries?"

"Really? Where did you find them?"

"A small guesthouse in Paharganj. One of the whore—" Mohite noticed Chance and checked himself. "—one of those disreputable ones."

"Good!" Ravinder thumped the table, happy at the break. "Where are they now?"

"They'll be here any minute."

"Take them straight for interrogation. We'll be down right away."

"We?" Mohite threw a glance at Chance.

Chance took the hint. "I was just leaving." He got up.

"No, that's all right, Chance. Please stay." He turned to Mohite. "We *are* batting for the same side, Govind."

Mohite nodded, clearly unhappy. Ravinder sensed he'd be hearing more on this from Thakur soon. But now he had bigger fish to fry; if he managed to grab the terrorists and stop a strike, even Thakur would leave him alone for a time.

An hour later, the excitement turned to shit.

The only thing the two South Africans were guilty of was having picked the wrong day to visit the wrong whorehouse. And they'd compounded their error by trying to fight off the cops and make a break for it when the whorehouse was raided.

The inspector who led the raid was a vindictive type, which was aggravated by their breaking his nose in their attempt to escape. And that both South Africans were solidly built ex-soldiers had convinced the furious cop that these were the two mercenaries wanted by ATTF.

Unwilling to talk openly with Mohite around, Ravinder waited till he was alone before speaking with Chance again. "I am going home now. Let me see what Ruby is up to."

"Do that. Keep her with you as much as possible."

"Where are you headed?"

"Back to the hotel to check out the deployment again. I am still not happy with how the security guys are responding to the emergency drill."

He was walking away when a thought struck Ravinder. He felt sure it would work, but it would require more than a single pair of hands. He also knew he could trust Chance to help make it happen.

"Chance, one second." Calling him back, Ravinder explained what he had in mind. "What do you think?"

"Using decoy delegates in case of an attempted strike on the summit is a brilliant idea." Chance sounded excited. "It will keep them safe and also, if we use armed decoys, give us a chance to take down the attackers."

"Great! But we'll need more people."

"You can count me in," Chance assured him. "Who else do you have in mind? Mr. Mohite?"

"No. He already has too much to do."

Chance had already sensed Ravinder's disconnect with his second-in-command. "What about Jennifer?"

"She should do, but don't brief her just yet." Ravinder saw the query in Chance's eyes. "The fewer who know, the better." Pause. "Right now, women from the West are not too high on my list of trusted people."

They both laughed, happy for that respite.

"Right." Chance nodded. "How about Ido Peled?"

"Yes, he should be good. I'll speak to him right away."

"Cool. Later, when the time is right, I can speak to Jennifer."

"Yes. Between the four of us, we can ensure both floors are

sealed off and all the delegates guarded. I will detail four of my people . . . people I can rely on totally, to act as escorts."

"Fair enough," Chance concurred. "What about the decoys?"

Ravinder ran over his options. "I think our best bet is the National Security Guards. Kaul, the NSG Director General, is my batch mate and a good friend. He will give us the thirteen decoys we need."

Once again, that bloody number. Ravinder pushed it away.

The two men quickly ran through the plan once more, fleshing it out to ensure nothing had been overlooked. The minute an attack was mounted on the summit, the delegates would be moved to another conference room, secured by Ido Peled. Chance would man the eighth floor and Jennifer the seventh, while Ravinder took charge of the control room. The thirteen decoys would be moved under armed escort to the alternate venue, the Samrat Hotel. The decoys would be used to draw out the attackers, who could then be neutralized.

Satisfied that they'd covered the critical points, they went their separate ways: Chance to Ashoka Hotel and Ravinder to call Kaul. He briefed the three guards at his house not to allow anyone out without clearing it with him. And also tasked a plainclothes team, three men including the driver, to mount surveillance on his house from sunrise to midnight.

"You must not let my daughter Ruby out of your sight even for a minute, and at the same time ensure she does not know you are watching her." He noted the unspoken query on their faces. "There have been some threats," he explained, "but she refuses to accept protection, hence . . ." He left the rest unsaid.

Ravinder's mind was in turmoil as he started for home.

As the car hit the road, he checked his watch. The delegates would be arriving soon. For the games, athletes had already been landing in droves. There were uniforms and guns everywhere. Delhi, he sensed, was a city under siege. And not just Delhi.

India was leaving nothing to chance. From Kashmir to the borders in Punjab and Rajasthan, the army had swamped every possible infiltration point. The Indian Navy had more ships and boats along every foot of the coastline than there were fish in the waters. The airspace over Delhi was closed, and even scheduled commercial flights were being shepherded by the Indian Air Force. Paramilitary forces had barricaded every road and dirt track into the National Capital Region. The Delhi Police had borrowed every available cop from neighboring states; and had swept the streets clean of criminals. New tenants in every residential colony were visited by a beat constable and their credentials verified.

As Mohite had succinctly put it to Ravinder, "The NCR is locked down tight, boss. Tight as a virgin's cunt."

Ravinder had winced. A city the size and shape of Delhi could *never* be locked down completely. And the fact that the danger may already have penetrated the fort was a possibility he now could not ignore.

Coupled with this were the unprecedented rains that had not only flooded most roads, slowing traffic to an abysmal crawl, but had also brought an outbreak of dengue and conjunctivitis, which had laid low many of his cops. Everything that could had started going wrong.

Ruby was back home by the time the surveillance team deployed outside the Gills' gate. Despite the run of bad luck, her day had been productive. She had not only finalized her attack plan, but had also briefed Ontong and Boucher, and mated them up with their vans and rocket launchers.

Both had balked when she told them what she expected them to do. But their objections faded when she pointed out that with Mark and Gerber out of the running, she was doubling their payout.

That settled, Ruby returned home, satisfied that things were back on track. Her new, abbreviated plan was as good as it could get in the altered circumstances.

When Ravinder arrived, Ruby was sitting with Jasmine on the lawn; the two were chatting merrily. Jasmine, in the thick of her final-semester exams, appeared to be sharing her excitement and stress with her sister. Ravinder could hear Jasmine narrating some incident about the moot court she was in at college.

Ruby broke out in laughter. Everything looked so *normal.* Looking at her, Ravinder found it hard to believe that she could be the one targeting the summit.

"What are my lovely girls up to?" Concealing his troubled thoughts with a warm smile, he walked up to them.

They both rose and hugged him. If there was anything else on Ruby's mind, she hid it well. Doubt assailed him.

Am I being paranoid? Just because Rehana and her brother Yusuf were gung ho about Palestine, is it fair to tar her with the same brush? Could I be overlooking some other threat? Some other more real threat?

"I want to take Ruby shopping," Jasmine's voice intruded. "She wants to pick up some Indian clothes before she leaves."

"Leaves?" Ravinder was surprised. "Where are you going, Ruby?"

"Home." Ruby's reply was tentative, as though she was not really sure what that word meant anymore. "I can't stay here forever." She laughed, a soft, almost embarrassed laugh.

"Oh!" Ravinder sensed she was watching him closely, but he was feeling stunned. Already worried about her possible involvment in the threat to the summit, this latest news added to his turmoil. He missed hers altogether.

"But before that we were planning to catch a movie." Jasmine's voice tugged at Ravinder. "Would you please have your office book the movie tickets?"

"Which movie?" Ravinder could still feel Ruby's gaze on him. She was looking . . . confused? Expectant? He wasn't sure. He sensed she was waiting for him to say something to her. *What?*

"Would you, please?" Jasmine again.

"Sure." Ravinder nodded, glad to be able to focus on something practical and mundane; this continued emotional turbulence was getting too much for him to handle. He was feeling exhausted.

"Thanks, Daddy . . . you're a sweetheart. We were thinking of *Sex and the City* . . . the new one. If you could book it at the Select Citywalk mall, then we can shop there after the movie."

"I will take care of it, princess. You can use my car too."

"But we'll be out late. I don't think we'll be back before nine or ten."

"No problem. I'll tell my office to send another car if I need it, but I don't think I'll be stepping out now. From tomorrow I'll be staying at the hotel till . . . for the next few days."

"You won't be coming home at all?" Jasmine asked.

"No. Not till this event gets over. I need to ensure things go smoothly."

"I am also going to be tied up at college for the next three days, moot court in the mornings and then we're all planning to go to the various cultural events that are being held."

"And you, Ruby? What are your plans?"

"Nothing special." She now looked strangely subdued. "Just catch up on some more sightseeing . . . maybe take in a movie."

"Why don't you go with Jasmine for the cultural events? A lot of Bollywood stars are here for the games."

"Maybe I will. Let's see."

"That'll be fun." Jasmine smiled. "Come, Ruby, let's get ready." She took Ruby's arm and tugged.

"Okay, girls. Have fun."

He gave them a hug each and watched them walk away. When out of earshot, he called his office and told them to book two tickets for the girls and two more a couple of rows behind for the surveillance. Then, knowing where they were going and which car they would be going in, he briefed them.

Ravinder ascended the stairs, a little confused, feeling he had missed something back there, but also happy that Ruby would be under close watch till late at night. Abruptly, an insiduous thought angled in. *Will Jasmine be okay? If Ruby has indeed turned rogue, she could be dangerous. . . .*

He froze, then continued climbing up; something in his heart refused to believe that Ruby would harm Jasmine. But he could not push away a little niggling doubt.

Watching Ravinder as they walked away, Ruby was hurting and puzzled. In light of his guarded behavior since that eventful lunch with Chance, she had expected . . .

Expected what? Ruby considered that. *Is it only my guilty conscience at work?*

Willing herself to focus on Jasmine, Ruby got engrossed in their conversation again, but deep inside she was far away; hurting but no longer sure if she was on the right path; he *was* her father, after all.

But he could have asked me to stay? He didn't even offer it. If he had just offered it once . . . She felt like crying. Then. *Am I being fair?*

Doubt continued to breed. But as they drove off, Ruby picked up on the surveillance car.

So, he is having me followed. Her feeling of betrayal came back. Then on second thought, *Maybe it's normal procedure for the ATTF chief's family. Maybe it's just a security team.* Doubts began to resurface.

Caught up in an annoying thrum, she tuned out Jasmine's chatter, leaned deeper into her mind, and called on her inner reserves.

He didn't even ask me to stay. The painful thought nagged her again.

Minutes later, her resolve was firm again. The hate was back. Ruby *knew* she could not falter.

Her eyes went to her wristwatch. Barely twenty hours left now. Soon the delegates would be in place.

The time to kill was rushing toward her.

Tuning in again to what Jasmine was saying, Ruby threw herself back into the game she was playing . . . *I am being forced to play.*

A firm head shake.

He did not even want to me stay. . . . What kind of father is he?

When Ravinder entered the bedroom, he could tell that Simran was worried. Several times in the past few days, she had tried to talk to him, but he'd pulled away, not knowing how much to share with her. Now he knew his silence was not helping her or the situation.

After closing the door, he sat beside her and began to talk. Starting from the beginning, he shared his story with her . . . and his fears.

When he finished, the house was silent. Neither realized the sun had set and darkness had crept in.

"I know how you must be feeling." The caring in Simran's voice reached out to him through the darkness. He realized that there were depths to her that he had not yet fathomed, despite all their years of togetherness.

Not fathomed or not wanted to fathom? He could not ignore this thought. Had he really given all to their marriage? *Or have I let Rehana's memories come between us?* Guilt seized him.

"This must be so difficult for you." Simran reached out and cupped his face in her hands. Her hands came away wet. "Don't worry. I know you well, Ravinder. I know you will always do the right thing. Just trust your instincts."

Ravinder felt an ache in his heart; he realized how deeply he cared for her, despite her bickering and nagging.

Then something inside him stirred. He reached out and folded her in a tight embrace. Their lips came together. The kiss soon became fierce. His fingers moved as though possessed with a life of their own. One by one her clothes came off. Simran moaned with joy as he entered her.

She moaned again as he came, her body arching up as she joined him. Then they lay together. Content. Surrounded by a shield of love.

Somewhere below, he heard a loud bang. Perhaps a door carelessly closed. Perhaps the wind. Reality returned with a thud.

"Do you think it is safe for Jasmine to have gone out with her?"

Ravinder shivered as Simran voiced the same fear he had felt. He did not know. Worse, he did not know how to tell Simran that he did not know.

They heard the front door open and the sounds of young girls in animated conversation floated up. The clattering of feet followed as Ruby and Jasmine came up the stairs.

"The next time they go out, I will also go with them," Simran said as they heard the girls go into Ruby's room and their voices died away.

"I was thinking of asking Jasmine to take Ruby to the opening ceremony of the games," Ravinder mused out loud. He looked at Simran, as if for her approval. "There is nothing anyone can do to anyone there. It will be safe."

"Yes. I will also go with them."

Silence returned. A short while ago, it had been warm and full of love. Now it was cold and forbidding.

Ravinder shivered.

Ruby was exhausted by the time Jasmine decided to call it a night. Then, no matter how hard she tried, she couldn't sleep. After a while, she stopped trying and parked herself in the bay window overlooking the front lawn.

A full moon rode high, playing hide-and-seek between the fluffs of clouds. Ruby saw it all with unseeing eyes.

Her mind was far away, watching a happy little girl playing hide-and-seek with her parents. She could see Rehana and Ravinder hunt for her, walking slowly through the house.

"Come out, come out, wherever you are. . . ." Their singsong chants rang out, making her giggle as she hid in the bedroom cupboard.

Then Ravinder was no longer there. Only Rehana, and she did not seem happy. And the girl was no longer happy either. They both were quiet and subdued.

And soon Rehana too had vanished. The little girl was alone. Only not so little now. And she was angry. Really angry. And she felt betrayed.

Across the corridor, Ravinder also tossed and turned, dead tired by now, but unable to sleep. It was that nagging feeling of having missed something. Perhaps the feeling that he should have gone with the evidence and taken Ruby into custody. Perhaps that he could not reconcile with the fact that his daughter might be the enemy. Perhaps that look in Ruby's eyes when Jasmine had mentioned she was leaving.

He felt an increasing foreboding that something awful was straining to be unleashed.

His uneasiness reached out to Simran. Lying awake beside him, she was so aware of the unhappy young woman who had disrupted their lives, who also might be in distress.

They lay in silence, almost touching.

Both waited for the endless night to recede.

Seven miles away as the crow flies, in his room at Ashoka Hotel, Chance was also unable to sleep. Though lying in bed, he was wide awake and wired. Finally he gave up. Having pulled out a Coke from the mini-bar, he parked himself near the window, watching the moon outside. The beauty of the calm October night slipped past unnoticed.

Like an erratically choreographed movie, bits of the past flowed through him. And always, hanging like a dark cloud over them, was the morrow slowly approaching. He wondered . . . *hoped* . . . that the days ahead would pass peacefully and it would all end well.

A few hundred miles to the north, standing on the porch of a LeT safe house near the Pakistani town of Muridke, Pasha also watched the same bright moon. He restlessly patrolled the porch, wondering how his assassin was faring. The shocking assault that had taken out Anwar and the total absence of communication from Ruby sickened him. The agent provocateur knew that even the best-trained and motivated agent could falter. But he also knew that the battle had already slipped out of his hands; as it always did once the mission had been launched.

Nothing to do now but wait. He knew. So he waited.

The neatly dressed man got out of the car and walked up to the main gate of the Gill home. He had a piece of paper in his hand and was referring to it as he approached, checking house numbers. Barring the occasional streetlamp, the street was dark.

"Excuse me," he said to the guard standing outside, holding up the paper. "Can you please tell me where Mr. Mahajan stays?"

The sentry shouldered his rifle and held out his hand. "Show me the house number."

The man drew closer.

The two other guards heard the exchange and came closer, curiosity more than anything else. Now all four men were just a few meters apart.

The sentry was taking the paper, so he failed to see the man's right hand creep up to his waist. There was a soft click, which registered with none of the guards. And the bomb wrapped around the man's waist went off with a thunderous roar. Nothing within six to seven meters remained standing.

All three guards and a part of the metal gate blew apart.

The bomber himself disintegrated. Only one of the guards was far enough away to survive, but even he was knocked unconscious.

The roar of the explosion had not yet abated when the door of the car in which the man had arrived blew open and another man leaped out, carrying a Type 56 Chinese assault rifle.

Rushing past the body of Aslam, his former cell mate, who had taken out the guards at the cost of his life, Javed Khan headed straight for the Gills' front door, his rifle on the ready. The mission given to him by the Jaish-e-Mohammed chief was clear: He would kill the ATTF chief. Or die trying.

Leveling his rifle at the door, he fired a long burst, shattering the lock. After kicking open the now useless door, he entered the house. He saw no lights on the ground floor. The curtains were drawn and the house was swathed in darkness. Pitch-black darkness. Cursing, Javed began to feel his way forward, trying to find a light switch.

To Ravinder, the sound was so loud, so close, that he knew the house was under attack. The popping crack of an assault rifle confirmed it. Not pausing to think, he leaped out of bed, grabbed the Browning from the bedside table, and clicking off the safety, headed out.

"Go to Jasmine's room and lock yourselves in!" he yelled at Simran as he ran. "And call the control room." In the heat of the moment, he forgot about Ruby.

Simran ran for Jasmine's room.

Jasmine too had been jolted awake, but she was befuddled. Then she saw her mother rush in, wild-eyed.

"We're being attacked!" Simran screeched with fear. She reached out and grabbed Jasmine, and began to blubber hysterically. The panic multiplied, feeding off both of them.

Simran was still wailing when she reached for the phone and dialed 100, the police control room, managing to get the message across before again rushing to Jasmine. The two women clutched each other, terrified. Simran had forgotten to lock the bedroom door.

Sitting in the guest bedroom's bay window, Ruby saw the blinding flash of the bomb. She froze. The rifle burst galvanized her. Instantly, her training took charge. She ran for the weapon that should have been by her bedside. But her hand came away empty. Then she realized where she was. The pistol in Jasmine's room flashed on her memory. A dozen quick steps, and she burst into Jasmine's room.

Jasmine and Simran screamed when the door blew open. Then they saw it was Ruby and some of their panic receded.

Ruby took in their condition at a glance. Without breaking her stride, she raced to the jewelry box, snatched out the pistol, her hands instinctively checking if the magazine was loaded. It was. She chambered a round.

A loud metallic clang from the living room spurred her on. She swiveled around and ran out.

Javed was cursing the darkness, clawing the walls to find a light switch. He had taken about ten steps when he collided with a large brass lamp. It toppled and hit the ground with a loud clang. He froze. *Hell!* By now someone would have called the cops and they'd be on the way. He was deciding what to do when . . .

Ravinder hit the head of the stairs as the brass lamp hit the floor. The gun steady in his right hand, he hit the light switch with his left. Fingers of light flashed into the living room. Immediately he saw the intruder. The rifle in the man's hand began to rise. Ravinder's weapon was already up. He fired. And missed.

From thirty feet away, the assault rifle roared to life. It was set on automatic. Like pinpricks of light, a volley of bullets flew at him.

Ravinder threw himself down, forgetting that he was standing at the head of the stairs. His head hit the wood, hard. Though the stairs were carpeted, it was hard enough to knock him unconscious.

Javed saw Ravinder fall. He heard the body hit the stairs and start to slide down. He assumed he had hit him. Needing to confirm if it was really the ATTF chief or only one of his minions, Javed raced up the stairs.

Racing forward, Ruby was chambering a round when the pistol shot rang out, followed closely by the roar of an assault rifle. Then she heard the thud of a body hitting the floor. She erupted out of the corridor that led to the bedrooms.

The sight before her eyes froze her.

Ravinder was in a heap halfway down the stairs. Coming up was a man with an assault rifle in his hands and a crazed look.

My daddy! Her heart plummeted. *He's killed my daddy!*

Javed saw Ruby at the same time and began to align his weapon on her.

He's killed my daddy!

Something inside Ruby broke. She fired. Again. Then again.

The first two bullets, delivered to his chest at close range, brought Javed to a dead halt. The third blew him backward. He was almost dead as he hit the foot of the staircase.

But Ruby did not stop. The killing heat was upon her, compounding her rage at the unknown man who had orphaned her. At a few feet from him, she saw that the intruder still had some life in him. Kneeling next to him, she prodded his face with the pistol. Javed's eyes fluttered open.

Ruby leaned closer, right into his ear, and whispered. "You-will-*not*-kill-my-daddy. No-one-will-*ever*-kill-my-daddy." Each word shot out separately, unforgivingly. Placing the pistol against his forehead, she pulled the trigger. Again. And kept firing till the weapon was empty. And the intruder's head a gory, pulpy mess.

In the distance, she heard the wailing of police sirens. She heard it, but it did not register. She felt empty. Completely hollow. Drained.

Then she heard a moan behind her as Ravinder regained consciousness.

Shocked, she turned and saw that he was sitting up, holding his head, where it had struck the stairs. He looked dazed but unhurt. Something inside her began to sing again. Something cried. Something snapped.

Dropping the pistol, she ran to Ravinder. "Are you all right, Daddy?"

He nodded, still dazed.

Just then Simran appeared at the head of the stairs with Jasmine in tow. They saw Ravinder's head was cradled in Ruby's lap.

"Ruby saved all of us today," Ravinder called out to them. He had tears in his eyes.

Both women started to cry as the aftershock struck.

Ruby sat silent and still. Stroking Ravinder's hair, softly, lovingly. Her eyes were blank and silent. Something inside her head had fragmented. She no longer knew who she was. Where she was. Why she was.

Vehicles came to a screeching halt outside. Cops burst into the house.

Ruby did not see them. She heard nothing. She motioned to Jasmine to come closer. Made her sit beside her and gently moved Ravinder's head to Jasmine's lap. "Look after Daddy. No one must hurt him." After getting up, Ruby returned to her bedroom, seemingly oblivious.

Simran, Ravinder, and Jasmine watched her go. None of them knew what to say. Or do.

Ruby collapsed on the bed. For once, her mind did not trouble her. It couldn't. Something inside had broken loose. A Rubicon had been crossed.

Unaware of the turmoil awaiting them, from seven different countries, thirteen different men began to move.

From Washington, London, Tel Aviv, Cairo, Damascus, and Amman. One by one, their aircraft slid through the skies, sweeping closer to Delhi.

In their hands lay the fate of millions of people. Hope for Palestine and peace for Israel. Their success would mean the return of peace to a land troubled by bloodshed for so many years. Each one of them was keenly aware of it.

Though none of them had any illusions about the gargantuan task, they had hope.

DAY NINE

A new sun was rising when Senator George Polk's flight touched down.

Thakur met the silver-colored USAF jet at the VIP area of Palam Air Force Station. Slightly balding, ruddy-faced, yet with an aura of power, the senator had a wide smile as he descended from the plane, no doubt looking forward to playing a key role in the historic summit. He was miffed that there was no press there to meet him and hail America's critical role in this event.

Mohite was hovering around Thakur. Jennifer Poetzcsh was there too, the senator being her responsibility. Suspicious of everything and mistrustful of the security cover provided by the Indians, her hand never strayed from her gun.

Thakur, also eager to make his presence felt, accompanied the senator to the hotel to make sure he was comfortably settled in.

Ravinder joined them there a bit later, still groggy from the events of last night. His head now hurt less, dulled by painkillers. But he was also still reeling from the emotional jolt. Ruby's actions had him completely confused. However, still unable to ignore the evidence against her, he would continue the surveillance till the delegates left India; that seemed the sanest course.

They had barely settled the senator in, when the Saudi delegate, Prince Ghanim Abdul Rahman al-Saud walked in. Despite his short, stout build and bushy eyebrows, his regal robes and aura left no doubt that he commanded instant obedience. Two hard-looking, well-built, retired SEALs were flanking him. Ravinder noted that both bore a striking resemblance to Mark Leahy.

And, my God, yes, the two South African mercenaries were still at large. And Ruby. *What is she doing?* He looked at his watch, a quarter to eleven. The surveillance team was to report every hour on the hour, so the next call would come at eleven, or if Ruby left the house.

That morning Ravinder, then Jasmine, and eventually Simran had gone to check on her. All three had encountered a locked door. The only response was her voice, telling them she was okay and they should not worry. But she sounded far from okay. Ravinder was concerned. He hoped it was nothing more than the shock of having had to kill someone.

He was still thinking of Ruby when Chance strode in with Sir Geoffrey Tang, the British delegate. Tang was extremely tall, fit, and totally smart in his tailored, gray, pin-striped suit. Despite his sixty-plus years, he had a full head of hair, with only touches of white at the temples. With deep-set, coal black eyes, chiseled features, and long sideburns and goatee, Tang looked the epitome of royalty.

"We heard about last night . . . are you okay?" Chance asked in an undertone. Ravinder nodded. "And Ruby?"

Ravinder nodded again. But both were keenly aware that the danger was far from over.

When Ruby came down for breakfast, she found Simran and Jasmine at the table. Jasmine gave a big smile and went running to give her a long hug. Jasmine appeared to have recovered completely. Or perhaps was in complete denial. At Simran's insistence, she was even going to college. Ravinder had agreed, realizing it was better for her than to sit and mope at home.

Simran also smiled at her, a warm smile, aware that none of them might be alive today if it had not been for Ruby.

"You are just in time, Ruby." Jasmine pulled Ruby to the seat beside her. "Come. Mom is helping me prepare for today's moot court. Would you also like to hear my contentions?"

"Why do you want to bother her?" Simran replied before Ruby could respond.

"If that is what you want me to do," Ruby replied tonelessly, ignoring Simran.

"Are you sure?" Jasmine queried. Ruby nodded. "Great!" Jasmine pulled out a sheaf of papers. "The case is a real one— *Mausami Ganguli versus Jayant Ganguli*. I am representing the father and my best friend Rekha is representing the mother." Jasmine began to read, giving details of how she would defend the case in the college moot court.

Ruby was staring at the plate of eggs on the table, and did not appear to be listening. Simran was watching her, a worried look on her face.

"So when the wife, Mausami Ganguly, deserted her husband, she moved to another city." Jasmine flipped a page and continued. "From there she managed to obtain an ex parte divorce. She also managed to get legal custody of their four-year-old daughter. The husband, Jayant, contested that in the high court . . . the divorce and the custody."

"Did he win?" Ruby's sudden question, delivered in that same flat monotone, shocked both Jasmine and Simran.

"What?" Jasmine asked.

"So did he get it? The custody, I mean," Ruby repeated, still staring at the plate of eggs.

"The father? Yes, he did get custody, but only later, from the Supreme Court."

"I see." Ruby had still not looked up.

Concerned, Jasmine exchanged a rapid glance with Simran, who, equally confused, shrugged.

"You can if you want to," Ruby said as she suddenly got up and began to walk away, heading back up to her room. "You can if you want to. . . . You have to want to," Ruby called without stopping.

Simran and Jasmine heard her go up the stairs with a heavy, dragging stride.

"Daddy did not want to. If he had, he would have found me." Ruby's tearful voice rang out from halfway. "Only Mom loved me."

They heard her bedroom slam shut.

Silence descended on the Gill house.

Mom?" Then more insistently. *"Mom!* Where are you?" Ruby was sitting on the edge of her bed, her face still blank. "Why is this happening to me? What have I done?" Nothing. "Have you also abandoned me? Please. I need you."

"I am right here, Ruby. I am always here, you know that." From the recesses of her fragmented mind, Rehana reached out and began to stroke Ruby's head.

The shock of the night's assault struck now. Hard. Ruby began to cry. Deep, shuddering sobs.

"He was going to kill my daddy." The words came brokenly, through the sobs. "I couldn't let him . . . even though daddy did not want me. If he had, he would have found me. He does not even want me to stay. If he did, he would have asked me to."

"I know, child, I know," Rehana said. "Hush! Don't worry. Everything will be fine soon."

"What should I do, Mom?"

"Do what you have to, Ruby. Your duty."

"But—"

"No buts, Ruby. Nothing has changed. Our lives mean nothing if we falter from our duty."

"But he is my daddy. I cannot do anything to him, even though he—"

"You don't have to, Ruby. Just finish what you started." Rehana began to talk slowly, insistently: cajoling, pleading. All the while, allowing Ruby to cry, allowing her pent-up feelings to flow.

Hours later, when the tears stopped, Ruby felt whole again.

The terrorist back in control. The embattled, shattered woman had gone underground.

Over the next few hours, one by one, the remaining delegates arrived. Ravinder's team was busy settling them, and Thakur, unwilling to be out of the limelight, ensured he spent time with each of them, assuring them how India was delighted to have them.

As soon as the last delegate arrived, Thakur took all of them for a grand tour of the secure zone, like a man showing off his firstborn child.

Ravinder was half-listening to Thakur when he saw Mohite waving at him from across the room. Quietly peeling away, he went to him.

"How are you, sir? That was horrible . . . what happened last night." Mohite paused. "I want you to know that we really tried to catch them . . . trying everything since the first guy tried to take out my car."

"That's okay, Govind. Even they get lucky sometimes."

"Well, we have taken out all three of them now, so maybe not so lucky after all. Your daughter did a very brave thing.

"I know. Thank you. Tell me, why did you—?"

"The officer in charge of PM security is here. He wants to speak to you."

"What about?"

"The idiot says he will only talk to you."

Ravinder groaned inwardly. Mohite must've done or said something to piss him off.

"Where is he?"

"In the control room."

"Okay."

"I will go with you."

"No." Mohite might just add fuel to the fire . . . *if* he was the one responsible.

As it turned out, Ravinder's intuition was spot on. The PM security man was livid.

"I cannot believe this, Mr. Gill. Your deputy actually told me to . . ." Ravinder allowed him to vent before smoothing things over. It cost him the better part of an hour.

Ravinder then went back to the eighth floor and buttonholed Mohite. "How can you tell the PM security man to bugger off, Govind?"

"You are always in a hurry to judge me and condemn me, sir. He was being such a nuisance and interfering with everything. I—"

"Come on, Govind, he was only doing his job. The PM will be here tomorrow morning. And they need to do what they need to do. That's their regular drill."

"How are you, Gill?" Thakur, having finished his networking with the delegates, was calling it a day. "I heard about the tragedy last night. Glad to see you are okay."

"Thank you, sir."

"I believe your daughter did a fabulous job. Brave girl. You must be proud of her."

"I am, sir."

"Excellent. Give her my best." Thakur threw a pointed look at his watch; he seemed to be in a hurry. "Do you mind if I have Govind for a bit?" Without waiting for a reply, Thakur gestured and Mohite sauntered off behind him like an eager puppy.

Free, Ravinder returned to his room on the seventh floor. He needed to lie down; the painkillers were making him groggy. A bank of monitors displayed the feed from all the cameras set up to maintain a 24/7 watch on all entry and exit points and, more specifically, the seventh and eighth floors. The master feed was being piped into the control room, to the left of the elevator bank, which was manned by four ATTF men per shift.

Ravinder lay on the bed and began to watch the live feed. He saw Chance and Jennifer emerge from the elevator. They said something to the guard. It must have been a joke because all three laughed. Leaving the guard still grinning, the two headed for their rooms: Chance to the one immediately opposite Ravinder's, and Jennifer to the one next to it.

I wonder if they will use the interconnecting door later. Ravinder smiled at the thought.

He remembered when he had been about that age. Rehana flashed into his memory. Hard on her heels came Ruby. Stress returned. He fretted about her, wondering how she was doing now; Simran's call about her strange behavior at the dining table had alarmed him, he would have gone to her if he could. His eyes flicked at his watch. The last call from the surveillance had come in twenty minutes ago; Ruby had not left the house the whole day.

There was a knock. He looked up at the monitor scanning the corridor. Mohite was outside. He let him in reluctantly, hoping there was no other problem he had created.

"I want your permission to have the city hotels checked again tonight, sir. Maybe we can now get hold of the South African mercenaries."

"Won't it take away too much manpower . . . we need every man we have to secure the games villages, the stadiums, and this hotel?"

"I think it is worth making the attempt."

"Let me check how Ashish feels?"

"He is okay if you say it is. I already checked with him."

"I will appreciate if you go through me in future." Ravinder did not hide his displeasure.

Mohite did not reply, merely nodded. "I wouldn't have done it, but Thakur sahib agreed that we need to keep looking for the terrorists."

"You discussed this with him?" Ravinder confronted him. "How many times have I told you to—?"

"I didn't, sir. We were just talking and he asked me, so I gave him my opinion."

Realizing it was futile, Ravinder ignored him and considered. "Okay, go ahead, but use only personnel on noncritical duties."

Ravinder went back to watching the monitors. He could see the delegates moving around on the eighth floor. Several of their PSOs were also mingling on the seventh floor. The guards on the stairwells and elevators were alert and in position. Everything seemed normal.

But will it last? His instinct was somehow warning him that a storm was about to break.

Unable to sleep, and despite the pain and grogginess, he went down to check the guards at the lobby and the hotel gates. Everyone was alert and in position. Then he walked down the street to the roadblock five hundred meters away. To his surprise, he met Mohite and one of the control room officers walking back.

"What are you two doing here?"

"Checking the guards, sir." Mohite gave his hard-at-work look.

"And him? What's he doing here? I made it clear that no one is to leave his post."

"He is just keeping me company sir." Mohite's expression was sheepish, but it had a defiant edge.

"Get back to your post." Ravinder waved the control room officer away, then waited till he was out of earshot. "You have to stop doing this, Mohite. No one—I repeat, *no one*—is to leave his post even for a second. I shouldn't be having to tell *you* that."

They walked back, a sulky silence between them. They were parting at the elevator when Ravinder realized that now only one man was guarding it instead of two.

"Where is the second man?" he asked the guard.

Before he could reply, Mohite jumped in. "I have reduced all nonessential posts by one man each and am using them to beef up the hunt for the two terrorists. I spoke to you about it, sir."

Ravinder could not believe his ears.

"Only from the nonessential ones, sir," Mohite continued, almost smugly.

"You consider the main access points nonessential?" Ravinder was seized by an urge to hit him. "How long will it take you to call them back?"

"Call them back, why?"

"Mohite, which part of my question didn't you understand?" Ravinder was on the edge now, on the verge of losing it. If he did not rein himself in, Mohite would be missing a few teeth. He forced himself to calm down. "Call them back. *Now!* I want every damn post in the hotel at full strength. Clear?"

"Right, sir." Taken aback, Mohite recoiled. "I will have them back in one hour." He scooted toward the control room.

One bloody hour! Pulling himself together, Ravinder called Chance and without giving him the reason asked him to keep an eye on the eighth floor. He himself began to patrol the seventh. Hand never too far from his weapon.

When the security posts had been restored he retired to his room and, taking another pill, lay down. He finally dozed off, but the unease stayed with him, and he did not sleep much that night.

DAY TEN

The morning light of summit day was but a pale streak on the horizon when Ruby exited the Gill gate. She was dressed in her dark maroon jogging suit with NIKE emblazoned across it, her hair tucked inside a matching maroon baseball cap; a bouncy ponytail jutted out as she began to run.

The events of the last thirty-six hours had faded. Having stayed cooped up since the attack, Ruby was raring to go. No trace of the stunned zombie of yesterday. And her mind was at rest, allowing only operational matters to be dwelled upon.

Her pace increased slowly as strong, muscled legs began to chew up the distance. Eager for exercise, her lungs sucked in the slightly chilly, early-morning air. Soon she got her second wind and settled into a steady, loping run.

Her mind was clear. It ticked through the list of actions that she needed to take.

The shrill ring of his mobile startled Ravinder awake.

"She is doing what? Jogging?"

"Yes, sir," the surveillance commander replied. "Just like before. Following the same route."

"Stay with her." Ravinder pushed sleep away. "And keep me informed." In a way, he was glad Ruby had emerged from her room. Perhaps she was getting over the shock.

He headed for the bathroom. It took several splashes of cold water before he was fully awake.

Today is the first day of the summit . . . the thirteenth. . . . Damn that fucking number. . . .

Throwing off his stupor, he quickly got ready and headed out. There were again a million things to check. To secure. Whatever was coming at them, it had to be stopped.

The surveillance team was crawling along in fits and starts—to ensure Ruby did not stray from their sight, yet not get close enough to be spotted.

Not once did Ruby turn to look over her shoulder. She had heard the car start and knew she was being followed. Slowly, imperceptibly, she began to pick up her pace, but staying on the road, where it would be easy for them to keep an eye on her. The car speeded up commensurately, as though tied to her with an umbilical cord.

Barring the occasional vehicle and a handful of other walkers and joggers, the four-laned road, with a green, waist-high, metallic barrier in the middle, was almost empty. Ruby swerved around an elderly couple, chancing a quick glance over her shoulder; sure enough, the cop car was there. She stayed the course for another two hundred meters. Now no break in the metallic divider for maybe a mile on either side. She slowed her pace and began to bide her time. A minute later, the opportunity presented itself.

She could see that the auto rickshaw coming on the other side was empty. She waited till it was closer and confirmed that. Timing it till the rickshaw was almost abreast, she put on a burst of speed and headed straight for the barrier. By the time she hit it, she was sprinting. Her left hand reached out, landed on the top rail, and leveraged her body across in a neat vault. Ruby landed almost in front of the rickshaw. She grabbed a five-hundred-rupee note from her pocket and thrust it in the startled driver's hand.

"Hyatt Regency. Fast. *Very* fast."

The money did wonders for the rickshaw driver's driving skills. Like Schumacher hitting the home stretch, the vehicle shot away, as fast as its rickety engine would allow. By the time the surveillance car accelerated and made a U-turn at the next traffic island, her auto was no longer in sight.

The surveillance team took two swift passes on both sides of the Ring Road, even stopped several auto rickshaws, but every time drew a blank.

Ruby had vanished.

At the hotel, she jogged in and headed for the sky blue Maruti van left by Mark in the basement parking lot. Three minutes later, she drove out. This was a part of Delhi she had familiarized herself with and knew that to get to Ashoka Hotel, she had to take a U-turn, go down the road till the next traffic signal, and then turn left. At this time of the morning, it would be ten or fifteen minutes at best. In no hurry, handling the manual gearshift a trifle gingerly, she drove at a sedate pace, ensuring she drew no attention.

The 84mm Carl Gustav rocket launcher and ammunition box kept under a tarp in the luggage section made dull, thudding sounds as the van crossed the rough patch just short of the Chanakya Complex.

Ashoka Hotel now lay dead ahead.

What do you mean, you lost her? How the hell can you lose a person jogging on the road at this time of the morning?" Ravinder struggled to regain his composure. "Do everything you can to find her and call me back." Then he dialed Chance's room. "Ruby is on the loose. They lost her." He could sense the man's muttered curses more than hear them.

"I'll ensure the top floor is secure with Ido." Chance was now fully alert. "I'll tell Jennifer to man the seventh."

"Good idea," Ravinder replied. "I'll join her in a minute. No, let me go down and ensure the lobby and gates are secure." He stopped at the control room to order a Code Red alert. "No, just a drill," he replied when the duty officer asked him why. "I want to check things before the PM gets here. *Move it!*"

Not that there was any real need. The security detail was still fresh.

Satisfied that nothing could get past the gatekeepers, Ravinder raced down. He had an urge to call Ruby and ask where she was. Not unusual for a father to do.

At this hour of the morning? Why not?

Then deciding to give it a little more time, he headed for the security posts at the gates. Both were alert.

Everything seemed normal. So far.

The next hour passed slowly. Code Red was on. Guns were at the ready. Fingers close to triggers.

From across the road, driving slowly in front of the hotel, Ruby caught a glimpse of Ravinder as he paced between the two gates. The security men at both gates were buzzing around, weapons at the ready. They had adopted an all-round defense, ensuring anything coming in could be covered and, if required, cut down immediately. A couple of handlers with sniffer dogs prowled in front of the porch.

So they are all alert. She had expected no less.

She watched Ravinder with mixed feelings till her van had moved past. Before any more ambivalence could set in, she pushed away all thought and focused.

Rehana has to be avenged. And Uncle Yusuf . . . and those thousands of others. I will not let these bastards sell us down the road.

Her hardness returned, bringing with it the clarity she needed.

How long will these buggers stay alert?

She was veteran enough to know that nothing could be guarded in totality.

Especially not if the attacker no longer cares for her own life.

The last thought caught her by surprise. She let it turn in her head as the van headed back the way it had come, with Nehru

Park on her right. By the time she had taken a U-turn and brought it to a halt in the parking lot near the park gates, that thought had crystallized. She was not afraid to die. If that were the price to be paid for the conference to be ruined, she would pay it.

I will make Rehana proud.

After locking the van, she made her way back on foot toward the hotel, stopping when the main gate came into view. Confirming that none of the security cameras on the hotel's walls were pointed at her, she settled down against a tree. To wait. And to watch.

Now that her mind was not acting up, she could have sat there the whole day.

Soon she saw things at the hotel gates begin to settle down and return to normal. Body postures became less aggressive. Rifles were slung back on shoulders. Even the dogs stopped patrolling.

Code Reds cannot last forever.

Ruby knew that. She had planned on it.

Ravinder was pacing between the gates when Mohite came out, looking sharp in a new, perfectly fitted and ironed uniform.

"You called a Code Red, sir? What is the problem?"

"That was almost thirty minutes ago, Govind."

"I know, sir. The control room officer called me, but he said it was only a drill." There was no hint of contriteness on his face. "I was getting ready to receive the minister, sir."

"Just a drill, Govind?" Ravinder gave a soft sigh. *Does he need to be reminded that a drill means everyone responds? Especially at his level? Oh, fuck it!* "Yeah. Just a drill," Ravinder repeated.

"Oh!" Mohite gave a pout, then a shrug. "Would you like me to call it off now?"

"No. The PM is due in shortly." He checked his watch; it was almost eight.

"That is a good idea, actually. Thakur sahib is about to

arrive. . . . I just spoke to his aide. It is good if he sees everything at high alert."

Ravinder was about to unleash a scathing retort, when Thakur's mini-cavalcade drove up, a security vehicle in front and two behind Thakur's cream Toyota Camry. Ravinder could not see anyone but the driver in the last vehicle, but this did not surprise him. He had learned early on that the Home Minister was superstitious; he did not consider the number three auspicious, hence the fourth car.

People and their eccentricities. Ravinder's smile faded as he remembered his own phobia for thirteen. He went forward to meet the minister.

Mohite was already four steps ahead.

Ravinder's smile had faded well before the minister entered the elevator to the eighth floor. Ruby's absence worried him. He bit back on his disinclination and dialed her mobile. It rang and rang but no one picked up. He tried again a minute later. The result was the same. Wherever she was, Ruby was not answering.

Sitting in the park, camouflaged by the tree she was backed up against, Ruby watched the Home Minister's convoy zoom down and enter the hotel. It was just a few minutes past eight.

A bit later, she felt the phone vibrate in her pocket. She gave a quick glance at the calling number and returned it to her pocket. The next time it rang, she ignored it.

Maintaining watch, she was observing the patterns of movement at and between the gate security posts, and the roadblocks on either side.

Sirens rent the air again. A longer cavalcade swept in, led by two motorcycle outriders. A dozen-odd cars swept past the gates and came to a sharp stop in the porch. Security men leaped out. Hard, alert eyes raked the area. When it became certain there was no threat, one of them opened the rear door of the Mercedes 500 SEL in the center of the convoy, and the Indian PM emerged, a bespectacled, slightly built, white-clad Sikh with a light blue turban. Ruby caught a brief glimpse of him before a ring of Kevlar-clad bodies closed in around him. They vanished into the hotel.

Both the gate security posts, now reinforced by the PM's men, looked alert and keyed up, their stance aggressive and weapons ready. Any move toward them now would be met with a firm, fiery response.

But she was in no hurry. Rocking back on her heels, she settled down to wait. Her yoga-hard body ensuring she was at rest. Her eyes stayed riveted on her target.

An hour later, the PM emerged, once again surrounded by armed men. He vanished inside his Mercedes, and the cavalcade disappeared. Within minutes, she noted a change in the security men at the gates. They did not all sit down, but a softening was apparent. Here and there, a cup of tea emerged. Even the occasional cigarette.

Ruby smiled; it was the same the world over.

An hour later, she took out her mobile phone and—using a spare, till-now-unused SIM card—called the police control room. Her whispered bomb threat provoked an instant response. The change in stance of the security details was instanaeous. A beehive of activity erupted. Teams of security men armed with metal detectors and sniffer dogs began to sweep the hotel.

Ruby knew it would be a while before the alert was called off. They would have to scan and clear the hotel. She was doing what she could to tire them out. To make the red alerts common. So they'd get used to them. *That* was when lapses would occur.

Satisfied, she returned to the van, dropped it off in the Hyatt's parking lot, walked across to the crowded passport office, and caught a cab back to the house.

She is back? When?" Ravinder heard the man out. "How did she get back? Did you speak to the cabdriver, then? Where did he pick her up? I see." With the bomb threat having proved to be a hoax, the delegates safely tucked into the conference room, and the summit now under way, Ravinder had been returning to the control room when the surveillance leader called. Having given up trying to find her, the team had fallen back to the house to wait for her to resurface.

He mulled this for a minute and decided it was time to change tactics. He again dialed Ruby's mobile. *Where in hell has she gone and what has she been up to?*

A grim smile crossed Ruby's face as her mobile rang; she had been expecting the call.

"Where did you go, Ruby? I have been so worried. I have been trying to call you for some hours now."

"I went out for a run, Father. Sorry, I had left my phone behind. I just got back."

"Why did you ditch the security car? We were so worried about you."

"I didn't realize there was one with me."

"Come on, Ruby. . . . After the night's fiasco . . . do I need to spell it out? No more risk . . . we never know who else is out there."

"I am sorry, Father. It will not happen again."

"But where did you run off like that?"

"Well, I got tired of jogging and did not want to return . . . too much on my mind, I guess . . . Then I remembered Jasmine telling me that the Red Fort is worth a visit early in the morning, so I caught an auto rickshaw and went off to see it."

"But—" Ravinder broke off, realizing he could not let her know that the driver of her cab had told them that she had hailed him from near the passport office in Bhikaji Cama Place—nowhere near the Red Fort. "Anyway, I am glad you're safe. From now on, whenever you wish to go anywhere, just tell the team and travel with them, in their car. That will make it easy for everyone."

"Not a problem, Dad. I will do that. Thanks."

The distaste of deceit and lies lay heavy with both when the call ended.

Ruby wondered how much he knew. *He has to know some-*

thing, else why the surveillance? But if he had been able to confirm whatever Chance may have told him, he would not be
allowing her to run free. Would he?

Is he just concerned about me—like any other father would be?
Ravinder wondered what she had been up to.

Am I just tarring her with the same brush because of Rehana?
Maybe she does not really know the reality of Rehana . . . and
Yusuf.

Ravinder returned to his room and went to work. The next few
hours passed as he coordinated between Ashish and Mohite,
ensuring that things at both ends were proceeding smoothly.

The spate of false alarms, sightings, unidentified bags, and of
suspicious people was keeping the cops busy. For several months
now, Delhi Police had been conducting awareness training for
waiters, cabdrivers, private security guards, shopkeepers; all had
been told to keep their eyes and ears open and report such things
and it seemed a lot of them had taken the briefings seriously.

Each call had to be investigated. But so far, none had resulted
in anything meaningful. Nothing, however, could be ignored.

Much as he tried not to think of it, he could not forget that this
was the thirteenth day.

Bad things happen on the thirteenth.

Ruby spent the rest of the day in her room. She was now waiting.
"The wait is always a bitch." Mark's words to her in the
Congo came back to her. She grinned and then remembered
Mark was dead and gone. The grin evaporated.

The summit had made no real progress on day one, but the ice
was broken. Both sides had at least acknowledged that the
killing would end only if they talked. As the day progressed,
hope brightened.

Ravinder's tension escalated as the day wound down. Though he tried hard, he was unable to forget that today was the thirteenth. The hourly calls from the surveillance team that Ruby had not moved should have helped, but didn't.

Have I been so wrapped up with Ruby that I have missed some other more real threat?

With every passing hour, new questions arrived to plague him. As darkness closed in, his anxiety deepened.

In Muridke, Pakistan, his eyes and ears riveted to the news channels, Pasha awaited word of his assassin's strike. Anticipation turned to disappointment and then to fury as the curtain came down on the first day of the summit. He was unable to sit still any longer.

DAY ELEVEN

The new dawn brought with it an overcast sky. The first sign of that heavy fog that paralyzes most parts of North India during winters appeared.

Again Ravinder woke up early and got ready. Some primal, or cop, instinct was gnawing at him. Powered by it, he dialed his home phone, a direct line to his bedroom and study. Simran was the only one who answered it when he was not home. She picked up on the first ring. As though she had been waiting for it.

"Are you all right?" she asked.

"I am fine, love."

"I was worried. I wanted to call, but I did not want to disturb you. I know how busy you must be right now."

For a moment they shared the comfort of silence.

"Simran, I wanted to check on Ruby. How is she?"

"I think she is okay, but . . . other than her morning run, she has not left her room, not since . . . I even had to send all her meals up. Not that she ate much."

"I see. Is she at home?"

"I think so. I have not heard her go down. You want me to check?"

"Could you, please? But carefully. I don't want her to know you are checking on her."

"Hang on, then."

He heard Simran put down the phone and walk to the door. Then a silence. He was starting to worry when he heard a crackling sound as she picked up.

"She is there. I peeped in and she is still sleeping."

"Hmm. Okay." Something was tugging at his mind. He was not sure what. "Right, then. I will call again when I can."

"And take very good care of yourself."

"I will."

"Have you eaten?"

"I will now."

"Don't forget. You get headaches when you skip a meal."

"I won't forget."

"Ravinder, if you want, I can check on Ruby again."

"No. Don't fret about it. The surveillance car is at the gate. They'll let me know if she steps out."

He sensed Simran wanted to say more. He did too, but somehow this did not seem the time. He forgot that there is never a wrong time to say nice things to someone we love.

After putting down the phone, Ravinder went out to run a check on the security setup. And he did forget to eat. And got a headache.

Ruby counted to thirty after the door closed, before she threw off the bedcover and left her bed.

She had heard someone walking up to her door, the footsteps muted, as though the person was trying not to be heard.

Someone up to no good.

She'd pulled the bedcover over her, right up to her neck, making sure she left her face uncovered.

She glimpsed the door crack open silently and Simran peep in. Ruby pretended sleep. Then Simran's face vanished.

Ruby now ghost-footed it to the door and listened. She felt only silence outside. Sliding open the door, she peered out. Six quick steps and she was at the door of Ravinder's bedroom. The murmur of Simran's voice came through as she placed her ear against it.

"Ravinder, if you want, I can check on Ruby again," she heard Simran offer. Then she heard the phone being put down. Ruby returned silently to her bedroom, filled with anger.

So, they are checking on me. They suspect. A moment later. *But maybe Daddy is just worried.* Some more thought. *Bullshit! Then he would have called me, not Simran. So be it.*

She sent a text to Ontong and Boucher. It was short. Delivery confirmation arrived seconds later; there was no sound, since the phone was on vibrate. Ruby deleted all the messages and started to dress.

Within minutes, she was in her usual baggy, black jeans and an equally loose, full-sleeved, blue cotton shirt. Her hair was tied back in a neat ponytail, an almost exact replica of what she had worn in the Congo. But the bulletproof vest was missing. As were her weapons. She missed them, but knew that even if she had them with her, she would not have taken them. Not today. Not where she was going. Today everything would be improvised, on the fly. She had a plan, not so foolproof as she would have liked, but the best she could evolve, given the constraints.

Deep in thought, Ruby missed the sound, aware of it only when the door began to open. Jasmine's head peeped in. Ruby started, no time to make it back to her bed.

"Ah! You are awake." Jasmine smiled. "Good. I wanted you to wish me luck. Today is—" Then she noticed Ruby's outfit. "Wow! You are dressed so differently. You look so . . . so cool. . . . Where are you off to so early?"

It seemed to be an innocent question. *Is it?* Her instincts told her it was, but . . . could she take a chance? *What difference does it make? I cannot . . . will not harm her.*

"Nothing much." Ruby held her gaze. "Thought I'd step out for some exercise."

"Hmm!" Jasmine's mouth puckered up. "You look so different . . . so deadly . . . like some kind of spy." She laughed. "Anyway, I must be off. Am late for college. Have to rush. We are winding up early today." She pattered on. "You are sure about not coming for the games? I still have all three passes . . . just in case you have changed your mind."

"I am sure, Jasmine. Thanks anyway." Aware of the ops clock ticking away, Ruby was aching for Jasmine to leave. "And all the best for your moot court. I am sure you will blow them away."

"Thanks a lot. Have fun." Then Jasmine was gone.

It took a moment for Ruby's breathing to return to normal.

Now time to eat and move. In the distance, she heard the gates swing open and Jasmine accelerate out the drive. Silence returned to the Gill house. Then she heard the dull clang of a bucket. Perhaps in the kitchen. Moments later, the distant hum of a lawn mover began.

Ruby turned to her ops checklist.

Eat and move.

But she felt no hunger. Generally she wolfed down a healthy breakfast, no matter what lay ahead. Now she forced herself to eat. She had to be at the top of her faculties. Finishing the cold chicken sandwich Simran had sent up last night, she washed it down with a glass of orange juice. By the time she finished, it was time. She checked her watch to reconfirm. Ontong and Boucher still had some time before they started out.

Grabbing the black tote bag she had packed, she silently went down to the security—*or surveillance?*—car at the gate. She had to time this part perfectly. No other way could she succeed.

No one heard her descend or exit the door. Then she approached the surveillance car boldly.

"I need to go to the hotel." She told the surprised driver of the surveillance car. "Father needs some stuff." She held out the tote bag.

Ruby saw the driver exchange glances with the cop beside him, obviously the surveillance team commander. He thought it over, and then nodded.

Ruby could almost hear his thoughts. He had been told to keep an eye on her. *What harm can there be if she is with us?* The boss's daughter, after all. They'd been told to keep her secure. With them, she *would* be secure.

"Fine, miss." He held the rear door open for her. "Please get in." Minutes later, they were off.

The sound of the bath shower hid the sound of the surveillance car driving off; Simran had no idea Ruby had left.

Mohite too had risen early. Ravinder ran into him when he emerged from his room. Again, he was dressed up in his Sunday best.

"You going down to meet the minister?" Ravinder asked, though he already knew.

"Yes, sir. He is on his way."

Ravinder checked his watch, twenty past eight. The delegates would be finishing their breakfasts and soon going to the conference hall.

"Fine. Have a look at the lobby security, Govind," Ravinder instructed, "and both the gates and roadblocks. I'm going up for a round of the eighth floor."

He was heading for the elevator when he realized he had forgotten his digital radio in the room. Turning, he went back. He'd kept it next to the bank of monitors in the corner. The monitors were still on; he'd forgotten to switch them off. Ravinder surveyed them for a moment as he slipped the radio onto his belt.

On one of the monitors, he saw Mohite emerge from the elevator and head across the lobby. The men on the other monitors looked alert. Nothing unusual. Satisfied, Ravinder switched them off and went to the eighth floor.

So, on the hotel porch camera, he failed to see Mohite walking out of the hotel gates, heading toward the security barrier down the road, and the surveillance car Ravinder had deployed at his house, drive up to him.

———

Despite her best effort to time her arrival, Ruby had arrived a bit too early. The problem was that she could say only so much to the driver of the surveillance car she was in. And asking him to halt outside the hotel might have alerted them that she was up to something.

Seeing Mohite walk out of the hotel and head toward the security barrier down the road, she spotted an opportunity and improvised. Telling the driver to slow down beside him, she powered down the car window.

Mohite turned and spotted her.

"Good morning, Miss Ruby. How are you?" Mohite was all smiles. "That was such a brave thing you did the other night. . . . We are all so proud of you."

"Thank you." She gave a bright smile. "It all happened so fast that . . ." She shrugged.

"So, how come you are here?"

Getting out, she pointed at the tote bag on her shoulder. "I just brought some stuff along for Dad. He has not been home since yesterday, so I thought—"

"Ah. The dutiful daughter." Mohite gave a big smile, the one he toted when he needed to impress someone. The boss's daughter was definitely fair game; she could put in a word in her father's ear whenever she wanted. After all the fuckups—*just bad luck as far as he was concerned*—Mohite was eager for a helping hand. "Come, Miss Ruby, let me take you up to him."

Ruby turned to the surveillance team commander. "Could you please wait while I go up and meet my father?"

Mohite chipped in helpfully, pointing at a vacant slot beside the gate. "You can park there."

"I should be back soon," Ruby added with a smile and then went with Mohite, hoping that the surveillance team would now have no qualms or call Ravinder.

Together, Mohite and Ruby began to walk past the hotel gates. With the men from the PM's security now gone, the detail seemed thinner. Ruby did a rapid head count. Ten armed men. Entrenched behind sandbag fortifications. Enough to stop even a

well-organized assault. At least long enough until reinforce-
ments clocked in.

The guard commander saluted as Mohite walked past; he,
however, was diligent. "Excuse me, madam," he called out to
Ruby, "that bag needs to go through the scanner." He pointed at
the tote on her shoulder.

"But of course." Ruby placed it on the X-ray machine that had
been installed at all major hotels since the November 26 Mumbai attack. She watched it disappear inside the machine. No worries. It contained nothing except some snacks. It was simply her
excuse to get in. Even if Ravinder had been called and questioned
her, Ruby had an answer ready; she needed to see him since she
was planning to return to London that evening.

The surveillance team leader had been explicitly ordered to call
Ravinder, but lulled by Ruby and also Mohite's presence, he
did not do so. Perhaps it was also the fact that while tasking
him, Ravinder had ordered him to keep Ruby safe; inside the
hotel, he knew she'd be safe. The car pulled into the slot Mohite
had indicated, and the surveillance team settled down to wait.

Mohite and Ruby had passed the X-ray machine when the
whooping of a cop siren became audible. The sound grew in
intensity. Ruby knew what it signified, Thakur arriving. Just as
she had planned.

Thank God he's on time.

As Mohite sprang forward to receive him, Ruby checked her
watch: ten minutes short of nine.

Perfect. Ruby permitted herself a small smile. *By time we reach
the eighth floor, the delegates will be settling down to their talks.*

Thakur's oily face broke into his politician's smile the minute
he got out of his car and set eyes on Ruby. "Ah! So we meet
again, young lady. Ruby? Right?" Returning his smile, she nodded. "How have you been? What you did the other night was

wonderful. So brave! The whole police force is talking about it. Good, good . . . So? What brings you here today? . . . Really? Off already? Why? . . . Come, come . . . let's get you to your father. . . ."

Still talking, the party—now comprising Thakur, his two PSOs, Mohite, and Ruby—headed for the elevators. Seeing the minister *and* their DIG, the elevator guard did not question Ruby's presence.

The mistakes were accumulating.

The assassin had now broken past the barrier, into the secure zone. Hunting season was now open.

Ruby strode forward. She could feel her body gird itself.

Just a few minutes more . . .

Someone else had also been watching for Thakur's arrival. Dressed in faded jeans and a full-sleeved, blue sweatshirt, the burly, ruddy-faced, nearly bald, and profusely sweating Ontong was at the same spot in the park where Ruby had taken position the previous morning. The stress was bothering him more than anything else; something did not feel right.

Ontong saw the minister's cavalcade pull up at the lobby. He immediately called the only number stored in his mobile; it was a new phone with an unused SIM card, purchased specifically for this operation. He'd drop it in some convenient gutter on his way to the airport.

Separated by the hotel between them, parked one klick away from the roadblock outside the hotel, the one farther away from Ontong, Boucher took the call.

Taller, whiplash thin, long-limbed, deeply tanned with close-cropped hair and hooded eyes that were never still. Like Ontong, Boucher too was in jeans and a dark green sweatshirt. He too was using a new phone and SIM card.

"Five minutes," Ontong said tautly. "We are on."

"Roger. I'm rolling in five." Boucher dropped the phone on the seat. He was tense. But far more confident than Ontong. Perhaps because Boucher did not think or worry too much.

Both men collected their thoughts. Both rapidly replayed Ruby's instructions in their heads. Both knew they had a short yet decisive role in whatever she had planned. Both hoped it would be painless.

Adrenaline was pumping in Ontong's body as he left the park and made his way back to the Maruti van with the rocket launcher inside. He had already checked it and both rockets. Both were ready to go.

Ontong kept his pace slow and easy. He knew he still had a few moments. Boucher was going into action first.

Boucher was moving by the time Ontong finished rechecking his weapon. He drove at a steady pace. He did not have to go far. The shooting position he'd selected was just ahead.

The 84mm Carl Gustav produced by Saab had an effective range of approximately 1,100 meters against troops in the open and could also take on an armored target 700 meters away. Unlike other such weapons, it used a rifled barrel to spin stabilize its projectile. Both Boucher and Ontong were comfortable with it, though, like most Aussies, they preferred to call it the Charlie Gusto.

A rocket launcher team normally comprised two men and could get off four to five rockets in a minute. With just one man firing and reloading, the rate of fire dropped to less than half, since the user had to bring down the launcher, crack open the rear, slide in a new rocket, close the breech, and hoist it back onto his shoulder.

Boucher was aware of this, but it did not bother him. He needed only to fire twice before he dropped the weapon and melted away. With surprise on his side, it would be a cakewalk. Ontong, coming into action minutes later, might not have that working for him, but he would be able to exploit the shock of the opening assault.

Boucher pulled over in the spot he had reconnoitered; it was on a curve, a blind spot from the security post in front. Not the optimal position, but keeping in view the security deployment, it was the best possible one.

Quickly moving to the rear of the van, Boucher reached for the already loaded weapon and also the second rocket, to be ready for an instant reload.

Taking position off the road, clear of the vehicle, he raised the launcher to his shoulder.

Mohite halted the elevator at the seventh floor and held the door open for Ruby. "Please go to Mr. Gill's room . . . that one," he pointed out, forgetting that Ruby had had a tour of the seventh floor a couple of days ago. "I will let him know you are here."

Ruby walked past the elevator security guards and headed for Ravinder's room. The ping of the elevator door behind her let her know it had closed. She threw a quick backward glance.

Both elevator guards had turned to see off the minister and had their backs to her.

Altering direction, she swiftly crossed to the other side of the corridor and headed for Chance's room. Using the red access card she had purloined earlier, she eased open the door and entered.

The guards did not see which room she entered. They had heard Mohite tell her to go to the boss's room and assumed she had. In any case, they did not perceive her as a threat; there was scarcely a cop in Delhi who'd not heard of the attack on the ATTF chief's house and how his lionhearted daughter had responded.

Jennifer, returning from checking the stairwell guard at the end of the corridor, did see Ruby enter Chance's room. She noticed that Ruby did not pause at the door, which to her implied that someone had opened the door for her or—

Chance? Isn't he supposed to be on the eighth floor? Or does Ruby have an access card to his room? Neither thought felt good. Her relationship with Chance was still too new; she had yet to understand him or feel secure about him.

But Ruby's presence in the secure area alarmed her, even though she was not privy to Ravinder's and Chance's suspicions. And this unrestricted entry into Chance's room perturbed her. Frowning, she headed down the corridor.

If Chance is two-timing me . . . She felt a surge of anger.

Caught up in an admixture of alarm and jealousy, Jennifer forgot to radio her sighting to the control room. Or to call the reserve guard to back her up.

Both were big mistakes.

After letting herself in, Ruby halted in the center of Chance's room. She did not switch on the lights; with the curtains pulled back, there was enough light.

A black hard-shell suitcase was on the wooden rack beside the TV. It had been with Chance as long as she could remember. Having lived with him, she knew his habits. The suitcase was locked. Chance was also forgetful; especially when it came to numbers. He always used his birth date for the suitcase. Ruby rotated the numbers of the combination lock. The case clicked open. She sighed with relief. Chance hadn't changed.

Hasn't he? She pushed that thought away. *Not now, damnit! Focus!*

The pistols were exactly where she had known they would be; at the base, wrapped in a piece of thick, soft cloth. She quickly unfolded it and found a pair of classic Browning Hi-Power pistols.

His choice of weapons has not changed.

Chance always carried a spare pair. Ruby had banked on it. Picking them up, she tested their heft. They fit with the comfort of an old sweater.

A silencer and two spare magazines were also wrapped in the same cloth. The magazines, each with a capacity of thirteen rounds, were full.

Ruby did the math. A total of fifty-two rounds in the four magazines.

If that is not enough, nothing is. . . .

Swiftly loading one weapon, she chambered a round, clicked on the safety, and slid it into her waistband. After thrusting the spare magazines into the pocket of her baggy jeans, she loaded the second pistol, again chambered a round, and began to screw on the silencer. Her fingers were confirming the silencer was fitted on securely when she heard the door behind her open. Ruby swung around, holding the pistol behind her.

Jennifer strode into the room, spotted Ruby, and ground to a stop. Behind Jennifer, the solid wood door slowly swung shut. Its click masked the snick of the safety catch being pushed off by Ruby.

"What are you doing here? Where is Chance?"

Before Ruby could reply, a thunderclap rang out. The windows' panes rattled as the 84mm HEAT rocket fired by Boucher boomed out.

"What the hell was that?" Jennifer instinctively turned toward the sound, alarm on her face. Then another boom, as the rocket struck and exploded. This one was closer, much louder. Jennifer ran to the window.

Ruby stood stock-still. In her mind's eye, she could see Boucher bring the launcher down from his shoulder, crack open the loading port, and shove in the second round, then raise it to his shoulder and place his eye to the sights. Her body tensed.

Jennifer saw the expression on Ruby's face. That Ruby had shown no surprise at the explosions registered with her. Jennifer halted again in midstride, and her hand reached for the gun on her belt. It was moving like a blur of lightning.

Equally fast, Ruby's hand came out from behind her back.

The sight of the silenced weapon almost froze Jennifer, but

the point of no return had been crossed. She clawed out her weapon, going for it, *knowing* it was futile, yet *hoping*.

Jennifer's weapon started to come level, aligning on Ruby. Her finger had already completed half the trigger squeeze.

Boucher's first rocket slammed into the roadblock on the road to Ashoka Hotel. Fired from four hundred meters away, the FFV551 HEAT round punched through the waist-high wall of sandbags and ravaged the men behind. There were no screams. None of the four men survived long enough to scream.

The six at the other end of the road were alive, but overwhelmed by the shock and by the debris that billowed out and now lay like a dark cloud over the roadblock. They were trying to figure out where the attack had come from when there was another massive flare of sound and light.

Boucher had fired again.

The second shot, an FFV441B HE rocket, was aimed at the hotel's eighth floor. It slammed explosively into the wall of the hotel, missing a window by inches. The thick stone walls stopped the HE round, but Boucher's job was not to cause damage. It was to cause a diversion.

The explosion echoed harshly through the eighth floor, rattling the windows, shattering some. Bits of plaster broke free from the ceilings.

The second explosion masked the plop of the silenced pistol in Ruby's hand. The 9-millimeter round caught Jennifer in her face, just above the upper lip. She was thrown backward. The pistol in her hand fired. The bullet thudded into the ceiling, sending out gouts of plaster.

Jennifer hit the ground with a sickening thud. Life deserted her.

The smell of blood rose, mingling with the smoke curling out of the Browning in Ruby's hand. For a second she froze, but her training took over.

Time was short. She raced for the door.

Ravinder was pacing the corridor on the eighth floor when Boucher's first rocket demolished the roadblock. Galvanized, he ran for the elevator; he had to get to the control room. He was halfway there when the second rocket struck, just a few windows away from the conference hall.

Silence returned. But he knew the attack had just begun and that rockets fired from a distance could only be a diversion.

From the other end of the hallway, he saw Chance and Peled racing toward him. They had only one thought: The delegates needed to be secured.

"Code Red." Grabbing the radio from his belt, Ravinder snapped into it. "I say again, Code Red. Lock down the floors."

Outside. Boucher dropped the rocket launcher and raced away, headed to the cabstand two hundred meters down the road. He would commandeer a car from there. In his head, he had already begun to race toward the airport.

What Boucher had not factored in were the snipers on all sides of the hotel roof. Ruby had known of them, but had conveniently forgotten to mention them when the two Aussies showed some reluctance during her briefing. Their lives meant little to her, considering she was putting her own on the line.

Despite the confusion below, the Indian Army sniper manning the side from which Boucher had fired was watching his area with eagle eyes. He spotted Boucher when he started running. Though he had seen the flares of the launcher's back blast, he had not seen Boucher due to the overhang of a tree. But the minute Boucher ran for the cabstand, that cover had been removed.

The sniper did not hesitate. Rocket launchers going off and men running away from the place they'd been fired. For him, the picture was clear. The weapon in his hands steadied. His crosshairs sought out the running man and homed in. He took a lead to compensate for the target's motion. His finger curled around the trigger of his Dragunov sniper rifle and began to squeeze.

Its 7.62 × 54mm rimless round raced forward at a velocity of 830 meters per second and covered the distance before Boucher had managed to take one more stride. The bullet smashed into Boucher's back, tearing out his heart.

No second shot was required.

Having dropped Thakur off at the conference hall, Mohite was returning to the control room. He was in the elevator when the rockets exploded. The canned music playing kept him from hearing either of the blasts. Unaware that the summit was under attack, he was entering the control room when Ravinder's voice erupted out of the radio.

"*Code Red!*" Ravinder's voice was strident with urgency. "I say again, Code Red. Lock down the floors."

"What the hell is happening?" Mohite asked the men at the monitors.

The minute Ontong heard the first rocket fired by Boucher explode, he grabbed hold of the rocket launcher from his van. He knew Boucher's second one would soon be on its way.

He had already loaded the launcher, with a second also ready to go. After double-checking everything, Ontong shouldered the weapon and stepped out of the bushes as the second rocket fired by Boucher slammed against the top-floor walls.

Starting the count, Ontong steadied the launcher on his shoulder and took careful aim.

Ten, nine, eight . . . Ontong fired.

Ontong's HEAT round smashed into the security post at the hotel's entry gate. Its boom, much closer now, echoed dully through the control room.

Mohite ran to the monitor for the main gate. It had suddenly gone dark.

Unaware that the rocket had killed the camera, Mohite thumped the monitor, trying to will it back to life.

"What the fuck happened?"

Reloading swiftly, Ontong was now in a hurry to get it over with and get clear. He had no idea what had happened to Boucher, but didn't wish to tarry here a second longer than he had to.

Moving swiftly to his left, he got the security post at the hotel exit gate into his gunsight. Hurriedly steadying himself, he fired again. But in his hurry to finish and get away, he forgot that the Maruti van behind him was on his left when he had fired the first time. When he moved left to acquire the second target, he had strayed too far to the left. The van was now directly behind him, just meters away.

He'd made a small mistake, but a fatal one.

The furiously flaming back blast of the rocket launcher caught the van head-on. Ontong had reversed the van before he'd parked it, so he could take the weapon out from the luggage compartment and bring it into use instantly. So the back blast caused the fuel tank to explode, smashing the van into smithereens. Flaming shards of metal sliced out in every direction, scything through everything in their way.

Ontong was one of those things.

Ontong's second rocket destroyed the security post at the hotel's exit gate. Another monitor in front of Mohite went blank as its camera too succumbed. However, the carnage at both gates was still visible from the peripheral vision of the cameras mounted in the porch. He could see that both posts were in serious trouble.

Galvanized, Mohite grabbed at his radio and screamed, "We are under attack! Both gates are down. All seventh-floor security personnel and reserve guards move down and reinforce the lobby." His voice was shrill with anxiety. "They must not get through. Seal everything off."

He kept shouting instructions into the radio as he ran. Accompanied by the three men held in reserve in the control room, he ran for the elevator. As it opened, he grabbed both the elevator guards also and hauled them inside. They all went down. And responding to his orders, the guards at the stairwells on either side also grabbed their weapons and headed down.

Yet another mistake had been made. *This* was a cardinal one.

Silence fell upon the now unguarded seventh floor.

In Chance's room, Ruby was hurrying past Jennifer's body when an idea struck her. She grabbed the baseball cap Jennifer had been wearing. Her fingers immediately felt its sticky wetness. The touch of blood sickened her. She fought off the nausea, but could not keep her eyes from Jennifer's face. She saw blood all over it.

Then Ontong's first rocket exploded. She stiffened and began to pull off Jennifer's flak jacket. Some blood had seeped onto its collar. But this time, Ruby's face stayed expressionless as she quickly wiped it clean on Jennifer's shirt.

She is wrong. I am right. Isn't that reason enough for me to pull the trigger? Is it! Of course it is. That is all there is to it . . . nothing to fret about.

The sound of the second rocket explosion goaded her into action.

Slipping into Jennifer's jacket, Ruby raced to the door. The ping of the elevator closing greeted her. She peered out.

The floor was empty. Even the elevator guards had vanished.

Not believing her luck, she ran out, the red master access card in one hand and a pistol in the other. She'd have to move fast if she was to exploit the opportunity Boucher and Ontong had provided.

"Just as a precaution . . . not that we are expecting any trouble . . . but just in case of some emergency, we have also secured the top two floors of Hotel Samrat and duplicated all the same arrangements there." Mohite's briefing to the Home Minister echoed in her head as she used the access card to open Ravinder's room and slipped inside.

The bank of monitors was what she wanted, to know when they began to evacuate and which route they would take. It had to be either of the two staircases or the elevator, though that was less likely; one elevator would not hold all the delegates, and the security team would be reluctant to split them.

So far, things were working out, yes—better than she had hoped.

They are wrong. . . . I am right. . . . The words now played like a litany in her head. One by one, she began to switch on the monitors.

Waiting impatienty for the elevator on the top floor, Ravinder, Chance, and Peled caught Mohite's transmission loud and clear.

Anger exploded through Ravinder.

That fucking idiot! He did it again. Instead of waiting for the attackers to come to us, he . . . How can he even dream of abandoning the control room? That fucking . . .

Cursing, Ravinder reached for his radio set and began to speak when he realized that Mohite was still talking. Realizing that he would not be able to transmit until Mohite released the transmit button, and itching to get to the control room, Ravinder headed for the stairs. The floors needed to be resecured, no matter the cost. And he needed eyes on the floors; that was why the control room needed to be manned by a senior officer at all times. His every instinct was screaming that the security breach had already taken place, that the rocket attacks on the gates were no real threat.

They have to be diversions. So where is the real attack coming from?

He suddenly wished he could check on Ruby's whereabouts, but no time. Now he had time only to react and counter her.

We need to draw out the attackers.

"Activate Plan Bravo!" he yelled at Chance and Peled.

Chance and Peled ran to the conference hall and herded the delegates to the conference room at the other end. Peled took position outside the door. Chance ran down the corridor to activate the second part of the plan. The decoys were ready and waiting.

The first set of monitors that Ruby switched on showed the confusion in the hotel lobby. The second set remained black. Ruby did not know it, but they were the ones that had covered the hotel gates.

Next, the ones watching over the seventh floor flickered to life. Ruby noted with surprise that both stairwells were empty.

Where are the guards? Is this some trick?

Her mind ferreted forward to spot a trap. She was activating the next monitor when she saw Ravinder rush out from the stairwell on the left and charge toward the control room.

Then the eighth-floor monitors came alive, flickering a bit before the picture stabilized. Chance hove into view. Weapon in hand, he was in the lead. Behind him was a ragged line of men in a variety of outfits. Bringing up the rear was one of the Palestinian PSOs. Ruby saw the two ex-SEALS traveling with the Saudi Arabian prince come running up. They took positions at the head and tail of the column, headed for the staircase closest to the conference hall.

Bingo!

She began to study the deployment of the security personnel and to freeze them in her head. She also took note of their firepower, a formidable array of Uzis, Glocks, Magnums, and Brownings. She evaluated her options and decided.

From the rear, that's where I'll attack. I just need to take out the guards and two or three of the delegates.

She tarried to study the stairs, especially the landings. She needed a place to hide . . . for one moment.

In the control room, Ravinder too was studying the secure zone; his attention, however, was not on the party moving behind Chance. He was searching for some other movement. *Any* other movement.

"Come out, come out. . . . wherever you are," he muttered aloud. "Whoever you are . . ."

That reminded him. He needed to find out if . . . His eyes continued to track the monitors as he reached for his mobile. "Where is Ruby?" he asked when the surveillance team leader answered.

"In the hotel, sir. Haven't you met her yet? She went up with Mr. Thakur and Mohite, sir."

Ravinder went still. He couldn't breathe. Suspecting was one thing. Having it confirmed was another. He did not know when he ended the call.

Somehow, he'd kept hoping that Ruby would not be involved in something so heinous. Now, no room for doubt.

Why, Ruby? Why?

His heart began to spin.

Not now. Right now you have a duty to perform.

From somewhere within, a quote from the Bhagavad Gita echoed through him:

And do thy duty, even if it be humble, rather than another's, even if it be great. To die in one's duty is life: to live in another's is death.

"I know you well, Ravinder. I know you will always do the right thing. Just trust your instincts. It will all work out in the end." Simran's words from two nights ago returned to him. He no longer knew how this could end well, but he was determined to take charge.

On the monitors, he began to scour the seventh floor. It lay still and silent. But he knew. She was out there somewhere. Waiting for the right moment to strike.

"Ruby, come out, come out . . ." He did not know when his lips moved. "Come out, come out . . . wherever you are. . . ."

His ears did not hear them.

His eyes remained riveted on the monitors.

His hands now held a gun.

The hide-and-seek game had turned deadly.

Satisfied with what she was going to do and how, Ruby withdrew both weapons from her belt and calmed herself. Her eyes stayed riveted to the monitor, watching for any change in the deployment of the men she meant to ambush.

Chance's party now had reached the stairwell between the two floors.

Perfect. Ruby forced her metabolism to slow down, but her adrenaline had peaked. Her body now was craving to catapult forward.

She knew the next few minutes would be her last. But it was okay.

Mom is waiting. She . . . they . . . are banking on me. I will not let them down.

Drawing another long breath, she again stilled her nerves and started to turn.

That was when the third man behind Chance looked up, an inadvertent glance, not even aware that the camera was directly overhead, in front of him. But it was and he had looked straight into it.

He was dressed like Sir Geoffrey Tang and made up like him, right down to the slightly graying, long sideburns and pointed goatee. But he was *not* Sir Tang. Having traveled with him for a week, Ruby knew the British MP. Enough to know this man was an impostor. He was too . . . young . . .

Yes! That was it.

Ruby held back. She began to reexamine all thirteen men behind Chance. Then the subterfuge became obvious. Despite their clever makeup, she now could tell they were not the delegates; they were decoys. As she intensified her scrutiny, she noted the weapons carried by the decoy-delegates. Concealed, yes, but each was carrying one.

Ruby's mind changed gears.

If these are decoys, then where are the real ones?

The answer came with a snap.

In one of the other conference rooms on the eighth floor.

Her mind began generating a new plan.

If that guy had not looked up, I would have flown right into their trap.

A new feeling of respect for Ravinder swept through her. One hell of an adversary.

Like father, like daughter? But he does not want me. . . . Stop! Think!

The minute they launched the decoys, hadn't they also given her an open playing field?

Every tactic has a weakness: the more daring it was, the more crucial the weakness. That was the nature of the beast.

Ruby could not see any security personnel on the eighth floor. She knew they would be there, but not many. A lot of guards on a supposedly abandoned floor would have been a dead giveaway.

Adapt!

Ruby reevaluated. If the decoys had been deployed, then they knew she had penetrated the secure zone, no other reason.

Now the decoys had crossed the seventh floor and were continuing down. Ruby watched Chance peel away at the landing and head for the control room. She waited till he pushed open the door and entered. The door began to swing shut behind him. The corridor was clear.

Now!

Strike!

Ruby raced out, headed for the stairwell on the far side, away from the control room. She was moving silently, as fast as her feet could carry her. Straight for the eighth floor.

Going for the kill.

The control room door was swinging shut behind Chance when Ravinder saw Ruby charge out of his room. Pistols in both hands, she was sprinting down the corridor. He knew her destination. That she was moving *away* from the decoys showed that she had seen through them and spurned the bait.

He ran out of the control room, shouting at Chance to follow him. As they ran, he explained. A few words were enough. The two put on a burst of speed, knowing that the delegates now were in mortal danger.

They were passing the elevator when its door pinged open and a harried Mohite stepped out. He was about to say something, but Ravinder pulled him out of the way and dived into the elevator with Chance behind him. Chance stabbed at the eighth-floor button, frantically willing the doors to close. They took forever. Then it began to rise, slowly and sedately as always. The two men inside strained to be unleashed.

The doors pinged open and they dashed out on the eighth floor.

Not a soul in sight. Only a deserted corridor.

Ruby raced up, taking the stairs two at a time. She was in peak condition, but her breath nonetheless burned through her lungs in short, ragged bursts. But her mind was sharp and focused. Her fingers were curled around the triggers of the Hi-Power Brownings, itching for the delegates to appear in her gunsights. Nothing else mattered.

She arrived a split second after Ravinder and Chance. She heard the ping of the elevator doors before she saw them. Swiveling, she changed direction, heading for the two smaller conference halls across the floor. It had to be one of those two rooms.

Chance saw her blur of movement and shouted. The two turned and chased after her. Despite those daily hours in the gym, Ravinder was not moving as fast as he wanted to. The younger, fitter Chance began to pull ahead. But he too was not moving fast enough. Summoning up his reserves, he ramped up the pace.

Suddenly Ruby spun around and fired. Twice. Then she was off again.

Both shots went wide, but they'd forced Chance to drop. Coming up from behind, too fast to stop, Ravinder blundered into him. By the time they got up, the distance between them and Ruby had increased.

Ruby was flying, her feet skimming over the carpeted corridor in long, flashing strides. As she skidded around a corner, she spotted Ido Peled standing at the door of the conference room on the right and knew the delegates had to be behind it. Like a linebacker, the tall, fair Peled stood with his back to the door, his weapon in hand. He tensed as she charged around the corner and came at him full tilt.

The body armor and baseball cap must have confused Peled. He'd seen Jennifer wearing those just a while ago. So he hesitated a second before bringing up his gun. That fraction of time cost him his life.

Ruby fired the unsilenced gun in her right hand, for its longer range and accuracy. The shot boomed and reverbrated, spurring on Chance and Ravinder.

Peled was dead before his body hit the floor.

Chance, now within range, raised his weapon and fired, twice. The first bullet buzzed past Ruby's head and thwacked into the thick wooden door of the conference room. The second hammered into Ruby. Jennifer's jacket limited the damage, but the high-velocity shock made her stagger. Still, she managed to throw open the door and charge into the conference room. She hit the door hard with her heel after she sprinted inside. It slammed shut behind her with a bang.

That was followed by more bangs, sharper, louder, and so close together that Ravinder could not tell how many shots had been fired.

Then Chance was at the door. Without checking his stride, he shouldered it in and ran inside.

Ravinder burst in hard on his heels.

Chance ground to a halt, the pistol in his hand still half-raised. He froze; the slightest move and Ruby would put a bullet in his head; her weapons were up and smoking. Ravinder again blundered into him.

Ruby's left-hand pistol was pointed straight at Chance's head. Her face was alabaster. Frozen. Immobile. Bereft of emotion. Only her eyes hinted at the turmoil inside her. Tiny seething dots, tense with concentration.

She was about eight feet away, her chest heaving, but the Brownings in her hands were rock steady. The weapon in her right was placed against Senator George Polk's head. And now no charm or smile on his face, just sheer panic. A low, almost inaudible keening sound crooned out of him.

Raj Thakur, Ghazi Baraguti, and Prince Ghanim Abdul Rahman al-Saud lay in grotesque poses around the conference table; they had been the closest when Ruby stormed in and opened fire. It did not matter to her. Every delegate was fair game. And she had gone for the headshot with all three.

Thakur's body had slipped to the floor. The top half of his pristine white kurta now bright red with blood. Baraguti was half in his chair and half across the table, rising when he stopped a bullet. Thick treacly blood was seeping out from his head and onto the teak tabletop. With his face blown away, there was nothing regal about the Saudi prince now. Bits of blood, brains, and bone were sprayed across the other delegates—all frozen in horror. Gun smoke furled in the stark room.

For one tiny but endless second, everything came to a standstill.

"Ruby, don't do it. Please." Ravinder's voice broke the frozen tableau. He was having trouble speaking; he could have sworn it was Rehana standing in front of him. "Don't! It's over. No one else needs to die."

"No, Father, it's not." Ruby's voice was pitched high, as though drawn from a tightly strung wire. Her face a grim mask. "It will never be over till our people are allowed to live in peace and with dignity. The killing has to stop."

"That is why they are here. To stop the killing." Despite her fiery posture, he could sense an uncertainty inside her. Somehow he had to keep her talking. *As long as she is talking, her guns will stay silent.* His mind lanced out, seeking the right words.

"No," she intoned, "they are not here for justice. They will sell us out, the way they have always done. This summit cannot go on." Still that same high-pitched Rehana-like tone, flush with emotion. "Our people cannot be sold out any longer."

"But no need now for more killing, Ruby." Ravinder's voice had taken on a softer, neutral but firm negotiator's tone. As he spoke, he inched slowly to his right, trying to ensure Chance was no longer in his line of fire.

"Stop that, Father." Ruby gestured with her weapon. A sharp flick. "Don't move."

"Fine, I won't." Ravinder slowly raised his left hand, palm forward, in a placating gesture. His right was at his side, still holding his revolver. "Don't you see how pointless all this is? The dust will never settle . . . neither for the Palestinians nor the Jews . . . not until they sit down and talk." Ravinder pleaded, "Drop your weapons. I promise I will do everything possible to defend you in court."

"No, Father, I will not be taken alive." He heard the sorrow in her voice, but her tone was steady, though he also sensed flecks of indecision.

Ravinder now *knew* he would be able to talk her down.

"Ruby—"

Without warning, the door flew open and Mohite burst in with a gun in his hand. His eyes widened as he took in the scene. His gun hand began to rise.

Ruby's eyes narrowed into sharp slits.

"No!" Ravinder yelled.

But too late.

BOOM! POP! BOOM! BOOM! POP!

Ravinder's cries were drowned out by gunfire.

Both Ruby's weapons had blazed into action, the soft pop of the silenced one submerged by the booming roar of the other.

The gun in her right hand had remained planted right against the senator's head. It disintegrated, spraying the table with chunks of bone and blood. Some of it sprayed onto the faces of Yossi Gerstmann and Ghafar al-Issa, the Jordanian, across the table. Both recoiled. Someone else screamed. But the continuing roar of gunfire drowned it out.

The gun in Ruby's left hand missed its mark. Instead of shooting out Chance's throat, it caught him high on the collarbone, just above the upper lip of his body armor, and spun him to the left. Ruby's gun had meanwhile moved on to Mohite. The bullet slammed into his face and made the back of his head into a bloody fresco all over the door he had just raced through.

Simultaneously, Chance jerked up his gun hand and fired. He got one shot off before he too was hit. But as his body took the hit and spun to the left, he fired again. Both bullets took Ruby in the middle of her body. And once again, the body armor shielded her. But the double blows delivered at this close range threw her backward. And Chance kept firing till his clip ran out.

As Chance spun to his left, Ravinder's field of fire cleared. His hand came up like a flash, and the gun in it thudded to life. Once. Twice. Thrice.

In the confines of the conference room, the boom of gunshots was endless thunder.

The terrorist was down. And still.

Ravinder watched Ruby being thrown back as bullets pounded into her. She hit the wall behind. Then slowly slid to the ground. For a moment she lay still, and then slowly curled up in a fetal ball.

Now the Rehana-like harpy who had terrified them vanished. Ravinder saw only the little girl who had once loved pink frocks and lollipops.

The pistol in Ravinder's hand felt like a block of ice, but heavier . . . much heavier. He did not know when his hand let go, and it hit the carpeted floor with a thud.

Then someone moaned, and reality struck like a sledge-hammer.

Ravinder the cop then stepped forward and kicked the guns away from Ruby. And Ravinder the father knelt beside her.

The door blew open, and a horde of security people rushed inside.

Kneeling beside Ruby, Ravinder was oblivious of the hullabaloo around him. He had zoned out. The cop had done his duty. He had been made to walk the hardest path that his karma could have called for, and he had not flinched.

But the cop was no longer there. Only the father.

Ravinder wished he were dead. He wished he had not fired. He wished *he* had been the target for Ruby's guns. Not the delegates, not Chance, not Mohite—just him. He would have paid the price eagerly.

Ravinder cradled Ruby in his arms. As he did, her eyes flickered open. She was alive, but barely. Ravinder sensed time was abysmally short, and he wanted to be with his little girl. For one last time.

Ruby opened her mouth. She seemed to be trying to say something, but only frothy bubbles of blood emerged.

With her eyes, Ruby beckoned him closer. He went. Now his ear was against her mouth. The low whisper, when it emerged finally, was drawn out, barely audible.

"Jasmine told me . . . that whenever . . . she was sick . . . or hurt . . . you would always . . . hold her . . . and put her to sleep."

He nodded. Even if he had tried to reply, he knew he couldn't. Everything in him had choked up.

"I am . . . hurting . . . Daddy." The words emerged in broken gasps. "Will you . . . put . . . me to sleep . . . Daddy . . . please?"

Ravinder managed to speak, a bare whisper. "Yes, princess." He knew his Ruby needed him to . . . for this one last time. "Of course I will."

Ravinder could feel her slipping away. Never had he felt so helpless. He held her close. Really close. And he could feel her breath mingle with his; it felt cold, like her blood, which soaked his shirt. Her lips closed in on his cheek. For a moment they were one again. Father and daughter.

The pressure on his cheek tightened. Then lightened. And Ruby lay still in his arms. Cold. Lifeless. Heavy. Empty. As empty and cold as the void inside him.

But he could not let go of her.

By time they managed to get Ravinder to release her, the light had faded from Ruby's eyes.

His precious princess was gone. Again. And this time she would never be back.

THE DAYS AFTER

With five delegates dead, there was no hope that the peace summit would proceed. The surviving, shell-shocked men departed within hours.

People—those in the know and those who would make decisions and could influence change—knew that the dust would never settle . . . at least not anytime in the near future.

Till sense and compassion took hold. *If* it ever did.

Safely ensconced in Muridke, Pasha was thrilled to hear of the carnage. And the fact that the British had trained Ruby made his victory all the more sweet. How gratifying, after all, to kill an enemy with his own sword. And it was also poetic justice, since Pasha believed that it was the British who had destroyed the Ottoman Caliphate and were primarily responsible for the plight of the Palestinians. After all, it was on their watch that Israel had crushed the Palestinians.

Pasha was jubilant when he shared the news with Saeed Ahmed, the LeT supremo.

"We must extract maximum mileage from this," Ahmed asserted.

"True," Pasha agreed. "Operations with such massive propaganda value rarely happen."

"Also use this opportunity to strengthen our ties with Hamas. There is much we can do for the jihad if we work together."

"What do you have in mind?"

"Why not go down to Damascus and see what they have in mind?"

Pasha agreed it was worth pursuing.

Miles away, in Tel Aviv, a Mossad duty operator put down her headset and reached for the phone.

Two days later, when Pasha left Muridke, a select group of men and women from various cities in Europe moved. Several had traveled to Dubai a few weeks ago.

The Kidon team was in place when Pasha's flight landed at Damascus. The deadly ring closed around him as he exited the airport and headed for the safe house his hosts had arranged.

"This one is for you, Ean Gellner," the lean, hard-faced Kidon, who had once painted BORN TO KILL on his army helmet, muttered as he cleaned the blade of his knife on Pasha's headless body.

As Pasha's body slumped to the floor, a few thousand miles away, in the holy North Indian city of Haridwar, a gleaming, black BMW 750Li came to a halt.

Retired Inspector General of Police Ravinder Singh Gill emerged, draped in white. He had lost weight, acquired a decade of wrinkles, and had a gaunt look. It was as though everything he had ever had, had been lost.

Jasmine, also in a pristine white salwar kameez, alighted and followed as they made their way to the edge of the water. She was sticking close, keeping a sharp eye on him; she knew he needed her.

Simran did not leave the car. She could not bring herself to.

She could not forgive Ruby. But she had traveled this distance with Ravinder, because him she *did* care for.

There were thousands of people clustered on both sides of the holy river. An endless sound rumbled on both banks. However none of this impacted on Ravinder and Jasmine. They felt alone.

They strode into the water, stopping when it was ankle high. It was icy cold. But neither seemed to notice; their cold within was icier.

Ravinder's hands shook as he tried to untie the string holding the red cloth to the mouth of the small earthen urn, which he carried. Jasmine came to his aid. In the past week, he had retreated into a cold, silent zone, and his silence scared her. She could feel his pain as their hands met at the urn.

The red cloth finally came free.

Together the two of them tipped over the urn. A swirl of gray ashes tumbled out. Most fell into the water. Some were blown away by the wind.

Soon no traces remained. Neither in the air, nor in the water.

Yet neither looked away from where the ashes had first hit the water. They just kept looking, as if trying to clutch on to them. Both believed that in this release lay salvation for the soul that the ashes had once represented.

The chill from the water rushing around their ankles began to seep into their bodies, merging with the chill in their hearts.

After a long time, both bade a silent farewell to the lovely young woman who had entered their lives . . . so recently . . . so briefly . . . so sadly.

As one, Ravinder and his second-born turned and slowly made their way back to the waiting vehicle.

Just before he got into the car, Ravinder turned and looked back at the gray waters of the swiftly flowing Ganges.

But all he saw was a pretty three-year-old girl in a pretty pink frock.

She seemed to be waving at him.

That brought a small smile to his lips.